About t

Decima Blake has a long-standing interest in child protection and is deeply passionate about child victims of crime. *Hingston: Smoke and Mispers* is the second in the *Hingston* series.

A percentage of royalties will be donated to the charity Embrace Child Victims of Crime.

Photography Seamus Ryan

By the same author

Hingston's Box

HINGSTON: SMOKE AND MISPERS

Decima Blake

HINGSTON: SMOKE AND MISPERS

Pegasus

Dedication

In recognition of all who strive to protect children
from becoming victims of crime.

Chapter One
Do You See What I See?

The first door on the Advent calendar had been opened. Piccadilly glamorised the crowds of Christmas shoppers whose cold, sullen faces could be ignored if, like Hingston, you were tall enough to look above them. He was close enough to Fortnum and Mason to hear the clock bells acknowledge six p.m. over the rhythm of taxi exhausts, bus brakes wheezing and the clamour that surrounded him. Stood outside the coffee shop he waited, looking at the wreaths and drapes that spanned the Burlington Arcade opposite. *Burlington.* That name, however elegant its display or its association with prosperity, would always remind him of the murder of Daniel Clarke last year. He sighed into the frosty air and pulled out his phone.

'I'm half an hour early,' Hingston explained. 'If you're nearby, I'll order yours.'

'I'm on a bus, just past Oxford Circus,' Uncle Zack replied. 'Traffic's solid.'

'You might have to get your own then!' he laughed and his brown eyes glistened in the winter chill. 'See you soon.'

Uncle Zack had travelled up from Dartmouth midweek. They'd booked tickets for a piano recital at St James' Church: Schumann at seven thirty, performed by the daughter of Zack's golfing partner.

Hingston turned to the coffee shop. Its white, star-shaped window stickers lacked the sparkle across the road at Old Bond Street but the drinks were good enough and Zack couldn't miss it directly in front of the bus stop. Hingston did not delay in getting inside.

The queue was bulked out with thick coats, carrier bags held in tandem and a rucksack that was reversed into his chest by the silent customer in front.

'Mind yourself,' Hingston responded.

An adjustment of the rucksack with one hand and a shoulder shrug was the result.

With a frown, Hingston averted his eyes from the rude man's balding head and scanned the tables for a free seat. In doing so, he logged the faces that were before him should any match those of persons previously arrested or interviewed, or those currently wanted. There was a space at the bar table that looked out across Piccadilly and someone began to rise from their stool; two spaces would be ideal.

'Yes, sir.' The barista caught his attention.

'Oh, an Americano, please.' He turned back to check the bench. The "someone" had sat back down. She had one hand up to her mouth and bending forward she thrust out her arm, striking the window. With both hands now grasping at her throat she turned silently to reveal her desperate eyes, her rising colour and the white and beige mass inside her mouth that spilled over her lip. Getting to her feet, she knocked over her stool which was lost to the noise of the Christmas pop music and the conversations that engrossed everyone but Hingston.

He strode across, got a grip around her upper arm and asked, 'Are you choking?'

The teenager nodded in a frenzied manner as she reached her fingers into her mouth, pulling at the glutinous saliva that clung to her tongue. Still no sound came from her.

As Hingston ordered the nearest person to call an ambulance, the shop began to notice the emergency growing in the corner.

The teenager's dark hair flicked time and again across her blue lips following every failed attempt to force the blockage out.

'I'm not giving up!' Hingston tried to reassure her and the only sounds to be heard were the solid thuds to her back and his breaths as he heaved his fist into her abdomen, willing the Heimlich manoeuvre to work.

The barista's manager was searching the girl's bag for her identity. 'Leanna Snow,' she blurted to the woman who was updating the ambulance dispatcher. 'L... E... A...'

Hingston felt the tension in Leanna's back loosen and her weight pulled hard against his arms as she lost consciousness. One last abdominal thrust: gravity and a relaxing trachea could help dislodge this now, Hingston hoped. The few remaining members of the public stared and exclaimed in hushed voices as he lowered her to the floor and swept back her hair.

Burst blood vessels freckled her swollen nose and mouth from which a violet stain had leached out to saturate her skin like dyed silk.

He opened her wet lips and felt for the obstruction with his finger. A claggy, slimy plug had sealed her throat.

'What's she eaten?' he directed to the manager. Whatever it was, it was immovable and he began to perform chest compressions whilst waiting her answer.

'Hot chocolate and marshmallows.' The receipt was in the manager's trembling hand.

The paramedics arrived and took over from Hingston. On the bench stood the large cup with soggy, bulbous marshmallows within it and two from the cup were oozing their sweet, gelatinous glue in pools of hot chocolate on a separate saucer.

'You gave her extra marshmallows?' asked the manager of the barista.

'She wanted extra.' The barista's eyes were glassy with tears.

Zack arrived and the barista prevented him from entering. Hingston excused himself from the scene, stepping between bewildered customers and explained, 'I just need to speak with him outside.' He stepped onto the pavement.

'What's going on, Jason? Is someone ill?'

'A girl has most probably choked to death. I tried to save her.'

Zack stared between the window decorations and saw the paramedics with Leanna. 'They were parked up on Regent Street. I saw them from the bus. Only had a short distance to come,' Zack rambled.

'The police will be arriving next. I'm not going to make it to the concert.'

***

By 8.35 p.m. he had finished his statement: typed, printed and signed in the local sergeants' office at the closest police station he could access in Mayfair.

Leanna Snow could not be resuscitated. *Seventeen years old.* Hingston replayed the catastrophe: her panic; his determination; her flailing arms and the scratches she drew down her neck; her soundless desperation that conflicted with the silent words scribed on the back of her till receipt:

insignificant pathetic
insignificant pathetic
insignificant pathetic
insignificant pathetic

Her fight for survival may have been instinct kicking in and overriding what could be considered

13

suicidal thoughts. Hingston couldn't reason upon it any further. He'd done all he could and the coroner would determine the circumstances, but it would take some effort to put Leanna Snow and those eight hopeless words into the vault in the back of his mind.

***

'Still missing, sarge,' DC Rob Barker confirmed to Hingston whose presence could be heard by the clinking of mugs being transported a little too quickly.

He set down the tea tray on Rob's desk and distributed the first round of the day with only a couple of words given to each of the DCs. Unlike his own, their mood was light as they were settling into the seven a.m. shift.

Hingston met eyes with his own reflection in the cold, dark windowpane which after sunrise would afford a view into Chiswick Police Station's yard. He picked up his "Best Detective" mug and looked over Rob's shoulder at the updates on Emily Britton's missing person report. If the head teacher at Thomas Sprigge High School hadn't cited the death of Leanna Snow as a likely reason for Emily's disappearance, Hingston would not have been feeling preoccupied by this investigation. Emily's photograph, embedded at the top of the report, evoked carefree times full of youthful excitement with her wide smile, bright eyes, sun-blushed skin and bobbed brown hair which was swung heavily to one side with a cheeky tilt of her head. Five months ago, her mother had taken this photo. It gave no suggestion of her self-harming behaviour.

According to Emily Britton's form tutor, when Saturday's tragedy was conveyed to Leanna Snow's year group at an impromptu assembly, Emily's reaction was, 'Different.' The other students were registering the news with bleak eyes fixed on the head teacher or by turning in shock to the student next to them. Some began lunging forward or leaning back to see the reaction of friends who were sat in different rows, separated by form group and alphabetical order. Emily raised one hand, directing her phone towards the front of the hall and took a photograph, 'Like you would at a music festival.' Her expression was pensive and with a glance at the student next to her, she slipped her phone into her bag. The form tutor decided to check on Emily's behaviour at afternoon registration, but she did not attend.

The Thomas Sprigge receptionist reported the absence to Emily's mum, asking whether Emily had gone home or to an appointment the school was unaware of. This "ludicrous" question inflamed Mrs Britton who reminded the receptionist of her own role within the Parent Teacher Association and of Emily's aspirations for Oxbridge.

Mrs Britton's subsequent calls to Emily's mobile went to voicemail or were cut off. She discovered the photograph of the assembly had been posted on social media by Emily at the start of the lunch break. No comment was attached to the photo.

Mrs Britton was insistent the absence was out of character and indicative of abduction. "My daughter has been kidnapped" were the opening words she delivered to the police control room after hanging up on her accountant boyfriend who had said such an eventuality was unlikely. Mrs Britton knew that too, but she wanted action. Indeed, the police action began yesterday afternoon, but without any sightings or contact with Emily last night, more needed to be done on this brisk Tuesday morning.

***

Thomas Sprigge High School had retained the austere appearance of the original grammar school that had occupied this sizeable corner plot in Acton until the 1960s. Off the back of the three-storey Edwardian brick building were modern additions including a heated swimming pool, a dance studio, and the sixth form block. All of these were largely hidden when viewing the school from the street, even when looking between the bare winter branches of the London plane trees.

Hingston had arranged an appointment with the head teacher for midday. Whilst the head was concerned about managing the impact of Leanna's death and Emily's disappearance on the other students, he was most concerned by the gossip, grumblings and accusations that parents had bandied about on social media last night. As the head's secretary led Hingston into the office with its large sash windows, original fireplace and cosy Bordeaux red wallpaper he discovered the most notable development of the morning was the presence of an unexpected third party. He concealed his surprise when the secretary introduced her as Mrs Britton.

Mrs Britton wore a tailored dress and was sat in a leather wingback armchair, legs crossed, her sheer black tights visible well beyond her knees, and she glared at Hingston.

He shook hands with both the head teacher and Mrs Britton.

The head teacher spoke first. 'DS Kingston…'

'*H*ingston.' The correction was prompt and he noticed a strange pouting smirk that faded from Mrs Britton's lips when her eyes reached his.

She darted her attention to the head teacher who was making his apology and there she fixed a determined stare, tilting her head away from Hingston.

The head teacher, William Cochrane, asked in his warm Scottish accent if Hingston cared for a cup of filter coffee, breakfast tea, or Earl Grey.

After the secretary closed the door with a slow and well-practised turn of the doorknob, Mr Cochrane smiled and thanked Hingston for meeting at the school.

Hingston leant forward in his seat. 'No problem.' Opening his notebook, Hingston launched into the purpose of his visit. 'You have access to the parents' comments that concerned you and the students who spoke to you this morning, are willing to speak to the police?' he asked.

'Yes.'

A loud smoker's cough from the wingback armchair interrupted them. 'Thank you for inviting me, DS *Hingston*,' Mrs Britton's sarcastic, commanding voice rang out. Her haughty expression worsened as she looked Hingston in the eye and bulked out her top lip with her tongue, an unattractive combination of gloating and goading.

Hingston paused. 'Mrs Britton. There are a number of matters related to Emily which we will discuss presently, and that saves the need to repeat them to you on a separate occasion.' He nodded a perfunctory thanks to the head teacher. 'Thereafter, the business of other parents and students will be discussed with Mr Cochrane, *alone*, as per the terms of our meeting agreed at nine fifteen this morning.'

'I *am* a member of the PTA,' said Mrs Britton.

'And I am obliged to conduct this investigation professionally.'

Mr Cochrane gave a laugh like a henpecked husband. 'Okay... Mrs Britton is naturally very distressed about Emily. I have shown her the parents' comments, but I have only given a flavour of the students' accounts.' This was exactly what he had told Hingston over the phone at nine fifteen and therefore

Hingston wondered if he was lying, repeating himself to warn Mrs Britton not to say too much.

Hingston studied the surplus blinking that Mrs Britton was performing, tearlessly, to the ceiling, and decided he should have sent Rob or another of the DCs instead.

'Have you a printed copy of the Facebook messages?' Hingston asked.

'My secretary's an angel.' Mr Cochrane supplied a number of sheets with an involuntary twitch. The sheets, along with a Post-it Note inscribed "William—police copy, T" were held together with a dainty bulldog clip.

Hingston read down the first page and flicked to the last. 'If you could ask… T?'

'Tina,' Mr Cochrane advised.

'Tina, to email me the details of each of the individuals who have posted these comments. If she can also include the names of their children and how their children are linked to Emily, for example, friend; in the same form group or shared classes but not friends, that would be helpful.'

Mrs Britton interjected again. 'Well, they certainly are not the parents of Emily's friends. Emily is intelligent. She studies mathematics, history, psychology and sociology. She is naturally very attractive…' Mrs Britton skimmed her eyebrow with her index finger, '*not* like the trollops who have written this *profanity*!'

Mr Cochrane fidgeted. 'Now, it's best not to bring opinion into this, Mrs B.'

She glowered at Mr Cochrane and in defiance, turned and crossed her legs the other way.

Hingston could not see any profanity in the messages. There was reference to self-harm and to bullying. 'When you reported Emily as having been abducted, you said that she had self-harmed,' he directed at Mrs Britton.

'It was years ago. When she was thirteen.'

Hingston nodded. 'You said it was current when you phoned the police,' he challenged.

'I was distraught! I wanted Emily to be found quickly, not put to the back of the queue!' Yesterday, Mrs Britton had failed to provide the police call handler with any reason to support her allegation of kidnap and her propensity to exaggerate was becoming more evident today.

Hingston challenged her no further. 'And, Mr Cochrane, the school haven't noticed any signs Emily may relapse and self-harm whilst missing?'

'No, but Emily has prompted some concern in the past year... Mrs B is fully aware of this.'

Hingston read one of the parents' Facebook messages: "Sadly the girl flipped months ago. I'm glad my Jess isn't in her classes".

Mr Cochrane seemed to be waiting for a prompt to continue.

Mrs Britton was displeased and huffed, 'It's nonsense! Safeguarding has gone mad in this school! I know my own daughter. We *do* talk. She's been fine!'

'Mrs Britton, it's important you are honest with me,' Hingston appealed.

Her glare softened. 'My daughter does *not* suffer from depression just because she chose to study that disorder for her psychology A-Level. She *does not* believe in psychokinesis because it's twaddle! Unfortunately, you can't prevent a creative, talkative child from discussing the curriculum! And less able students will get jealous.' Her frown lines deepened as she turned to Mr Cochrane. 'Go on! You've had this written on Emily's school record. You obviously want it on the police record too!'

'Mrs B, I'm just trying to help the officer understand where these Facebook comments stem from. If Emily has seen them it's not going to help the current situation.' He reached to a piece of paper and looked at Hingston. 'Emily's psychology curriculum included a module on anomalistic psychology—psychokinesis, exceptional experience.' He saw Hingston's look of unfamiliarity and explained, 'For example, moving objects without touching them, near-death experiences, sixth sense.'

'Okay,' Hingston confirmed.

'It was only a very small part of the course, but Emily became quite intrigued by these theories. During a lesson she remarked that "to bring punishment by the

21

power of the mind would give much greater satisfaction than to…"' He checked the wording on the paperwork. 'Than to "contaminate yourself with the distraction of a blade".'

Hingston masked his reaction to this whilst Mrs Britton remained silent, turning the ring on her right hand.

'Mr Cochrane, yesterday afternoon you said that you thought the death of Leanna Snow was the likely reason for Emily's disappearance.' Hingston did not want to pass comment on Emily's unusual remark about punishment or self-harm or whatever form of harm she may have been referring to.

'Yes. Emily wrote an essay debating near-death experience. Just before October half term. She focussed on perceived evidence of the afterlife and clearly had gone to great lengths to research the topic. It could be considered a morbid fascination. I have no answer for the photograph she took at yesterday's assembly, I must add, but perhaps Leanna's death has triggered a reaction that is much more intense than we could have anticipated? She and Leanna were in the same form group.'

Mrs Britton cleared her throat. 'They were close in the younger years until their A-Levels took them in separate directions,' she added without the offensive tone that had accompanied her earlier remarks.

The meeting continued for a further twenty minutes. It became of more value to the host and the uninvited guest than it was to Hingston who explained police processes, how to try to prevent further social media outbursts and who, to his frustration, asked questions for which limited answer was provided. The Facebook references to Emily bullying other students were quashed by Mrs Britton, and Mr Cochrane had no evidence to support the allegations. Hingston thought Mr Cochrane might disclose something after Mrs Britton left, but he did not.

Hingston received more information about the parents who appeared to have been slanderous on social media and then Mr Cochrane introduced him to the two students who had agreed to speak with the police.

***

It was encouraging to see the attentive expressions displayed by Harry and Chloe. They had sat for some time in the bursar's office whilst Hingston's first appointment overran. These two mathematics students were Emily's ex-boyfriend and her tennis partner. Both showed their concern and had impeccable manners, standing when Hingston entered the room and shaking his hand.

Introductions over, Harry spoke confidently. His striking blue eyes were held steadily on Hingston. 'We wanted to speak with you together, because we both got this text from Emily on Friday.' The pair produced their phones and Harry held them side by side to evidence the point, allowing Hingston to read the message:

> *I AM SORRY FOR WHAT*
> *I HAVE DONE. I PANIK.*
> *THAT IS MY FAULT!*
> *FORGIVENESS?*
> *FORGOTTEN? WILL*
> *YOU REMEMBER*

Hingston was drawn to the spelling error. "PANIK" did not tally with the Oxbridge aspirations reported by Mrs Britton, but that could be another exaggeration. He wanted their views first. 'Okay. What does that mean to you?'

Harry continued, 'We were going to ask her what she meant yesterday because she ignored the text Chloe sent in reply.'

Chloe had retrieved her phone and flicked her long ponytail back behind her neck. '"Called you but you're not answering. Love you Em. Forgave you last term. Forgotten." Three exclamation marks. "You didn't want to talk about it again. You OK?" Hugs and kisses, smiley face; you know.' Chloe read out the message, keen to convey to Hingston the emotion behind her words. 'Harry and me got together on the biology field trip in July. Em hated us for it, but she and Harry finished way back in Year Twelve, you know, October last year.'

Hingston had a momentary lapse in concentration as his memories of 1997 and his own schooling days flooded back... Back on task, he asked, 'So, neither of you have spoken with or heard from Emily since Friday?'

'No,' they replied in unison.

'And you think the text relates to your relationship?'

They nodded. Chloe elaborated, 'Em does worry, usually after the event and she can get panicked. She went round accusing me of stealing Harry from her. It nearly ended our friendship, you know, forever, but we managed to work it out. Harry and me spoke to Mr Cochrane this morning because we'd talked about it and what with her going missing... the text didn't sound like her really.'

Harry took over. 'Emily is *the* most *correct* person in the Year. I know it sounds a bit anal... sorry,' he laughed and ran a hand through his dark hair. 'But she'd never spell something wrong or end a sentence without punctuation. It's just not her way.'

'Do you think someone else sent the text?' Hingston asked.

'We don't know,' said Harry. 'After she went missing, we wondered if it could be that.'

'Or drugs,' suggested Chloe. 'I didn't tell Mr Cochrane this, actually.' She cast a doubtful look at Harry and her cheeks flushed. 'Something's disturbed her in recent months. I saw the inside of her pencil case

25

before she zipped it back up and glared at me, you know, like "don't you dare ask".'

'Yeah,' Harry agreed.

'She'd painted inside the case with Tipp-Ex and marker pen. It read "insignificant pathetic". Just those two words. *Over and over.*'

Chapter Two
Let Nothing You Dismay

'DS Hingston,' was the response he gave to all calls made to his desk phone. Variations in tone enabled his team to determine whether the number shown on the phone's display was recognised or not, and if recognised, whether the call was expected or not. This call, from the Control Room, was recognised but not expected. He said little, bar repeating the incident reference number and thanking the call handler for bringing it to his attention.

Rob waited for Hingston to relay the details.

'Male matching the description of Dr Sven Olson found dead,' Hingston said as he searched for the incident log on his computer.

'Shit. Where?' asked Rob.

'Hanging by the neck within the Egyptian Avenue at Highgate Cemetery.' He exchanged a look with Rob that acknowledged the unexpected location more than the death.

***

Hingston stared at the reams of photographs on the internet that showed inside the iconic West Cemetery at Highgate. The Egyptian Avenue was a popular feature in all seasons. The morning of Wednesday the 5th of December had begun with light snowfall. He imagined the approach of the solitary female tour guide who, at eleven forty-five a.m. set off up the frosty woodland path to unlock the Terrace Catacombs.

The gentle thud of her footsteps, steady, yet not solemn in their pace, were keeping the chill from her toes. Against the silence she was conscious of herself and of the thousands of feet that lay still in the Victorian cemetery. She looked at the names that, over her years at Highgate, had grown lovingly familiar and whose stories she gave life to on afternoon tours. In two hours the cold-penetrated catacombs, mausoleums, monuments and tombs would again be admired for their architectural splendour. Visitors would learn about the funerary symbolism used to remember lost loves long mourned by exquisite stone angels and guarded by loyal pets immortalised in stone.

She looked at the masses of tombstones that were situated in clusters between the trees, far back from the path she ascended. The stones were tilted and were gripped by dense ivy and random undergrowth that twisted around them with a strangler's hold. It was as if the souls they represented were vying for position, fighting to be remembered.

Scuffing her shoe against the icy gravel, she thought of London's poor who lay anonymously in common graves beneath the path she trod. She would acknowledge them too on the tour.

She soon came to the broader section of the path that opened out to the left and revealed the two weatherworn obelisks and four lotus columns. They were divided symmetrically by a broad, robust archway and they magnified the entrance to the Egyptian Avenue. She approached the closed iron gates. They were coated in thick black paint to match the sixteen substantial cast iron doors that sealed the vaults that flanked the avenue. The vaults themselves, long unopened, were not solely occupied by the dead; there was evidence of bats. These dark-loving mammals would squeeze in and out of the vaults through small door vents, pushing strands of cobwebs into messy grey clots of fluff that lingered inside the vents and dangled out. They would be quiet now, she knew. The moist, defrosting vegetation and trees that grew above and hung over the avenue held back much of the light. However, when compared to the original tunnel construction (its roof had been removed years before she came to Highgate), she had been able to convince herself that this was a hospitable gloom.

Pulling back the gates, she looked up the avenue and through to the Circle of Lebanon vaults beyond. The sun illuminated the pale stone pediment that faced her and this increased the illusion of the avenue's great length. She would often pause to admire the drama of the architecture seen from this particular spot at the entrance. It reminded her of the fabled ascent toward heaven's light, but this morning, her eyes were being drawn from the light toward the unfamiliar shadow that encroached at the left of the exit.

Stood still with her breath trapped inside her pounding chest, she computed the shadow's human form. The shoulder protruded sharply. The neck was held at a tilt with the face shying away from the daylight. The thickset body appeared of giant stature until she saw the feet drooping down towards the ground…

Hingston redirected his attention back to the incident log. Whilst it only summarised her actions, it was more than sufficient to enable any reader to empathise with the hysterical tour guide.

The desk phone interrupted with its mellow, warbling ring. It was the station reception officer.

'Got a young person in Reception for you. A Chloe Dandridge.'

'I'll be down in five minutes,' replied Hingston.

***

Chloe stood alone in Reception, engrossed in her mobile phone. Hingston saw her familiar eager expression reappear when he invited her to speak in the adjoining interview room. It was quite different to the interview rooms used in custody, but when Hingston advised Chloe to avoid walking into the panic strips on the walls, she was taken aback. She was further surprised by the tape machine, which unbeknownst to her was defunct.

'Do you need to record this?' she asked.

'Very unlikely.' Hingston smiled. 'But tell me why you're here.'

Chloe inhaled as though she was about to reel off a very long account. 'I called Emily and she answered.'

Hingston headed up the page in his notebook with the date and time.

'She said... "I'm fine. Stop calling me", and I started to say, "Just tell me where you are", but she cut me off. I rang straight back, and she'd turned her phone off. I've been a bit persistent. I'm sorry if I've made things worse. I was trying to help.' Wide-eyed and teary she looked at Hingston who hoped she wouldn't cry.

'You've not made anything worse,' he reassured her. 'You're a concerned friend and Emily's taken your call. Despite cutting you off, it's positive.'

Chloe nodded and appeared calmer.

'So when was this?' he asked, aware that no one else had achieved contact with Emily—including the police.

She showed him the call log on her phone. 'This one. 12.10 p.m. Call duration six seconds.'

He made a note of the time of the call and Chloe's number. 12.10 p.m. was just under an hour ago.

'And tell me how Emily sounded when she said those words,' Hingston directed.

'Just like normal, you know. A bit whiney because she wasn't happy with me, but she was calm. She wasn't whispering or shouting at me, or sounding strange or anything.'

'Could you hear anything in the background?'

'Um, no. But she's got a phone with one of those noise cancelling features. Harry's up on all that.' She smiled at the thought of her boyfriend.

'Harry. That's reminded me. Shouldn't you be at school?' he queried.

'It was Harry who drove me here. He couldn't get parked outside, so he's driving round to find somewhere. It's okay, we've both got study periods before and after lunch, so it was all right for us to come over here,' she said.

'You know you can call 101 and ask to be transferred to me. If I'm not here and the team are out, the Control Room will make sure the information gets to the right place as quickly as possible,' Hingston advised. 'But this has been helpful. I'll get someone from my team to take your account in the format of a statement for you to sign, if that's okay, while I get this information on our systems.' He reached for his mobile to call Rob.

'Oh, yes, I'll do a statement about it, but there's something else I wanted to tell you about. But it might not be helpful at all. I do have a photograph of it though.' She scrolled through her phone, engrossed just like she had been when stood in Reception.

Hingston held off calling Rob.

'This is it.' She handed her phone to Hingston. It was a photo of Emily stood with a group of girls at some type of social event. They were all laughing and looking liberated. 'Yeah, ignore all of us with her. We went out on the last day of term when we broke up for the summer.'

Hingston was studying Emily's face, wondering if her eyes looked as happy as her broad smile suggested.

'You can zoom in on it like this…' Chloe took back control of her phone and returned it with the focus directed on Emily's necklace. 'She got *that* towards the end of term and was showing it off all night. Never confessed who gave it to her.'

The necklace looked like a dark orange lump of plastic on a beaded chain. The shape of the plastic resembled a stick man of sorts; the "head" was in the form of a loop, the "arms" were long and held vertically, sandwiching a short torso that fanned out at the "feet" which pointed east and west. It was a memorable character, for Hingston knew he had seen it before… yes… in August… round the neck of a missing Chiswick woman pulled from the River Thames. *Dead*.

Chapter Three
Mark My Footsteps

'Jason,' called Detective Inspector Brace in her usual commanding manner across the open plan office. Hingston had just returned from the interview room, yet Brace's expression appeared impatient as she watched him walk over to her office. She made several glances at the notebook he held, but wasn't going to ask about it. 'Come in and pull the door over,' Brace directed with an unnecessary tone of superiority. She seated herself behind her desk and smoothed her blonde bob with one hand.

Hingston suspected someone of higher rank had annoyed her.

'Rob *Smythe...*' she began.

Hingston nearly smiled at the name of the bombastic detective chief inspector; clearly his suspicion was right.

'... has called about Dr Olson. It's believed to be his body in Highgate Cemetery. Suspected murder. CCTV shows an individual entering the cemetery via a gate at the top of Swain's Lane. They were carrying a small pair of steps and used them to get close to the CCTV camera and spray-paint the lens. This person is of smaller build than Olson and is presently the only suspect we have evidence of.'

'I'll prepare the handover,' said Hingston.

***

Back at his desk, Hingston first added Chloe's update to Emily's missing person record. Addressing the DCs, he requested one of them update Mrs Britton and ask her who gave Emily the necklace.

His attention back on Dr Olson, Hingston reviewed the information gathered and recorded before the body was found.

Dr Olson, fifty-two years of age, was a gynaecologist. He had practiced at numerous London hospitals and for the past fourteen years had predominantly worked out of a clinic called the White House in Hampstead.

Married with no children, his rounded, clean-shaven face appeared very content and kind in the photograph displayed on the missing persons database. Originally from Sweden, Dr Olson's blond hair and soft features had a warmth that seemed to radiate and his vibrant blue eyes shone as they gazed upwards towards the left of the photo. His wife described him almost poetically when she reported him missing yesterday and somehow his photo appeared more like a portrait of a saint than a recent holiday snap. Hingston wondered if it was the positioning of the sun and the colour of the ocean that had something to do with it, or whether Mrs Olson had electronically enhanced the photo to create a dreamy image of him. Certainly, she was more focused on praising her husband than answering the questions asked by the call handler.

Dr Olson should have arrived at the White House Clinic at eight a.m. yesterday. Mrs Olson was unable to reach him on his mobile at nine a.m. and therefore rang the clinic. The secretary said he hadn't arrived and by lunchtime Mrs Olson phoned the police, concerned by his continued absence.

When asked if he poses a risk to himself or to others, Mrs Olson said, 'Sven poses no risk to anyone. He is a people person. He's well respected in his profession. He's a gynaecologist, so he's wonderful with patients and they do think *so* highly of him. He's achieved a lot and takes pride in helping people. He wouldn't put himself at risk because he has so much to give others. No, that would be selfish and selfish he is not. I'm just worried he's been taken ill or has been involved in an accident.'

Dr Olson had not been involved in any of the day's road traffic collisions and he had not been admitted to any hospital. He, or a person now believed to be him, was found hanging in Highgate Cemetery less than twenty-four hours after Mrs Olson called police. Had he been a high risk missing person then more police resources would have been applied in that period, but he was not. There was no suggestion he was likely to become a murder victim.

Hingston thought of Mrs Olson who would be asked to identify the body, if the early indications were correct. Her love and admiration for her husband was tremendous and Hingston hoped that the victim may perhaps turn out to be someone else.

Handover documentation for Smythe complete, Hingston wanted to know the outcome of the call to Mrs Britton.

'Yes, sarge,' DC Coleridge said in her usual efficient manner. 'I got through to her and she was pleased with the update, but unable to even *guess* who may have given Emily the necklace.' DC Coleridge was cross about this. She had little patience with the parents of missing children when, as she put it, "They know bugger all about their offspring". 'I'm pissed off with her already,' she moaned.

'What did you say to her when she had no suggestions?' Hingston thought it best to check, in case her frustration had been voiced to Mrs Britton.

'That if she could think of anyone, to call back. I wasn't rude, sarge. Don't want a complaint.'

Rob, back from taking Chloe's statement, chipped in. 'You mean *another* complaint!' He laughed and pointed at DC Coleridge with a mischievous glint in his eye.

'One complaint is more than enough,' Hingston added. 'And that was many months ago. It's not going to be repeated.'

Rob let the matter drop. 'So this necklace looks a bit unusual, sarge. I got Chloe to email the photo of it to the team inbox.'

'Perhaps we should email it to Mrs Britton,' Coleridge interrupted. 'Might jog her memory.'

'It's not as unusual as you'd think,' said Hingston who had found the record for the woman drowned in the Thames. 'Look. Sheila Baptist. August suicide victim. That necklace she's wearing is virtually identical.'

Rob and Coleridge walked round to his computer.

'Let's see the one in the inbox,' prompted Coleridge.

There was no doubting their similarity. Hingston thought there might be reference made to the necklace within Baptist's file. It was worn in the photograph submitted to police when she went missing and was around her neck when she was pulled from the Thames a week later.

'I'll have a little look at this,' Hingston said, prompting Rob and Coleridge to return to their desks.

Whilst Hingston was aware of the case, it was not one of the investigations he had overseen. He accessed the electronic documentation that DS Brian Pye had compiled. The file was large and included reports, scanned statements and copies of emails sent between

DS Pye, the supervising officers based at Westminster and the Marine Policing Unit, and the Coroner's Office.

Sheila Baptist had lived in Chiswick and was an accountant at a local firm where she had worked for fifteen years. Aged thirty-nine, she was single and had good relationships with her colleagues, although she was said to have led a very quiet personal life. The colleague who reported her missing advised police that her only relative was her estranged father who lived in Spain. The only available photograph of Sheila Baptist was that taken at an office Christmas party the year before she went missing. Sometime during those eight months she had changed her hairstyle from the dark blonde ponytail held low at the nape of her neck to a short style dyed a deep chocolate brown. The orange "stick man" necklace was on full display, enhanced by her ruby red top.

Sheila Baptist had jumped into the Thames from Victoria Embankment wearing a jacket that was far too hot for the August heat. Inside the jacket, numerous cast iron kitchen weights had been sewn into the lining. Insufficiently heavy to pull her to a swift death, their presence was still taken as evidence of suicidal intent. There was no suicide note, however.

Hingston kept searching. The necklace *was* referred to. Her colleague who provided the photograph had told police that she *wore it every day*, and given its bold design, he believed it would be easily recognised. Either he wasn't asked or he didn't know if it had been gifted to her by someone significant. That said, none of the documentation Hingston had skimmed through so far referred to any significant person known to have been part of her life.

A meeting reminder popped up on his computer screen. Fifteen minutes and he would be attending the *Tasking and Co-ordination…* no, he was scanning through Sheila Baptist's file; he would check his calendar in a minute. Not many more documents now and all were easily identifiable. Their file names were compliant with the force records management procedure of date followed by document title, followed by surname in capitals, followed by initial. His eyes were drawn to this one:

03.09.12.MG11OLSONS

'Olson?' said Hingston as he double clicked on the file name and the witness statement opened. At the top were the basic details: Sven Olson, aged over eighteen, gynaecologist. Hingston read on. "I am the above-named person and I am a consultant gynaecologist practising at THE WHITE HOUSE CLINIC, 278 ADELAIDE AVENUE, HAMPSTEAD, LONDON, NW3 6RY. On Wednesday 22nd August 2012 at 1530 hours one of my patients, a SHEILA BAPTIST, date of birth 20/11/1972, of 96 BLENHEIM AVENUE, CHISWICK, W4 8BZ, attended THE WHITE HOUSE CLINIC for her biannual consultation with me. I now know that BAPTIST was reported as missing to the police the following day, Thursday 23rd August 2012, and that she died on Thursday 30th August 2012 having drowned in the RIVER THAMES. I was unaware of this until the police advised me and requested the statement I here provide. BAPTIST had been a patient of mine for three years. I confirm that BAPTIST presented in good spirits and did not say or indicate to me in any respect that she was depressed or troubled by a preoccupation which could have led to her disappearance or death. I do not know any details regarding her social or personal life and this includes any plans she may have made to follow her consultation. She engaged with me in light conversation after her consultation ended at 1550 hours. This lasted no more than two or three minutes and whilst I cannot remember exactly what was discussed, she did say that she wished she had taken a holiday abroad this summer but could not afford one or that she did not have the time for one. This seemed to be a small disappointment to her. I remain deeply saddened and shocked by her death. I am willing to be contacted again by police regarding BAPTIST should this be required."

Hingston reread the emotive comment that contributed nothing to the police enquiry: "I remain deeply saddened and shocked by her death". Olson must have been keen to include these words, but for someone who had only just been told of a death, to *remain* deeply saddened and shocked seemed a peculiar way to put it.

Hingston's meeting was looming. A quick check of the calendar... *ground floor conference room.* He looked again at the photo of Sheila Baptist aside the photo of Emily Britton supplied by Chloe. Emily, whilst wearing the peculiar "stick man" necklace, sported a chocolate brown bob which framed her broad, youthful smile with the hair ends flipped out and upwards. There was no photograph of Sheila Baptist with her hair styled that way, but the description Hingston had read on her missing person report came to mind and made him frown.

He collected his notebook and the Tasking Group meeting papers, locked his computer and headed towards the corridor while dialling a number on his mobile phone.

'Mrs Britton?' he queried as he descended the staircase. 'Nothing to be concerned about. Can you tell me, has Emily any health reasons that may have led her to see a consultant? No, I'm not asking for the details of her medical history... and the name, please. Yes. A Dr Olson.'

Minutes later, Hingston strode into the conference room, dialling another number. 'Apologies, I'll be back in ten,' he said to the chair of the Tasking Group.

An accepting nod was given and Hingston returned to the corridor.

His call was answered by a loud and impatient boom of a voice: 'Smythe. Make it quick, Hingston.'

Chapter Four
Yonder Peasant, Who is He?

When Hingston returned from the Tasking Group, Brace was waiting for him.

'Rob Smythe. Twice in one day.' She did not attempt to conceal her dislike of the muscular, bald-headed DCI.

Hingston followed her lead, back into her office.

'I take it he told you?' she barked.

'He said he would be seeking authorisation, ma'am.' Hingston struggled, but succeeded in remaining polite.

'Well, he did. You're posted to his investigation team as of this afternoon,' she complained.

Brace was gripping her coffee mug and put it down with a clonk on her desk. She did not usually show emotion, preferring to present an unflappable, albeit cold, disposition.

Hingston waited for her next instruction but it was not forthcoming.

'Ma'am, DCI Smythe did not state where the incident room was being located.'

'Hampstead,' she replied.

Hingston knew that Brace used to work out of this grand, Grade-II listed police station. It was soon to be closed and sold off in response to cost-saving requirements. The cutbacks involved numerous stations, plus the sale of New Scotland Yard. Innumerable disappointed officers were fond of these buildings and the memories they housed. Therefore, Hingston being posted to Brace's old stomping ground had needled her nearly as much as losing her best detective to Smythe for the foreseeable future.

'You'll be one of the last to serve out of Hampstead Station,' she reflected.

***

Smythe had moved from Hounslow Police Station to the London Borough of Camden at the start of November. Hingston had heard that Remi had made the same transfer and concluded his stunning Detective Constable ex-girlfriend, with those beautiful pale green eyes, must still be involved with the repugnant Smythe.

Hingston travelled from Chiswick to Hampstead, to arrive in readiness for an eight p.m. briefing. Smythe had taken over the first floor at Hampstead Police Station to house the Major Incident Room, two report writing rooms, an exhibit store, side offices for management use and a briefing room.

The briefing room looked out over the queue of traffic on Rosslyn Hill that polluted the dark December evening with a monotonous thrum of engines.

Smythe was stood at the front of the room, scanning the officers and police staff who were filling the rows of seats before him. His head was held high and he had positioned his arms behind his back as if he were on the parade ground. The artificial lights emphasised his muscular torso which filled out an entirely non-military lilac sateen shirt and his tie was loose at the neck. The lights also enhanced his unnatural tan, and its false colour looked particularly apparent when he spoke to Remi who was seated in the front row and smiled at her.

'Has he had them bleached?' Hingston muttered as an alternative greeting, having worked his way through the room to sit down next to Remi.

Remi looked Hingston in the eyes with a solemn expression, blinked and turned her head back to Smythe and his brilliant white teeth. 'The day before he transferred to Camden,' she answered in a regretful tone. She then gave Hingston a sideways glance that revealed her amusement at the gleaming set. 'He thought no one here would be aware he'd had them done,' she whispered. 'But then, when the third or fourth person mentioned Hampstead Heath during his first day on the borough, he got suspicious.' She put her hand up to her mouth. '"Don't you just *love* Hampstead Heath" were the words that really pissed him off!' Her eyes were twinkling with delight.

'You can't beat a bit of Cockney slang,' Hingston agreed whilst he wondered if Remi was the source of the gossip.

The room fell quiet when the first briefing slide appeared on the screen behind Smythe. *Operation PYROLITE* shone in large red letters. Smythe's deep voice boomed as he focussed attention on the scene footage taken at Highgate Cemetery. 'This is the entrance to the Egyptian Avenue at Highgate Cemetery West. Approximately one hundred feet away is the body of Dr Sven Olson, a fifty-two-year-old gynaecologist who practiced at the White House Clinic in Hampstead.' As the footage began to zoom in, Smythe pointed to the shape of a figure on the left side of the avenue which was suspended close to the exit. He paused the video. 'I'll explain the chronology of events as we currently understand it and what we know about the victim. Then, as per the agenda, I'll move on to what we know about the suspects, for we believe there to be *at least* two suspects working together; the scenes; associations and the media. *Ask* questions if *anything* is unclear. There is the opportunity to provide updates as we go, so speak up if you need to.' Smythe's forehead became deeply lined as he raised his dark eyebrows and nodded, giving a long stare that he directed across the audience. The air was electric, like that at the start of an athletics final. The serious faces that looked back at him were determined and ready for action. Content with their response, Smythe picked up a large photograph of Dr

Olson, the same saintly image Hingston had seen on the missing persons database, and he began the chronology.

'Dr Olson was last seen at approximately seven a.m. yesterday morning by his wife. She was in bed when he came in to say he was leaving for work. However, he failed to arrive at the clinic which he travels to by train from their home in Kensal Green. His normal routine would have seen him arrive there by seven fifty-five. We do not yet know if he caught the train, but CCTV has been seized and will be subject of review. Mrs Olson reported him missing at 1.23 p.m. yesterday, having failed to reach him at work and on his mobile. Mrs Olson was of the opinion that he had not prepared to go missing and that it was entirely out of character. There is then a gap in the chronology.' Smythe paused to check there were no questions brewing and continued.

'The billing data for Dr Olson's mobile has revealed just two calls made after he left his home address. One was made at 4.37 p.m. and one at 10.26 p.m. *Note*, no mobile phone was found post mortem, so it's probable the offender removed it. Going back to the calls made, both were of approximately thirty seconds duration and were made to a mobile number known to police: that of seventeen-year-old misper, Emily Britton. DS Hingston is dealing with this line of enquiry.'

Hingston nodded. 'Sir, cell site analysis indicates Dr Olson was in the area of south Islington at the time of the afternoon call, and had moved to Highgate Village by the second call. The analysis of Emily Britton's call data places her in Islington when both calls were received, as does a further call she took from a friend at 12.10 p.m. today. The cell-sectors differ each time so we're still looking at a wide geographical area. Unfortunately, live cell site has produced no hits since we obtained authority this afternoon; her phone is now switched off. We know from Emily Britton's mother that Emily has been a patient of Dr Olson for approximately two and a half years. High Tech Crime have begun work on her laptop now that it's been moved to the top of their priority list. I'll come back to Emily when we discuss Olson's associates,' Hingston confirmed. He glanced at Remi whose eyes were focused on his mouth as she listened. She noticed him looking back and turned away.

'Thank you,' Smythe acknowledged to Hingston and redirected his attention back to the room. 'Regarding Emily Britton, whilst we do not know the reason for Olson's calls, a very fair hypothesis is that he was having some form of inappropriate relationship with her beyond the parameters of consultant and patient. Again, DS Hingston will address this matter later, but we must consider whether Emily Britton was the reason Olson failed to go to work.'

Some disgruntled noises came from the audience; heads were shaken and noses upturned.

Smythe moved onto the next milestone in the chronology. 'Access was gained to Highgate Cemetery at 11.09 p.m. by an unidentified suspect. This male…' Smythe moved his presentation forward to a still of the CCTV footage, 'cut through the heavy-duty chain lock that secured the cemetery gates situated at the top of Swain's Lane.'

Photographs of the gates, the chain lock discarded just inside the cemetery grounds, and the damaged CCTV camera were on the next slide. 'He used spray paint to cover the camera lens, seconds after his entry with a pair of steps. As a result, we have another gap in the chronology. We don't know whether Dr Olson was present at this time, out of view of the security camera, ready to enter of his own free will. We don't know if he was lured there subsequently and accosted or whether he entered the cemetery under duress. Nor do we know if he had any expectation of the threat to his life.' Smythe began to puff out his chest, a sign that his frustration with what wasn't known was getting to him.

'We do, however, have an estimated time of death. Expert opinion from the scene places this between midnight and two a.m. The final milestone is the discovery of the body this morning at 11.55 a.m. when the tour guide, an Annette Hamish, was confronted with *this* scene on entering the Egyptian Avenue.' Smythe pressed the infrared control and the scene footage continued from where the distant, suspended figure was last made out.

The officers and staff remained silent as Dr Olson's corpse was approached by the scenes of crime officer who filmed the dingy, dank setting and slowly the details became clearer. A zoom shot showed the ligature that cut deep into Olson's neck. His skin was an insipid colour, exaggerated by the diagonal bruising that followed the line of the rope. Smythe's commentary broke the intense concentration.

'The pale skin indicates he died of vagal inhibition, not asphyxiation. This is where the heart is stopped by pressure being applied to the vagus nerve in the neck. The drop measures approximately twenty-five feet; a slip knot was used and death would have occurred within no more than a minute or two or quite possibly much less.'

The footage panned to the side of Olson's face that was dipped into the shadow. 'The grazing to his right cheek and the cut near his temple indicate a struggle had occurred. We'll come back to that point when we discuss the scenes. His hands are bound together behind his back.' Smythe watched the projection screen, waiting for the footage to catch up with his commentary and come to an end. A few members of the audience inhaled deeply when it did.

'So,' boomed Smythe, 'we have a male of five feet eleven inches who is of stocky build. To incapacitate him would have required some effort. It was dark and sub-zero. The snow had not yet fallen. The ligature would have been first tied to *this* cast iron water piping above the Egyptian Avenue.' Another photograph illustrated the scene. 'The ligature would have been slipped over Olson's head prior to manhandling him over this damaged, low, wooden screening—call it a low fence if you will, but it is relatively flimsy. He would then have been pushed over this narrow ledge to plunge to his death.' The next photograph showed the drop down into the avenue. It afforded a glimpse of the top of Olson's head and shoulder.

'Now,' Smythe continued. 'We know the majority of all murders are committed by a person known to the victim. This…' Smythe moved onto the still CCTV image seen earlier. '*This* individual who broke into the cemetery is estimated to be shorter than Olson and is clearly of smaller build. You can see little of their person due to the bulky coat, scarf, cap and hood. They are also wearing gloves. They have carefully prepared for this break-in, equipping themselves with chain cutters, a pair of steps and spray paint. Only the chain cutters have been found, presumably forgotten rather than intentionally left behind. The ligature is not seen on the footage. We have found no material to suggest the offenders' exit was different to the point of entry.' Smythe reached for the mug of tea that was cooling by his laptop. 'Indeed, aside from climbing over the wall by the main public entrance, which would have involved unnecessary effort and risked detection, there was no other means of exit due to the high brick walls, security spikes and the surrounding properties that box the cemetery in.'

'Sir,' called a female internal press officer, 'have we had any other break-ins at Highgate Cemetery in recent years?'

'No. The last was in nineteen ninety-four and the site was less secure then.'

'Thanks,' she said and made a note in her journal.

'I said earlier that we believe there are at least two suspects. To come equipped like this, a mode of transport would be required and it would have taken two individuals to commit the murder. CCTV footage in the area of Swain's Lane is being checked for suspect vehicles. Whether it was a third suspect who drove a vehicle to convey the equipment and the offenders to and from the cemetery, we are hopeful house-to-house enquiries may prove fruitful this evening. Whilst the suspect parameters remain broad at this time, forensic examination has secured some material that will assist. Barry, if you'd explain from here,' Smythe directed and Barry, the crime scene co-ordinator, walked to the front.

Barry was the opposite of Smythe in almost every respect. Wearing force-issue black trousers and fleece, his complexion was almost as pale as Olson had become. He had a mop of fair hair and a gangly appearance; his grey eyes were large and kind. There was something almost good-looking about Barry's face when he smiled, but whether anyone would describe him as attractive was debatable. He had a wiry voice and spoke slowly, but with conviction. His hand gestures were consistent and rigid, much like a string puppet. 'Okay. I'm going to start with the point of entry and exit, then the scene above the Egyptian Avenue and then...' he coughed, 'a scene that we suspect *is* connected to Dr Olson's murder, and if it is, it may indicate a motive quite unusual.' Barry was enjoying the drama and speculation he believed he had generated and nodded his head at Smythe for emphasis before moving on. 'So.' He cleared his throat with a wheeze and the audience understood that the December chill had aggravated his asthma. 'The offenders chose Highgate Cemetery West. It is *only* open to the public for organised walking tours. The gate that was secured with the chain lock is not seen on the walking tours, *so* when the offenders walked from this gate to the area above the Egyptian Avenue where the murder was committed, they either used one of the very poor-quality maps on the internet and navigated haphazardly, or they benefitted from having been on a tour and pieced that knowledge together with the map. *Or*, they have been, or are currently, employed here.' Barry paused to let this register with the audience. 'As you can see from this photograph of the entrance, there are some footwear impressions in the muddy path which are subject to forensic examination. We have not seen evidence of trampled vegetation. Nor have we seen disturbances in the mud or in the gravel that coats some of the woodland paths which could indicate anyone was running or

53

randomly rushing about. This suggests the Egyptian Avenue was a *predetermined* destination and the route to it was understood: planned as carefully as the method of entry and the spray-paint for the CCTV camera. Also, it would suggest that Dr Olson did not struggle upon approach to the area of the Egyptian Avenue. Of course, *as the DCI says*, the ligature was tied to water piping. What *I say* is why bring a rope to hang someone unless you're confident there's a water pipe to tie it to!'

There was a degree of fidgeting coming from Smythe. 'There were plenty of trees, Barry,' he snorted.

Barry wheezed again and smiled at him, enjoying his moment in the spotlight. '*Alas*, the trees are not strong enough and would have put the offenders in danger, whereas the piping was on the near side of the wooden screening. *Anyway*,' continued Barry with a sly glance toward Smythe that suggested he had only just started to show off his skills of deduction, 'above the Egyptian Avenue there is an area of around four square metres where a struggle did occur and there, we have found blood, fibres and hair that we are testing. Examination of the ligature continues, but the water piping has not yielded any material to assist in the identification of the person who prepared the scene.'

Smythe clicked through some photographs on the screen to support Barry's commentary and also, it seemed, to speed him up.

Another wheeze emanated from Barry, followed by an apology that sounded insincere. 'Which brings me on to the third scene.'

Smythe activated the next slide. It showed an off-white substance which had massed and pooled out over a small area of the path. Hingston's mind flashed back to the marshmallow that filled Leanna Snow's mouth and oozed stickiness onto his fingers. He realised he had missed the start of Barry's explanation.

'...from here, in the Circle of Lebanon, you are only three or four metres away from Olson. Wax has usage in magical practices and may indicate Olson was involved in something of this nature. Black magic, perhaps.'

'Can you tell us anything from the wax, *forensically*, that may assist in suspect identification?' asked Smythe with a flare of his nostrils.

'It will be limited and as it has melted, fingerprints are most unlikely unless it was touched whilst solidifying. We may find fibres in the wax. Of note, there is evidence of multiple wicks. We may be able to identify where this particular type of wax originated and from there, suggest where it may have been purchased,' Barry advised, 'but it will take time. What's *interesting...*' he threw another nod in Smythe's direction, 'is we appear to have very different levels of forensic awareness: the break-in was professional, the setting up of the ligature was professional, but the melting of the wax is amateur; quite clumsy, even *foolish*, like leaving behind the chain cutters. And potentially, we could have DNA evidence of one or more of the suspects from where Olson was incapacitated. The struggle on the ground appears quite...' he coughed, 'vigorous.'

Smythe stepped forward. 'Scene forensics continue and mapping of those scenes is underway. We await the post-mortem results and a search of Olson's home and clinic addresses will commence in the morning. Of course, we have stepped up resources to locate Emily Britton.' Having taken back full control of the briefing from Barry, he thanked him in a muted voice and launched into the next agenda item as vigorously as everyone now imagined Olson had been incapacitated. 'Associations, DS Hingston.'

Barry nodded, giving a discreet but cheeky American-style salute before striding his way to the back of the room. Hingston rose from his seat and turned to deliver his input without any slides, but with three large photographs. The first he held at head height. 'This is Emily Britton. She went missing on Monday from Thomas Sprigge High School in Acton, having failed to attend afternoon registration. She posted a photograph on social media of the morning's assembly at which the death of another seventeen-year-old student, Leanna Snow, was announced.' He raised the second photograph. 'This is believed to be accidental death by choking and the student was known to Emily; they used to be close friends. It was therefore considered the death prompted Emily's disappearance. Subsequently, we became aware that Emily and the deceased girl had both been writing the same demeaning words, "insignificant pathetic", onto items in their possession; the reason for this is presently unknown. Of note, Leanna Snow had written these words on a till receipt less than an hour before her death. There are additional concerns from the school about Emily's mental health including a non-recent history of self-harm. She developed a fascination with aspects of her psychology course criteria which involved unproven theories, for example, being able to move objects with the power of the mind and causing harm by such. If the melted wax at the cemetery *does* indicate magical practice, then this could be an interest that linked both Emily Britton and Dr Olson, and or those who murdered him. Emily is shown in this picture wearing a distinct necklace and her hair is styled in the fashion of a dark brown bob. *Another* of Dr Olson's patients wore a virtually identical necklace...' Hingston held up the third photograph, that of Sheila Baptist. 'No one has been able to advise where either female obtained the necklaces from. They are not fashion items, nor are they available on the high street, so we suspect Olson gifted them to both parties. When this patient, thirty-nine-year-old Shelia Baptist, was found dead in the River Thames in August—*note* the coroner's verdict was *suicide*—she had changed her hairstyle to exactly that now sported by Emily Britton both in colour and cut.

Furthermore, Baptist saw Olson the day before she went missing. Emily has been in contact with him whilst missing. Was Olson the reason for Baptist's missing episode and suicide? If so, is Emily Britton similarly at risk of suicide? Did she go missing because of Olson *instead* of the death of Leanna Snow? Whilst Olson's addresses are searched, we will be looking for material related to Emily Britton, Sheila Baptist, the necklaces, and we will be considering any other patients who may have been *involved* with Dr Olson. This is yet to be communicated to Mrs Olson and will be handled by Mel Stoker, Family Liaison Officer.'

Mel raised her hand to identify herself to those in the room who were unfamiliar with her. In her mid-forties, PC Stoker was a warm, motherly figure with a short blonde ponytail.

Hingston continued: 'Mel will also be facilitating a list of associates of Dr Olson who will be subject of witness interview. Uniformed colleagues,' Hingston nodded to the row in which the local neighbourhood inspector and sergeant were sat, 'will be seizing his computer equipment. We shall obtain an account from Mrs Britton about Emily's association with Olson, but it appears she is unaware of contact outside of her daughter's medical appointments.' Hingston pursed his lips together. 'Those are the key points.'

'Thank you, I'll move on to the final few minutes of this briefing and take any questions,' said Smythe whilst Hingston returned to his seat. 'Next steps. We've addressed most of these as we've discussed each agenda point. In summary, there is more work to do around suspect identification via house-to-house, CCTV and forensics, we have associations to identify, the line of enquiry related to Emily Britton, and a preliminary press release will be issued. The cancellation of the afternoon tour of the cemetery did not hit social media; is that still the case?' Smythe asked of the press officer.

'Yes, sir. Only half a dozen were on the tour, and it appears they were respectful of privacy,' she said.

'Makes a refreshing change,' snorted Smythe. 'The draft press release is endorsed. We're keeping the link to Emily Britton confidential *and* the matter of the wax. It's a murder and an appeal for witnesses; that's it. We don't want anyone speculating again about the Highgate Vampire or any sodding horror stories.' Smythe's irritable tone made some people start to become restless in their seats, eager to get back to the task in hand.

'Any questions?' he demanded.

The officers and staff remained silent, content with the details shared at the briefing.

'Okay, ladies and gents, good work.' Smythe grasped his hands together with a loud smack; his bleached smile concealed behind tight lips. 'Back here for debrief at eleven thirty p.m.'

Chapter Five
Brightly Shone the Moon

Hingston clicked the end of his ballpoint pen and sighed.

'I heard about you and the girl in the coffee shop,' said Remi. 'Makes Emily's case more of a personal challenge, I know.' She still had the knack of guessing Hingston's thoughts and touched his wrist. Her delicate fingernails gleamed soft pink and white. Her rosebud lips and sympathetic smile were just as fresh and inviting.

'Saturday was the start of a diabolical week, but it's great to see you.' He smiled.

She removed her hand. Presumably, Smythe would be keeping an eye on them.

'Zack came up from Dartmouth,' he added.

'How's he doing?' she asked.

Remi always got on well with Uncle Zack. Hingston had taken her on holiday down there several times when they were together, twice for the Royal Regatta. He thought of the shimmering expanse of the River Dart in the August sunshine: the elegant boats coursing about, mooring up; the delighted crowds and excited children; the impressive air displays; the fragrance of smoking hot street food; the fireworks; live music on the bandstand; and Remi dancing and laughing under the golden street lights that were strung with coloured lights and bunting, her arms silky and bare, pulling him close... 'Good,' Hingston replied. 'Yes, Zack's good.' He hoped his pause for thought appeared shorter to Remi than it felt to himself. 'But I've not been much company for Zack. Missed a concert Saturday night, which was the reason for his visit. So he had to go on his own. Rest days Sunday and Monday were a bit flat as you'd expect, but we carried on with a visit to Greenwich and to the Imperial War Museum. Ate out. Curry as usual.' Hingston smiled about Zack's love of a good curry. 'He's gone down to see Mum and Dad. Back to mine on Friday. We're going to the Magic Circle Headquarters that evening, provided we don't end up staying on late here.' He pulled an expression that conveyed little optimism.

Remi looked surprised and started laughing. 'It's nearly forty-eight hours away, Jason. I'm sure we'll have things well in hand by then. Besides, Rob and I are going there that night too. He hates losing money. *But hey*, what are the chances of the four of us booking the Magic Circle *and* for the same night! Seven thirty start,' she noted.

'Well, Zack will be very pleased to see you,' Hingston said, concealing his dislike of the term "Rob and I". He tried to stop thinking about the overbearing, smug Smythe lording it up with his muscular arm protecting Remi's shoulders.

'It will be nice to see you *both* too.' She smiled and glanced over in Smythe's direction.

'With all this cemetery black magic talk from Barry, if we ask the magicians the right questions, perhaps we can claim it as overtime,' Hingston jested. 'Talking of Barry... he didn't seem very pleased about being hurried along during his input.' Hingston detected a history between Barry and Smythe and was keen to find out more.

Remi rolled her eyes. 'Come on, let's head back to the office.'

They walked out of the briefing room and found a quiet spot out of earshot, down the corridor and round toward the women's toilets.

Remi spoke in a hushed voice. 'Barry moved to Camden about a year ago. He and Rob seem to follow each other around, unfortunately. They must stew on their dislike of each other too much, Law of Attraction and all that,' she mocked and rolled her eyes again. 'They clash over almost everything. It began about fifteen years ago when Rob was a DC and Barry a relatively young scenes of crime officer. You know Rob. He likes everything summarised and delivered yesterday. Barry has, apparently, *always* been methodical and one for detail, *and* if he has the mind to, he'll dig in his heels and make you listen to all the background information that relates, *especially* if you want him to cut to the chase. Rob says it's self-importance.'

Hingston smiled at the similarity he believed both men shared.

Remi continued, 'Sadly, Rob was particularly stressed on this occasion and Barry was dusting for fingerprints more slowly than Rob thought necessary. You can imagine the scoff that would have accompanied Rob's complaint of...' She moved her shoulders back, ready to mimic Smythe: '"For fuck's sake, Barry! Ken bleedin' Dodd would be more efficient with his tickling stick." Barry *swore* at Rob.' She paused to contain a laugh. 'I've never heard Barry swear, you know. Rob pretends he can't remember the exact words Barry used.'

A number of possibilities came to Hingston's mind.

'*Then* Barry downed his brush. For half an hour he refused to continue, adamant it was his lunch break. This was at *five p.m.* and he was going off shift at six!'

'And neither has forgiven the other,' Hingston concluded.

***

The report writing room at the rear of the station was tatty. The paint was lifting to the right of the window and the desks had not been cleaned for at least as long as the damp had been allowed to penetrate. The Emily Britton line of enquiry was going to be limited for the remainder of the evening unless there was a remarkable turnaround from High Tech Crime, a positive result from the uniformed officers patrolling Islington looking for Emily, or she turned her phone back on. The latter was the least likely in Hingston's opinion. As the desktop computer struggled with his first log on at Hampstead Station, Hingston tuned in his Airwave radio to listen for any live communication stemming from house-to-house enquiries at Highgate. The timing was perfect.

'Go ahead. Over,' a calm female voice requested.

'Silver saloon. Partial registration number. Hotel Victor Five. Over,' replied a male officer.

'Say again the registration number.'

'I say again registration number Hotel Victor Five. Over.'

'Thank you. Over.' She sounded cheerful whilst recording the details.

'Seen zero-zero-one-five hours. Repeat zero-zero-one-five hours. Over.'

'Received. Over.'

'Out.'

The partial index would assist in the CCTV search and an intelligence officer would soon be identifying possible vehicles and registered owners. Hingston hoped the witness was accurate in their recollection and that the vehicle was indeed suspect.

Remi had logged on at the desk opposite him and was already accessing the relevant log. 'That was fortunate,' she said, leaning between the computer monitors to see Hingston. 'A mother, up with her baby, stood looking out of her window which backs onto the cemetery where access was gained. Missed the action, but the car almost opposite the gates she didn't recognise.'

'Very observant of her,' Hingston remarked as Remi leant back to her monitor to read on.

'All the neighbours use those bays that run parallel to the cemetery. The unknown vehicle was parked in the bay at the head of the row. Guess she's been doing a lot of looking out of the window,' Remi surmised, swaying back to meet Hingston's eyes again.

The Airwave radio continued to chatter and bleep. Hingston's desktop screen began to load. He clicked the email icon followed by every pop-up screen thereafter in order to set up his inbox. With the loud clicks of the old mouse button his activity sounded more impatient than he actually was. *No* new emails.

'What do *you* think Olson's been up to?' he asked Remi.

She leant into the gap and contemplated. 'I think he's been trying it on with his patients for years. Why start in his fifties?'

'Okay,' said Hingston wanting to hear more.

'The whole same hairstyle and necklace link feels odd. A bit obsessive or perverse. Plus, a thirty-nine-year-old and a seventeen-year-old. Is he sexually interested in them both? I don't believe they'd both respond to *him* in the same way at all. He must have spent *a lot* of time grooming them, Emily more than the older woman, I'd say.'

Hingston posed another question. 'What about the motive for killing him?'

'If Olson has been having inappropriate relationships for years, a number of people may want him dead. *But* to kill him in Highgate Cemetery, you know—why not Hampstead Heath for instance? It's private but with public access. The cemetery must have significance to go to the length of breaking in. But *what* significance?'

Hingston watched Remi, waiting for her to continue.

'I don't understand the wax. I mean, the wax is surplus to requirements in terms of causing death. How many people would be *that* preoccupied with magic to spend more time at the scene than absolutely necessary? You'd just get out of there, wouldn't you?' Remi shrugged. '*Well*?'

'Unless the murder was carried out whilst someone else burnt the wax?' Hingston suggested.

'Ooh,' Remi straightened her back. '*Emily Britton*?'

***

The debrief was streamlined but comprehensive. Everyone was away before midnight, ready to start

66

again in eight hours. Smythe said he was satisfied with the progress made so far, in particular the house-to-house enquiries which demonstrated *an impressive community spirit* in Highgate. Those were the words Smythe stressed when concluding the debrief, before ending with a short, sharp dose of motivational speaking: 'There's an impressive community spirit in Highgate, ladies and gents. Up with the likes of Chiswick, wouldn't you say, DS Hingston?' Smythe had deployed a stereotypical well-to-do accent for this rhetorical question. Reverting to his brash tone, he said, 'We can work well with communities like that. Pricey postcodes cannot afford unsolved murders. *And nor can we.*'

***

Hingston withdrew his keys from the ignition with a clatter as the bunch fell into the footwell. The unexpected overtime had extended his shift to fourteen hours and his return home to Hatch End had just about exhausted him. His 1930s semi stood in darkness. A greasy takeaway had kept his energy up this evening, but now the aftertaste was as unappealing as the thought of getting back in the car in a little over six hours.

As he approached the front door the outside light illuminated, revealing a delicate whisper of frost on the bare rose bushes. The burgundy gloss paint gleamed, promising a warmth that would not meet him inside. He pushed his shoulder hard against its silky surface as he fumbled with the Yale lock and exhaled more body heat into the night air. Before he could flick on the hall light, the words "insignificant pathetic" slipped into his consciousness. Like a solitary snowflake prickling his forehead and skimming away stealthily, he found himself doubting what he had just thought he felt. A sense of uneasiness? He turned on the light, closed the door and kept his coat on.

'Too bloody cold and tired,' Hingston whispered and walked to the kitchen to make a cup of tea.

Upstairs he bothered with only part of his night-time routine: the new part that began less than a month ago when he returned from the elderly Peter Embling's house with the items that now accompanied his Victorian musical box. The sepia photographs, newspaper cutting and transcript of the Victorian journal sat with the musical box on his bedside table. Hingston was still astounded by the circumstances of his reinvestigation into the Victorian boy's murder, the restoration of justice for the woman wrongly hanged for the murder and the positive outcome delivered to the Clarke family as a result of the reinvestigation. Whilst fifteen-year-old Daniel Clarke was murdered, the Clarkes, unlike the Victorian family, did have their two remaining sons safely returned to them.

Hingston spent his last minutes before laying down in bed looking at the small 1860s sepia photograph of the beautiful Circassian girl with her blonde, pinned back hair and painted lips. Then, as he did every night, Hingston focussed on the tall, muscular, tattooed man stood next to her: her father, who despite his blond hair, bore a striking facial resemblance to himself. Peter Embling had said as much. Hingston only glanced at the accompanying newspaper cutting headed "Circus Death Horror" before flipping the photograph over to read and reread the handwritten words "To the one I can rely upon, with love". His emotional connection to the Victorian case had been reinvigorated since the cutting and the photograph had been left under his car windscreen wiper whilst it was parked on Peter Embling's driveway. He wanted to know more about the Circassian girl and her father: *much* more. The past few weeks at work had been very busy, leaving him insufficient spare time to commence any research. He looked longingly at the photograph before placing it onto the lid of the musical box. It lay there every night to be seen again every morning, unchanged, and with him feeling none the more enlightened. He *was* keeping an open mind, something he had learnt to do during the Clarke investigation, but it wasn't producing any more glimpses into the past or any notion that made him believe he would ever be able to conclude for certain *why* the Circassian girl's father looked so much like himself. His dreams, visions or whatever madness was going on in 2011 appeared to have ended now.

The elderly woman from Bayard's Cove also hadn't been far from his mind these past few weeks. Nor were his strange encounters with her around Dartmouth, which he remembered wistfully. He would ask Zack if he had seen her at all in the past nineteen months. He suspected not.

As he lay down and closed his eyes, his tense shoulders were soothed by the mattress and his thoughts drifted away… as if they were most… insignificant.

***

Thursday morning was as unfestive as Smythe's temper. Hingston arranged to meet Mrs Britton at her home address in Acton to take her statement regarding Dr Olson's association with Emily. Mrs Britton also offered to show him something belonging to Emily that she described as, 'Private, but appropriate for police eyes *in the circumstances*.' Hingston reminded Mrs Britton of the importance of being open with him; however, this was met with a gruff, 'I'll see you at ten,' and the phone receiver was put down.

Mrs Britton was smoking a newly lit cigarette when Hingston arrived. Her makeup was immaculate and her eyeliner very heavy. Her designer business suit, high heels and lofty expression conveyed her arrogance. Her disdainful glance toward his feet and the demand, 'No shoes past the lobby,' conveyed her dominance. She did not present like a normal mother whose child was missing. He almost wished DC Coleridge had given her a mouthful over the phone for knowing "bugger all" about Emily.

'Apologies,' he said as he stepped from the lobby into the hallway. 'Force policy to keep shoes on.'

She tutted, shut her eyes and ever so slightly shook her head as if to say *you are unbelievable.*

Arrogant, dominant and intolerant. Hingston decided these were the three words that best described Mrs Britton. As he followed her through to the kitchen where he was not offered a cup of tea, she stubbed out her cigarette into a lead crystal ashtray, opened a window and placed the ashtray on the window ledge outside. Hingston frowned at her unusual activity and covered for his expression with a request she show him Emily's possessions first and provide her statement thereafter.

'Your colleague asked me about Emily's necklace, so I searched her bedroom for it...' she called from the staircase on her way back to the kitchen. Her voice rang sharp and clear against the minimalist hallway with its high ceilings, uncarpeted floors and lacquered stairs. Her heels clicked on the ceramic Versace tiles that Hingston had spent part of his time studying whilst she was up in Emily's bedroom. As she marched in a clip-clop fashion back to the breakfast bar where Hingston sat on a bar stool, she was unaware that he now knew this was a skimmed milk household with a preference for deluxe microwave meals and Baileys Irish Cream.

She took the bar stool next to him, crossed her legs and looked challengingly into his brown eyes. Hingston ignored this and looking steadily back, said, 'And did you find the necklace?'

'I believe this is the one,' she said as she opened her daughter's jewellery box to reveal the orange stick man pendant.

Hingston had expected her to say no, given he'd convinced himself Emily, like Sheila Baptist, would have been wearing it obsessively.

She lifted it out of the box that contained a tangle of other chains, cords, pendants, chokers and dress rings. The stick man was placed carefully on the top.

'How often did she wear this?' Hingston asked as he felt the cool pendant and ascertained it was not plastic. It was a type of semi-precious stone.

'If jewellery was not routinely confiscated by the school, she would have worn the ugly thing there, I'm sure. Look. I've told your colleague, I don't know who gave it to her. Someone with atrocious taste, clearly.'

'Do you know what this figure is?' He pointed at the stick man.

'No idea,' she said.

Hingston examined the small beads which were also coloured stone and the large, modern clasp. There were no markings to identify a designer and the quality of the carving of the stick man was quite basic. He didn't say so, but the gift giver *did* have atrocious taste.

'So, if there are friends of Emily who you're confident *wouldn't* give her this necklace and she didn't buy it for herself, do you know of anyone who potentially *could* have bought it for her?' Hingston hoped some names may be forthcoming.

'I know you were interested to check whether Emily was under a consultant,' Mrs Britton batted her eyelids whilst re-engaging her challenging look, 'so if you're thinking Dr Olson gave it to her, I suggest you talk straight with me.' Her nostrils flared and she held her chin up.

'Emily and Dr Olson were in communication by mobile phone two days ago. It is possible he gave her the necklace, but it is also possible someone else did. That is why any persons you can name would be helpful,' Hingston appealed.

Mrs Britton was now livid. Her eyes were wide and her colour was rising beneath her soft tan foundation. 'My daughter is missing and she's speaking with her fucking gynaecologist!' She rose and snatched her cigarette pack from the countertop, lighting up whilst talking through the cigarette. 'Bastard! Abduction!' She took a deep drag on her cigarette and waved it about in anger. 'I said kidnap from the start. Why aren't you arresting him?'

'I was going to discuss Dr Olson a bit later. Importantly, Emily has since spoken with Chloe Dandridge. That was around midday yesterday. You know Chloe?' he checked.

'Yes.' She spat the word, still furious, and glared at him.

'Emily told Chloe she was fine. She asked Chloe to stop calling.'

'Is she with that fucking pervert now?' Mrs Britton raised her eyebrows and grasped her hair, infuriated by Dr Olson. 'Because if she is, she's not fine. You should be *arresting* him! Why haven't you arrested him?' She took another drag on her cigarette.

'Dr Olson has died.' Hingston watched her eyes. She looked confused and her colour faded.

'So, where is Emily?'

'Her phone has been switched off since she spoke to Chloe, so we are unable to trace her, unfortunately,' Hingston said. He was not going to discuss the circumstances of Dr Olson's death.

Mrs Britton stood with one hand shaking in front of her mouth and her cigarette burning away in the other. 'If Emily said she was fine, then she can't know Dr Olson is dead, then?' Her tone was soft and she contemplated her thoughts whilst her eyes scanned the kitchen units back and forth. 'Assuming she...' Mrs Britton frowned hard. 'But if he abducted her... and now he's *dead*, she wouldn't have been phoning Chloe, saying she's fine... she would've been calling me... or the police... or just getting herself back home...' Tears started to appear, quivering above her lower lids and bubbling over in streams that pulled mascara and eyeliner into long grey streaks. Mrs Britton's aggression and business exec pomp were disintegrating just as rapidly. She finally behaved like a mother who cared.

Hingston got up, opened the window and reached for the lead crystal ashtray.

'No, I'll get it,' she said and snatched it from his hand. Her eyelids were beginning to go blotchy and as she stubbed her cigarette out, she lost grip of the ashtray. It spun upside down and smashed onto her Versace tiles with a sprinkling of ash and three broken pieces of crystal skimmed to a standstill several feet away. 'Urrghh,' she wailed. 'Pathetic,' she sobbed.

Hingston studied her face and then the floor. There was a fracture in the tile where the ashtray had fallen.

Mrs Britton was dabbing her eyes with a tissue when she sat back down at the breakfast bar. The morning was passing by and Hingston had not envisaged spending so much time in her company. However, she appeared more amenable now and she presented a diary on the countertop.

'Emily's diary. I'm not happy to have read this. I'm even less happy to show *you*. I only discovered it this morning.' She opened the bright pink 2012 day per page diary and turned to Saturday the 1st of December. In red biro was a torrent of words that interlocked like a bizarre combination of *Scrabble* and an incomplete jigsaw puzzle. A professional artist would have struggled to create such a detailed impression of a disturbed mind. The page was almost entirely red. The word "PANIK" was scribed both horizontally and vertically, sometimes two lines deep, sometimes minute and it was heavily overwritten which had caused deep indentations such that the page had thinned in numerous places. The ink smelled strong. It looked like an intricate doodle that had taken hours to grow into an intense pattern and between the primary word "PANIK" other small words were dispersed. Statements could be made out: "I PANIK", "I become PANIK", "I am PANIK". Emily's text message sent to Chloe and Harry came to mind, but Hingston couldn't remember the exact wording. He would check once back at the station. It definitely contained "I PANIK" because that was the spelling error her friends had homed in on. Clearly it was no error at all. Was it instead a nickname?

Mrs Britton spoke in a brusque tone. 'You know that's the day Leanna Snow died? The 1st of December?' Her arrogance had returned. 'It's obviously upset her.'

'Yes, I am aware of that,' Hingston said. What he didn't want to highlight to Mrs Britton was the question mark that now hung over the order of events. Yes, Leanna Snow died on Saturday. The school assembly was Monday morning. Emily went missing at lunchtime on Monday. If she had only found out about Leanna Snow at the assembly, she would have returned home to spend considerable time using the red biro before going missing from home. Hingston suspected the page was graffitied *before* Monday. Perhaps Emily knew about the death before the school's announcement, which could explain her lack of shock, but then *how* would she have known? *Or* the diary entry did not relate to Leanna Snow and the date was coincidental. 'May I take a photograph of this page?' Hingston asked.

'If you must,' she replied. 'Don't ask me why she's misspelt panic,' she added.

'It's an unusual style of doodling,' Hingston remarked whilst taking the picture on his phone. 'Does Emily have any other doodles like this in her diary?'

'No.' Mrs Britton flicked through the pages and the neat handwriting was not decorated with anything bearing resemblance to that of the 1st of December. The ink was black elsewhere with not a trace of red biro.

'What does Emily normally write about?' Hingston probed.

'She's a teenage girl. I'm not going to give you the details of her private thoughts. *I* shouldn't even be looking at this.' Mrs Britton was taking the privacy matter too far in Hingston's opinion. He said nothing, prompting her to comment.

'School. A bit of opinion or gossip about other kids. Teenage angst. Nothing that gives rise to concern. I've skimmed enough of it. There's *nothing* about *anything* of significance.' Mrs Britton wiped her nose and sniffed. 'What I did want to show you was this train ticket to Cambridge. Emily and I are both independent types. I've brought her up that way. *But,*' she paused for additional emphasis, '*but*, I would have expected her to have told me about a day out in Cambridge.' Mrs

Britton placed the ticket in front of Hingston with a click on the granite and touched its surface twice as if she were confronting Emily with it instead. The date was in October. 'This was a Saturday when she said she was studying at Harry Whitson's, but clearly not.'

'That's the Harry she used to go out with?' Hingston checked.

'Used to?' baulked Mrs Britton. 'She *is* as far as I'm concerned.' Her tongue was pressing out her top lip again and it began to annoy Hingston.

Hingston shifted in his seat and presumed she was wrong. DC Coleridge's assessment returned to his thoughts. 'Does Harry feature in her diary?'

'No, but it's not that sort of diary. She sees plenty enough of him and need not waste her time daydreaming or writing mush. I've not brought her up to be soppy.'

Hingston realised Mrs Britton's opinion of men was lower than he had first thought.

'Emily only writes about the girls. She'll make a superb psychologist. She's very emotionally aware and incredibly observant.'

'Is that her aspiration?' Hingston seized the opportunity to find out more about Emily's interests and her personality.

'Oh, very much so.' Mrs Britton smiled. 'She already gives some very mature and sound advice.'

'Does Leanna Snow get mentioned in her diary by any chance?' Hingston was becoming curious.

'Yes. *Not* very flattering, but Emily will be Emily: very direct.'

Another result of how she was brought up, Hingston thought. 'Can you show me that section?' he asked.

'No. It's irrelevant to her going missing. It was written months ago. No,' she reiterated.

Hingston wondered if Emily was bullying Leanna or perhaps vice versa. The girls *were* connected by the words "insignificant pathetic"; albeit the offending pencil case could not be validated as it was in the school bag Emily went missing with.

'Going back to the ticket to Cambridge,' Hingston tried another angle, 'do you think she went with Harry?'

'Obviously I don't, otherwise why would I bother to show you the ticket? If she'd snuck off there with her boyfriend, I wouldn't have anything to worry about.'

Hingston gave her a puzzled look.

Mrs Britton rolled her eyes. 'Who's the detective here?' she scoffed and produced her phone. 'Facebook. October the thirteenth. Saturday. Harry Whitson's account. Evidence! Rugby tournament. *Ealing*. Not Cambridge and no sign of Emily in any of the photographs.'

'So, is Emily in Harry's more recent posts?' Hingston knew it would be unlikely and awaited Mrs Britton's reaction.

'Look for yourself.' She handed him the phone. There Emily was on a number of occasions, but so were numerous other teenagers, including Chloe. There was no public reference to him being in a relationship with Chloe, or Emily, or with anyone for that matter. No cosy boyfriend/girlfriend pictures had been posted. They all looked like mates; it was impossible to say if anyone was going out with anyone.

'Mrs Britton. I've spoken with Harry and Chloe. They've told me they are a couple and that Harry and your daughter ended their relationship in October twenty-eleven.'

'Emily is not a liar,' Mrs Britton shouted, slamming Emily's diary on the countertop. 'She would have told me if they'd split up.'

Hingston looked at the ticket which suggested otherwise.

Her eyes were welling up. 'Not that fucking Dr Olson. You think she went to Cambridge with him!' She slammed Emily's diary down again and it ricocheted off the breakfast bar into the ash and lead crystal that had been swept into a pile by the fridge. The bright pink cover was face up and the A4 pages had splayed out; all were bent and buckled underneath.

'Mrs Britton,' Hingston appealed, 'we cannot say it was Dr Olson she was with in Cambridge nor that he was responsible for her going missing. That is why any names you have of other associates would be very useful, please.' Hingston thought the head teacher's presence would have been a helpful calming mechanism at this juncture; he had managed to control her with his smooth and jolly pronunciation of "Mrs B". Hingston was not going to venture there and remained quiet.

Mrs Britton stood up and collected the diary, leaving behind on the floor a couple of pieces of paper which had previously been wedged between the pages. 'Sorry,' she said. 'I'm struggling to handle the situation. If her father hadn't divorced me to go and live in Australia when she was seven—never to bother with us again, I must add—I doubt Emily would have experienced her self-harming issues. I'm confident she would have had *no* interest in Dr Olson and she wouldn't be missing now.'

Hingston was empathetic. However, he was distracted by the papers that lay amongst the ash. 'It's okay,' he said. 'When Emily spoke with Chloe yesterday, she sounded herself. Her last known location was Islington so she's not gone very far. The public will be seeing her face on social media appeals and at localised bus stops as of this morning. Someone will recognise her and phone in. Maybe she will return of her own accord before then.'

Mrs Britton nodded and bent down to retrieve the papers. 'These must have fallen out of Emily's diary,' she stated.

'Yes, they did,' Hingston confirmed.

'How... oh...' Mrs Britton screwed up her nose and turned the papers over. A bright yellow tri-fold leaflet entitled "The House of Life" glared even more intensely into the room than Mrs Britton did at it. She slapped it onto the countertop. The second paper was a folded piece of A4. She opened it with a sharp whipping noise, huffed and then remained silent. 'Why have this?' she said and turned it toward Hingston. It was an article printed off the internet. The headline read: "Eight-year-old chokes to death".

'How?' asked Hingston.

'On marshmallows,' she said, bemused. 'How obscure.'

Chapter Six
Do You Hear What I Hear?

Hingston closed the front gate with a squeak and a clink of the latch. Mrs Britton's statement, Emily's diary, the internet news article and "The House of Life" leaflet, were all in his possession. The blue sky of the morning had begun to accumulate delicate clouds which were radiant and fluffy like those depicted on the ceilings of Renaissance chapels. Hingston's eyes moistened in the chill as he strode along the pavement to his unmarked police car. The street was long and he had been forced to park some distance away from the Brittons' address due to the "residents only" bays and the number of vehicles that crowded this busy Acton road.

He unlocked the Astra and opened the boot which was grimy due to the winter roads and the Murder Squad's neglect. The number plate had been given a good polish by some officer whose token effort had at least ensured the vehicle complied with the law.

Hingston looked across the road as he slammed the boot shut, securing Emily's property and her mother's statement inside. The semi-detached house opposite looked as neglected as the Astra and contrasted greatly with those at the Brittons' end of the street. As he looked at the flaking paintwork on the fascia boards and the cracks in the pebble-dash that reached down the side of the house like forked lightning, he noticed an equally tired car on the driveway. *Hotel Victor Five...* began the registration plate. It was a silver saloon.

Hingston called the Incident Room from the privacy of his driver's seat.

'Afternoon, Caryl,' said Hingston on recognising the assistant investigator's Welsh accent. 'Jason Hingston here.'

'Hi Jason,' she replied cheerfully. As a member of police staff, Caryl Pugh did not use his rank when speaking with him. 'How can I help?'

'Has the silver saloon been identified yet?' Hingston tapped his fingers on the steering wheel.

'No. We're working through the CCTV presently,' she said.

'Can you do me a check on a silver Ford Mondeo, Hotel Victor Five One Charlie Echo Tango.'

'I'll read that back to you,' Caryl said, 'Hotel Victor Five One Charlie Echo Tango. Ford Mondeo.'

'Correct,' Hingston stated and he waited for her to run the details through the Police National Computer database.

'Registered keeper is an Adrian Marchant, date of birth the third of February, nineteen forty-nine. I'll just find out a bit more...'

Hingston could hear Caryl's keyboard keys tapping and muffled voices from the office.

'Jason?'

'Yes?'

'Marchant's not known to us,' she confirmed. 'Anything else?'

'Yes. The vehicle's parked on the drive of sixty-eight Northbourne Road, Acton. Can you check that for me? Thanks.'

'Okay, just a mo,' she chirped. 'Sixty-eight Northbourne Road, you say?'

'That's the one.' Hingston looked at the semi. It was the shabby side of the partnership. The adjoining neighbour had double glazed units, a cleaned roof, a red ribboned wreath on their black front door and a Christmas tree that was visible through their downstairs bay window. In terms of festivity at Number 68, there was none.

'Right. Are you ready?' Caryl asked.

'Yep. What have we got?' Hingston said as he noticed a dim light visible through the stained glass in the old front door of 68.

'No warning markers. Burglary in October this year. Reported by a Hugh Marchant, date of birth the seventeenth of March nineteen eighty-one. Son of the owner of the vehicle perhaps?' said Caryl. 'No other crimes or incidents at the address. Hugh Marchant, no other records for him.'

'Thanks, Caryl. I'm going to see if anyone's in. I'll be back to the station after that,' Hingston advised.

'Okay, take care. See you later.'

Hingston took another look at the semi and returned to the boot to get out his public protection equipment and to notify the Control Room of his whereabouts.

Bulked out with his stab vest over his plain clothes, he approached the silver Mondeo and peered inside. Mud could be seen in the front and back nearside footwells. There was a jacket tossed on the parcel shelf. A sticker of a golden retriever was smiling at him above a National Trust membership badge. *Dog walking mud or cemetery mud?* Hingston thought.

As he approached the front door, he heard a growl which sounded drawn out and pained. He pressed the doorbell and stepped back a few feet. The howl that followed startled him. There was no sign of anyone coming to the door. He stepped around to the bay window and looked through the glass that was dusty and smeared from London's rain and the buffeting of foliage from the holly tree that had grown too large for the garden. Traces of birds' mess contributed to the filth. He could not see the dog which growled again with a high-pitched whine at the end. He knocked on the window to try to attract it into sight, but to no avail. Animal cruelty was not a possibility he had anticipated when crossing the street.

Hingston rang the doorbell again and it caused a scuffle to be heard in the hallway. He bent down to the letterbox below the stained glass and pushed it open, keeping his hand on the door and his thumb well back along the length of the letterbox. The dog did not fling itself towards him or snarl or snap, but a foul, nauseating stench hit his face. As he dropped the letterbox back into place there was another growl, but this time it sounded more like a heave.

Shielding his nose and mouth with his sleeve, Hingston opened the letterbox and looked inside. Twisted awkwardly and looking up at him was the swollen face of a man coloured the most garish yellow. Sunken eyes squinted through lashings of this dazzling substance which had smudged over his palms and the walls. His body was thrown across the floor like a broken marionette and knotted in agony. His mouth was open, grimacing wildly, and his tongue was peppered with powdery dots of golden canary yellow. Hingston watched him scratching at the carpet which was sodden and odorous. The man let out another growl as Hingston spoke to the Control Room to expedite an ambulance and assistance from the nearest police units.

***

Uniformed officers entered first. Access was gained via the bay window into the lounge which looked like it had been left untouched since October's burglary. They navigated their heavy boots around the delirious male and the bodily fluids that surrounded him in order to open the front door for the ambulance crew.

The incoherent man was presumed to be thirty-one-year-old Hugh Marchant. The house was now full of voices which were interrupted by his coughing or drowned out by his groans and painful, strangled wails. Above the commotion, occasional Airwave bleeps could be heard. Hingston gloved up in the lounge to help locate the origin of the yellow substance that covered the man's face and had entered his mouth. He glanced through the smashed windowpane at the emergency lights which spun relentlessly outside the address and at a nosy passer-by, who was being moved on by a constable.

Upstairs, in a bathroom that clattered with the sound of a vintage extractor fan fixed into the window, Hingston saw a splash of yellow on the floor. Around the corner, a spatula coated in the viscous, messy gloop was discarded on the floor, having dripped all over the handbasin. On one side of the taps was a bottle of artists' linseed oil and the other side had been used like a palette. A film of the yellow substance coated the ceramic and a brush had rolled into the sink. Hingston looked down into an open bin which contained used tissues that glowed with traces of yellow. He lifted the bin and gave it a shake. Something heavy was at the bottom. He removed the tissues, placing them into an evidence bag and revealed a small jar with a dusting of yellow powder inside. It was labelled "Orpiment Pigment". A skull and crossbones, were printed above the words "Acute toxicity".

Hingston alerted the ambulance crew which confirmed their diagnosis of poisoning. They were hurrying to decontaminate the man's mouth, face and hands prior to their rush to hospital.

***

The afternoon was ablaze with activity. Barry's team descended upon 68 Northbourne Road; Hingston returned to Hampstead to find High Tech Crime had completed their work on Emily Britton's laptop; a large number of Olson's associations had been identified during the morning—a credit to PC Stoker's caring manner with his widow; most of the investigative team were now engaged in speaking with those associations; Olson's addresses were being searched and Smythe had scheduled a debrief for six p.m. to review the day's developments.

Hingston discovered Remi was one of those tasked with victim lifestyle enquiries when he saw her Post-it Note affixed to his computer screen. Her curly handwriting read: "With Olson's secretary. I'll see you before 5".

To get intelligence checks completed for his return, Hingston had already phoned in the name of the House of Life organisation or society or whatever type of group it was. To his frustration, there was no trace.

The yellow leaflet itself supplied no details of the author, no points of contact and no means of seeking further information. There was limited text inside and based on its amateur appearance it could have been created by Emily for a non-important classroom exercise. Mrs Britton, typically, had no idea. He decided his priority was an internet search. If nothing could be found, he would make an enquiry with the school.

All websites on the first page of the search results related to Dante Gabriel Rossetti's sonnets about love and intimate relationships. They formed a collection that went by the same title as the leaflet. Hingston skim-read some of the pages. Nothing appeared relevant to the leaflet, the content of which he found quite perplexing:

The "Principles of the House of Life" were displayed on the yellow paper in a bullet point list and read "Love", "Protect", "Harness"—points that could tenuously be linked to Rossetti, followed by "Believe", "Communicate", "Revive" and "Justice". On the centre page a series of requirements were displayed in large, italic font with some words emboldened:

All welcomed to the House of Life uphold these principles.

***They** are achievers. They **commit**. They reap the reward. They **respect** their position. They **tread, swallow** and **inhale** in **selfless** pursuit of all that is **right**.*

It was the last line that Hingston read more than once with a strange constriction in his throat and an image of a mouth filled with wet marshmallow and another stained yellow with orpiment.

He continued to scroll through the internet search results and found a detox spa in St Ives that was clearly unconnected, as was a rescue centre for sloths in South America. He stared at the very next webpage summary and knew he had found something relevant. He read it aloud: '"The House of Life was an *Ancient Egyptian* institution where *magical rituals* were performed"…'

He turned his attention back to the leaflet. On the last page were the words "Rise Rule" printed four times: a set of eight words displayed in a familiar format on a leaflet Hingston believed was anything but insignificant or pathetic.

He picked up Emily's article about the eight-year-old's marshmallow choking fatality. The footer was dated 03/11/2012, some four weeks prior to Leanna Snow's death. How could this be coincidental? On the balance of probabilities, Hingston believed it was not. He thought back to the coffee shop. No one else was sat with Leanna on the bench that overlooked Piccadilly. He saw that for himself. It had appeared accidental, but could it have been suicide, the method of which suggested by Emily Britton?

He remembered the text message sent by Emily to Chloe and Harry. He needed to check what else she had said besides "I PANIK". In a few clicks of the mouse Chloe's statement filled his computer screen and there it was: "I AM SORRY FOR WHAT I HAVE DONE. I

PANIK. THAT IS MY FAULT! FORGIVENESS? FORGOTTEN? WILL YOU REMEMBER". Hingston felt his chest tighten. Was Emily seeking forgiveness for Leanna Snow's death? It appeared more likely than forgiveness for being jealous about Chloe and Harry's relationship. As Chloe had explained, that was many months ago, all had been forgiven and Emily had said she didn't want to talk about it any more.

"PANIK". He focused on the persistent, off-the-wall spelling ground into Emily's diary in red biro as if she were both obsessed and scared by it. He flicked to the offending diary page. "I PANIK", "I *become* PANIK", "I *am* PANIK". He glared at those letters like Mrs Britton had glared at the leaflet. Clicking back to the internet he typed "Panik Ancient Egyptology". The results appeared. First hit: "Panik—the demon".

Chapter Seven
Are You Listening?

'Are we missing anyone, ladies and gents?' Smythe was pleased by the silence and the facial expressions that indicated not.

The briefing room was near capacity, the old windows ensured it was still agreeably cool and as he opened his mouth to continue, an ambulance siren squealed into action on Rosslyn Hill. The rush hour queue delayed its passage and Smythe's introduction. Impatiently, he waited.

'Thank you!' he complained with a frown. 'Let's crack on with this.'

A few of those in the room turned to clean pages in their notebooks and a wheeze from the back was seen to irritate Smythe who gave the knot of his tie a squeeze and fixed a stare in Barry's general direction.

'Interesting developments today. *Unexpected* developments. I'll summarise and hand over to those dealing for latest updates. Any questions, you know the drill.' Smythe turned to the Operation PYROLITE slide and clicked forward to the intelligence analyst's network chart. It had become a much more crowded visual since the version circulated this morning and

Hugh Marchant's name and his father's silver saloon were the latest additions.

'Sven Olson's widow has provided details of his relatives, friends and colleagues. A number of those colleagues were also identified by his personal secretary. The names, et cetera, of his patients have also been requested and presently remain outstanding. Therefore, only Emily Britton and Sheila Baptist are shown on the network chart.' Smythe pointed toward the screen. 'We have identified our suspect vehicle. DS Hingston with his bloodhound characteristics… no, not in looks… well…' Smythe spotted Remi frowning at him, feigned a deep laugh and curtailed his joke. 'DS Hingston located the vehicle on the driveway of a house on the *same road* as Emily Britton's home address. Inside the house was a Hugh Marchant, aged thirty-one, who is believed to have made an attempt on his own life. *Potentially*, he did so as a result of his involvement in Olson's death and he has become our prime suspect. We also have the *presently* unidentified *House of Life* shown here on the chart linked to Emily Britton.' Smythe paused and could see everyone was up with him. They were all studying the branch that connected the seventeen-year-old misper with the mysterious House of Life.

Smythe explained: 'The House of Life appears to be some form of ideology related to an interest in Ancient Egyptian magical practice. Potentially, a group of individuals are linked to this ideology. We are not saying this is a religious group or a cult, but we must be alert to the possibility. Whatever we are dealing with, the House of Life may be linked to Olson's murder; to the chosen location of the Egyptian Avenue and to the wax located nearby.' Smythe paused and saw Barry nodding like he belonged on a car parcel shelf. 'Barry. Anything you'd like to say about the wax at this point?'

Barry cleared his throat. He was buzzing with anticipation and his slow voice was pitched noticeably higher than normal. 'Yes. The wax has been tested and found to be beeswax. Without jumping *too far* ahead, the address we attended this afternoon, that of Hugh Marchant, *that* address had four small wax figures on a shelf in the lounge. Each is poorly sculpted and each has four wicks to speed up the time in which it takes the figure to melt. They have been seized and we will be testing the wax to confirm whether it is an identical match.'

There was a note of interest hummed by someone in the audience.

'Black magic,' continued Barry just before a faint wheeze escaped from his narrowed airways, 'black magic, like I said *yesterday*, does involve the melting of wax. *Another* consideration: if our little pool of wax in the cemetery was originally a figure, made presumably to represent Olson, *who* do the other four figures represent?'

There was no note of interest hummed at this remark. Instead, breaking the silence, a hushed utterance of '*God*,' was heard as Caryl put her hand to her mouth and pulled a face. Raised eyebrows was the response offered from the person sat next to her.

'Back to the agenda,' said Smythe. 'Hugh Marchant will be discussed shortly. The House of Life came to our attention in the form of a leaflet located in Emily Britton's diary. Correct me if I'm wrong, DS Hingston, but this leaflet is not known to Mrs Britton or the school?'

'That's what I have been told, sir,' Hingston replied.

Smythe introduced a photograph on the screen that showed the leaflet with its three internal sections facing out. 'It's best you explain your observations from here,' prompted Smythe. 'Tell us about Marchant at the same time,' he instructed.

'Okay, I'll read out the content as it is a bit small for those of you at the back,' Hingston began. Afterwards, he proceeded to share his deductions, highlighting the marshmallow choking article, the likelihood that Emily had some involvement in the circumstances of Leanna Snow's death and Emily's diary entry in which she obsessed that she is "the demon".

At this point, the hushed exclamation earlier made by Caryl was replaced with the baritone reaction of another investigator: 'Fucking hell.'

'What we need to ascertain is,' Hingston continued, 'if the House of Life exists as a body of people, how many are involved? What is their perceived and *actual* purpose? How do they communicate? Where do they meet? What *is* Emily's role in it, *exactly*? Aside from living down the same road as each other, can we evidence a link between Hugh Marchant and Emily? He has wax figures in his possession as Barry explained. He was found today at his home address suffering from acute arsenic poisoning which was the result of ingesting orpiment pigment and painting it onto his face.'

'An arsenic compound,' Barry chipped in. 'Arsenic sulphide to be precise. Bright yellow it is. Like that bizarre leaflet.'

Hingston continued. 'Hugh Marchant *is* alive and receiving hospital treatment. He has not yet been arrested and it is too early for the hospital to give a prognosis.' Hingston glanced at Remi who was staring at Smythe. 'His father's car is the silver saloon suspect vehicle. In the last hour, it was found on the CCTV trawl, driving through Highgate Village on the night of Olson's murder, heading toward the cemetery.'

'Good work,' encouraged Smythe even though he was already aware of this.

Hingston nodded. 'Marchant's mother was contacted as next of kin. She volunteered she was in Yorkshire visiting friends for the week and said her husband, Adrian Marchant, was with her. They live in Cambridge. She alleged their son had borrowed the silver saloon from them a number of months ago and said he lives alone. We are not yet in a position to eliminate Adrian Marchant or Linda Marchant from the enquiry.'

Smythe cleared his throat. 'Marchant's poisoning,' he said. 'The house was secure, no one else was inside when officers entered and so far, we have no evidence of third party involvement. The question is, were the parents in Yorkshire on the night of Olson's murder or not? Tomorrow we will be speaking with them.'

'Cambridge,' Hingston continued, 'where Marchant's parents live, is also of note. Emily Britton travelled to Cambridge on Saturday the thirteenth of October. Her mother became suspicious of a train ticket that she found when searching Emily's belongings. It conflicted with Emily's account that she was studying locally that day. Emily's mother appears to trust Emily to be independent and doesn't check up on her daughter's version of events. She believed her daughter had an eighteen-year-old boyfriend, but in reality they've been separated for over a year according to both the boy himself and Emily's best friend.'

'Can Mrs Britton really be that out of touch?' voiced Remi. 'I mean, kids today are much more open about their relationships. They talk about their boyfriends and sex, don't they?'

Smythe contemplated this whilst running a hand over his bald head. 'You think Mrs Britton is lying to us?' he said with his tone adjusted to something less commanding and to Hingston's ears, more *coupley*.

Remi nodded. 'It's possible.'

Hingston's recent proximity to Remi had ignited feelings of jealousy that he was trying to subdue. He looked at her and questioned whether her dilated pupils evidenced excitement about the investigation or about Smythe. Her role in the Murder Squad meant a lot to her and she'd always been passionate about policing; *must be the investigation* Hingston convinced himself.

'What's your take on Mrs Britton, DS Hingston?' Smythe commanded in his husky voice.

'Erratic. Aggressive. Detached. Unmotherly. She broke down this afternoon which convinced me she cared for Emily. At least it did so at the time,' Hingston said. 'She volunteered the diary evidence and the link to Cambridge which she needn't have done. She seemed oblivious to the presence of the House of Life leaflet and the marshmallow article that were hidden in the diary.'

Remi turned in her seat to speak to Hingston. 'But if she'd *looked* through that diary to find the Panik stuff, she would have known the article and the leaflet were in there. If they hadn't fallen out of the diary, she wouldn't have shown you. I think there's more going on with that woman. *She* could be *part of* the House of Life for all we know!' Remi blinked at Hingston and checked Smythe's reaction. He looked impressed, possibly more by her direct challenge to Hingston than her hypothesis.

Hingston returned with a counter proposal: '*If* she knew the items were in the diary, surely she would have removed them before bringing it to show me. Or, better still, she would have destroyed them.' He looked Remi in the eye. She smiled and gave him a nod to encourage him to continue. It made him think.

'Unless,' he said, 'the ticket and the diary excerpt were shared to lead us in the direction of Cambridge, to portray her daughter as an innocent child upset by Leanna Snow's death and throw further suspicion upon Olson? Initially she did refuse me access to the diary's contents. The leaflet and the article *did* appear to fall out accidentally,' Hingston recounted. 'Perhaps Mrs Britton thought she should appear helpful to avoid suspicion. Perhaps she thought she could lead us away from the House of Life *and* herself?'

'So,' Smythe said, 'we need to consider that Mrs Britton *may* be a suspect.'

Agreement was voiced by a number of the team, including Remi and Hingston.

'Emily Britton,' Smythe continued with a hint of frustration tightening his voice, 'has not turned her mobile back on, has not used her social media accounts, has not been sighted and is of concern on a number of levels. If Leanna Snow's death *was* suicide, Marchant's made his attempt today, we've got Sheila Baptist's suicide to consider, Olson's murder and Emily remaining missing, *is* Emily at risk of suicide as well? It appears she has had some involvement with the circumstances of Leanna Snow's death. Is she involved in Olson's murder?'

Noises of agreement sounded again. Hingston confirmed that he was reviewing Emily's laptop, that Remi had just begun the review of the diary and that so far, there were no leads.

'*Who* else may be involved? We're lacking suspects ladies and gents.' Smythe's voice crescendoed as he appealed for more action, but the team were already equally determined. 'Come on, Barry, dazzle us with some science! What's your latest?' Smythe gestured to him to come to the front with the casual thumb of a hitchhiker.

Barry ignored the sarcasm and presented himself with a proud smile. He stood at ease which emphasised his lanky legs and enormous boots. 'Get your Ray-Bans ready,' he responded.

Remi smiled whilst looking down at her notebook. Smythe flared his nostrils and remained straight-faced. Oddly enough, it was the typical expression he wore to compliment his Ray-Bans, but they were in his drawer awaiting the first glimmer of sunshine next spring.

'Headlines,' said Barry. 'We've found prints on the chain cutters, so our forensically aware suspect was either accompanied by a numpty or the prints belong to someone unconnected to the break-in who had their hands on them previously. Their hands were quite small and could therefore be female.' A quick cough interrupted his flow. 'Footwear. Six sets of impressions at the entrance. Olson accounts for one. The cemetery workers' footwear prints are being gathered for comparison. Surprising how many volunteers they've got,' he remarked with wide eyes. 'DNA from the scene where the struggle took place matches Olson and there is DNA from two other persons.'

'I'll stop you there, Barry,' Smythe interrupted. 'We haven't got Emily's DNA, have we?'

'No, sir,' Hingston said.

'Something for tomorrow. Caryl,' Smythe pointed, 'a call round to Mrs Britton first thing. Hairbrush for Emily. Thanks.'

'Okay, will do,' she replied.

'Right. Barry. *Continue*,' Smythe directed.

'The ligature has some green fibres attached to it. A dark, forest-green. There were a few matching fibres in the beeswax, close to one of the wicks. There happens to be a dark green jacket in the suspect vehicle. That is now at the lab. The car is still subject of examination. End of headlines. Did I *dazzle*, Rob?' Barry may have given Smythe a wink, but Hingston's mind was on Mrs Britton. He could remember the sound of the lighter she had flicked impatiently to light her cigarette. His suspicion was bubbling.

Smythe hurried the briefing along. Tomorrow was going to be busy and time for the team to unwind tonight was important. Smythe advised that house-to-house enquiries were complete. A second resident had returned home around one fifteen a.m. and saw a silver saloon travelling unduly fast down Bisham Gardens, away from Swain's Lane and the cemetery. The resident watched it pass because he believed it was going to clip one of the parked vehicles. He had seen two occupants inside the car, both of whom were male and the passenger wore glasses. Smythe celebrated this moment by giving a thumbs up to the first sighting of suspect number two and the attainment of another milestone for the chronology of events.

Nine of Olson's associates had been contacted to date; most were doctors, two of whom, a Dr Bakshi and a Dr Janesen, practiced at the White House Clinic. Their accounts were similar regarding Olson's professional life. The private practice was in its twentieth year; Olson was very well regarded and had to turn away new patients due to demand. Olson's secretary, Dr Bakshi, and Dr Janesen appeared to know the most about his personal life. They all referred to Olson's passion for reading, ancient history and playing table tennis. For the latter, Olson was a member of a local league which played every Wednesday night. The ancient history interest was to be further explored, particularly with reference to Dr Bakshi's report that Olson had attended a number of talks this year at the British Museum.

PC Stoker raised her hand when Smythe drew breath. 'Sir, Mrs Olson made no reference to table tennis.' She frowned. 'I didn't see any trophies or photographs that would corroborate those accounts.'

Remi turned round to rest her arm on the chair back. She looked at PC Stoker. Her pale green eyes were sparkling. 'When I met the secretary, she showed me the calendar she managed for Olson. Table tennis was a recurring appointment.'

'Well,' snorted Smythe, 'whatever little game Olson's *really* been playing, does it involve his patients, the House of Life, or both?'

***

"What time will you be home?" read Uncle Zack's message. He was capable of asking standalone questions by text. Hingston presumed this was because it took Zack so long to type them.

After driving out of Hampstead station's yard, Hingston telephoned Zack on the hands-free. Zack's loud voice wouldn't be heard outside his car against the noise of the main road. Nor would the voices of his parents if Zack elected to put one of them on.

'Zack!' said Hingston.

'Jason, my boy! Did you get my message? What time will you be home?'

Hingston laughed. 'Should be in by five,' he replied.

There was a pause.

'Should be in by five,' Hingston repeated.

'It's gone seven now!' laughed Zack. 'I know you're working flat out, but wakey, wakey,' he chortled.

Hingston was stationary at a set of lights. 'I'm talking about tomorrow. I'll be back with plenty of time for us to eat before the Magic Circle open their doors,' he said and took a glance into the vehicle alongside him that was waiting to turn left. The driver was Barry. He was talking and nodding, or possibly singing. Hingston didn't stare.

Uncle Zack laughed. His timing amused Hingston. 'Jason, I text you this morning to say I was returning a day early. So, I'm in your house, dinner's prepared, table's laid, cheese and port are sitting here temptingly…'

Hingston cut in with a groan. 'I didn't see your text. Sorry. I'll be back for eight. One of those days! Sorry. It'll be great to see you. Saves me getting fish and chips as well,' he teased.

'Yes, not the same as my Dartmouth chippie either!' replied Zack. 'How you Londoners live without the sea air!'

Hingston continued to think about Dartmouth on his way home and it didn't take long into their fillet steak dinner for him to get onto the subject.

'I thought I'd visit you for New Year if that suits?' Hingston said.

'That would be wonderful. The last time you did that…'

'Yes. I brought Remi with me.' Hingston stabbed a sauté potato and hurried it into his mouth.

Zack looked at him. 'Any chance that might happen again this year?' His optimistic tone was dropped for his second question. 'Or is she still putting up with bald, old Ken?'

Hingston laughed through the piece of steak that had just joined the potato. 'Bald, old Ken,' he said having taken a gulp of water, 'otherwise known as *Rob* Smythe, has just paired his fake tan with a set of bleached teeth. His attempt to impress *Barbie* has backfired. But on a serious note, Remi and *Rob* will be there tomorrow night. So, don't call him Ken. And don't expect to see Remi for New Year or next year or any time with me.' Hingston sighed. 'Sorry. We're both working together as of this week and it's pissing me off.'

Zack lowered his glass of wine. 'Jason! Working together is a Christmas gift come early! Mark my words, my boy, enjoy her company, don't behave disgruntled, remind her what she's missing and Remi will be watching those New Year fireworks in Dartmouth instead of London.' Zack stared at Hingston who was not sharing his optimism. 'I'm looking forward to tomorrow night,' Zack said. He smiled and rubbed his hands together. 'Can't beat a bit of magic before Christmas.'

Hingston's eyes dropped to the candle flame that flickered between them. It had lit the pool of wax which surrounded the wick and slivers of gold danced in the reflections. Hingston watched the pool tremble as it released its first tear to roll down the edge. *Magic*, he thought.

Chapter Eight
Later on, We'll Conspire

'Ooh, Jason. Look at this.' Remi beckoned him round to her desk.

On her computer screen was the photograph of a turquoise-coloured rectangular grid. 'This is senet. An Ancient Egyptian board game.'

Hingston could see basic symbols on some of the squares and small playing pieces were dotted across it.

'Emily mentions senet on this page of her diary. *Wednesday* the twelfth of September. Says she loves senet. No other comments. Olson's alternative to table tennis?' she hypothesised.

'Mmm.' Hingston contemplated Remi's suggestion. 'Bit of a jump at this stage. See what else Emily has to say further ahead, but we've certainly got something to link to the House of Life.'

Remi gave him a knowing smile. 'And look at this…' She pointed back to the board game and zoomed out. The board was in fact a box with deep sides. It wasn't simply coloured turquoise: it was made of turquoise and Hingston saw a pattern painted on the side in black.

'*That's* the stick man,' he exclaimed. It was subtly more curvaceous than the pendant design, but otherwise identical. There were four of them on one side of the box, interspersed with something that resembled a palm tree.

'We need to find out what that stick man represents,' said Remi before Hingston could say as much.

***

The room was of modest proportions, yet Hingston felt overwhelmed and apprehensive, as if he were entering a labyrinth. The weak lighting and restricted airflow were inducing this condition, no doubt, but the artefacts that crowded the long, tall cabinets were so immense in volume and unfamiliar in nature that they were bewildering.

The archaeological treasures from Ancient Egypt were held back behind glass and secured within countless rows of shallow drawers. Fragments of pottery, vases and vessels, beaded jewellery, rings, amulets, combs, miniature figurines and hoards of tiny unrecognisable items filled shelves to capacity. Chunks of decorated masonry and damaged statues provided glimpses of deities, scenes of prosperity and an abundance of hieroglyphs. Patches of faded colours clung to once vibrant surfaces, yet a striking beauty was still retained in their carved designs.

Faces with bold eyes and immortal presence stared stoically from death masks, canopic jars, statues and reliefs, delivering every sense of the power and mystery conjured by the grandeur of the pyramids and the reign of the pharaohs.

Except here, stood in the Petrie Museum, with the present-day House of Life lurking in the London shadows, Hingston enjoyed little of that romanticism. It was being lost to a dark, undefined threat that appeared to have taken root within the sinister side of Ancient Egyptian practice. Slowly it was creeping into the peripherals of Hingston's consciousness, seeping into the silence.

'Good afternoon.' A well-spoken woman interrupted and greeted Hingston with a smile. 'Apologies for keeping you waiting. I'm Natasha, the curator. My colleague didn't make a note of your name.' She outstretched her hand.

'Jason Hingston, Detective Sergeant,' he replied with a handshake.

'If you'd like to follow me, I have a private office through here.' Natasha was an elegant academic, probably in her mid-forties. Her slender build and good posture combined with her sharply tailored black dress and designer glasses presented a youthful appearance. Like Hingston she was tall and she led the way with soft, vivacious footsteps which allowed no time to look at the artefacts en route. 'Can I get you a tea or coffee?' she asked once inside her office. She pushed a loose honey-blonde curl behind her ear. Her long hair was fashioned into a French plait that was tucked in on itself, disguising its length.

'No, I'm fine, thanks,' Hingston replied. 'I shan't keep you too long.'

'Not a problem. How can I assist?'

Hingston hung his coat over the back of a chair and sat down. 'A current investigation involves a missing teenager. She appears to have an interest in Ancient Egyptology. To help us locate her, we want to find out more about a necklace she owns and understand certain things she has written down. We hope an expert opinion will provide an important insight we presently lack.' Hingston placed his notebook and pen on Natasha's desk. 'This is the necklace she owns,' he said as he passed his mobile to Natasha to show a photograph of the stick man pendant.

Natasha displayed instant recognition and looked straight back at Hingston. 'That is an Isis knot design. It is a modern piece. The Isis knot looks like it is made of carnelian, a semi-precious stone commonly used in Ancient Egypt. Do you want to know about its symbolism? I can't tell you about the origin of the girl's necklace; it could have been made anywhere, I'm afraid.'

'The symbolism would be good to understand,' Hingston confirmed.

'Okay. Isis is a goddess. She is associated with faithful love, motherhood, childbirth and is often depicted holding her son, Horus. Additionally, Isis was a powerful sorceress and a protector. This leads me on to the Isis knot itself, also called the *tyet*.'

Hingston was jotting down key words as she spoke. She waited for him to finish, gave the spelling of *tyet* and continued. 'You will find amulets, such as that belonging to the girl, were used for protection. Knots were believed to bind magic. Isis knots had funerary uses and were also associated with pregnancy. They were used to protect and assist in the rebirth of the dead into the afterlife and to prevent miscarriages for those being born into this world. Some scholars refer to the Isis knot as a girdle-knot, some say it depicts a protective belt used by pregnant women or a cloth used whilst menstruating and another interpretation is that it depicts the female sexual organs.' Natasha paused. 'Is this too much detail?' she asked with her wide blue eyes magnified by her glasses.

Hingston was writing "sexual organs" and the saintly image of Olson, the revered gynaecologist, was persisting in his mind. 'No, the detail is helpful. Please carry on.'

'Carnelian, the red or orange stone that I believe this Isis knot is made of, was also of significance to the Ancient Egyptians. Firstly, carnelian was used for its magical properties to enhance love, passion and desire. It appears in amulets of various designs.'

For Hingston, it was now that Olson plummeted from physician, possible pervert, to predator.

Natasha spoke softly and swiftly. 'The red colour also occurs in the semi-precious stone jasper and both jasper and carnelian were thought to protect the wearer from bleeding. Hence its protection against miscarriages. Both stones were common materials for Isis knots. I think it's important to note here that the lines between magic and medicine were blurred in Ancient Egypt. *This* necklace is a positive, let's say, *holistic* item.'

'Okay,' said Hingston, not entirely convinced.

'The colour red, however, applied in its broadest sense, could have completely different connotations,' Natasha added. 'Red was also the colour of evil, so they used red ink to write curses. But here I digress,' she said and appeared apologetic. She smiled. 'Do you have any questions?'

Hingston visualised Emily's extraordinary diary entry for the 1st of December. The deeply indented red biro with its frantic repetition of "Panik", otherwise known as "the demon", haunted him with a new, vile aggression. 'We've done a bit of our own investigative work online and would like to check a few things. As regards the knot of Isis, or rather, the *Isis knot*,' Hingston corrected himself, 'no further questions. You've been very informative.'

Natasha clasped her hands together and leant forward on her desk.

'So,' Hingston continued, 'our missing teenager is very interested in senet. Is it still played today?' He gave her a doubtful look.

'The original rules are unknown so it would be an interpretation of the game. Some suggestions for play can be found online. It's by no means a popular game. An unusual choice for a teenager,' she remarked with a frown.

'I saw a board online decorated with the Isis knot,' Hingston said.

'The Isis knot isn't a standard part of the design. I'm unaware of any particular association between it and the game.' Natasha frowned again. Her lines showed her age.

Hingston could tell she was considering something, so he remained silent.

'Of course, the Isis knot and its association with rebirth does *make sense* here because senet was not just played by the living, it was one of the challenges presented to the dead on their journey to the afterlife. The *Book of the Dead* refers to it.' Natasha looked at Hingston for his next prompt, unsure if he wanted to know more.

Hingston did not like the sound of the *Book of the Dead* and did not stop himself from expressing it facially. 'The Ancient Egyptian fascination with death has always put me off learning much about them,' he admitted.

'Well, their desire to survive in the afterlife was the focus of their Earthly existence. Senet, by the Middle Kingdom, was played *with* the dead. It was a way to engage with family members who had been separated by death.' Natasha gave a faint smile to reassure Hingston that their belief system was not as morbid as he thought.

'Well,' said Hingston, 'if we could communicate like that with the dead now, it would make life much easier for the Murder Squad.' He laughed, but his banter fell flat with Natasha. If Remi had been here, she would have seen the funny side of it. 'Okay, back to business.' Hingston moved the discussion forward. 'We have a name that our missing teenager has referred to. It's "Panik" spelt as it sounds, but with a "K". Online it suggests this is "the demon". Is that correct?' Hingston hoped she would say it was not.

'*Oh*. That is correct, but I suppose I shouldn't express opinion here... I mean, I don't want you to think I'm being inquisitive about your investigation.' Natasha pushed her hair behind her ear again, except it had not fallen loose this time. It was a habit. 'I'm a little surprised your teenager is familiar with the name, that's all,' she said.

'I'm happy for you to express opinion,' Hingston replied. 'Don't worry, I don't think you're seeking information about the investigation,' he reassured. 'I won't tell you anything I shouldn't.' He gave her a smile and she blushed.

'Okay, in that case, I would expect scholars to know of Panik, also members of the public who are academic in pursuing their interest in Ancient Egyptology. In my opinion, your teenager is only likely to know if someone told her. It's not something one would find in regular documentaries or run-of-the-mill publications. Panik appears in the *Judicial Papyrus of Turin*.' She placed her hand on her bracelet watch and adjusted its positioning to check the time. 'I have an appointment at two thirty, but I'm available again from four if we run out of time,' she said.

'Thank you,' said Hingston whilst wondering how much Natasha had to say. His evening out at the Magic Circle also crossed his mind. 'Is Panik an integral player in this papyrus?'

'Panik was the name given to one of over thirty individuals found guilty of conspiring to assassinate Ramesses the Third. The *Judicial Papyrus of Turin* documents what is known as the Harem Conspiracy,' Natasha explained. 'The conspirators were punished and some had their real names either partly or fully changed to pseudonyms. This was not done to *protect* their identity. This was a punishment applied to *lose* their identity. As such, they *would not* be sustained in the afterlife. The term for this is *damnatio memoriae*, a Latin phrase which means a person must be erased from memory.'

Hingston nodded.

'Panik was one of the conspirators who was executed,' she continued. 'In answer to your question, Panik is not an integral player in the papyrus, but he was one of those whose actions were deemed most serious.'

Hingston had stopped writing and was busy processing the revelation he had been so unprepared for. 'This is intriguing, Natasha. So, what did Panik do to result in his execution?'

'That is where the papyrus leaves us uninformed. It's not a transcript of the trial. A lot is left unexplained. It has long been debated by scholars whether the assassination attempt was successful or not. However, very recent medical studies of Ramesses the Third's mummy indicate that he was murdered, but that report is not in the public domain just yet,' she said.

'So what do we know about the Harem Conspiracy and those who were involved in the murder? If you can give me the headlines, I'm happy to read up on it,' he added. Hingston was eager to achieve the answers he wanted before Natasha's next appointment.

'I can lend you a couple of resources from our library. In there you will get a feel for the conspirators. They were officials, people of status and women close to the pharaoh. The conspiracy was led by one of Ramesses' wives and their son was also involved. The punishments varied. Some, like Panik, were executed, others forced to commit suicide and there were mutilations.' Natasha's kind eyes scanned Hingston's straight face.

His mind was fixed on her last words and the complexities of such an investigation if forced suicide applied to Leanna Snow, Sheila Baptist and Hugh Marchant. 'Thank you, Natasha. Yes, if I could borrow those that would be fantastic,' he said and inhaled deeply. 'This is a long shot, but do the words *insignificant* and *pathetic* mean anything in the Harem Conspiracy?'

Natasha's expression froze. 'Unfortunately, yes they do,' she replied. 'I say unfortunately, not because I am averse to assisting you. It's not that at all. It's all these factors coming together in relation to your case. I'm starting to feel quite uncomfortable that a missing teenager is in some way linked to this,' Natasha explained with a troubled look in her eyes. 'I'm going to retrieve these books I'm lending you and will show you the reference to those words. Please bear with me for a few minutes.'

Hingston waited. University College London had done a better job of lighting the office, but it was just as airless as the museum itself. Bookshelves around the walls encroached into the small space and upon them a bustling secondary library existed with several statues of Egyptian gods standing guard. Despite serving as bookends, their visual strength exuded a much higher status. He recognised Horus with his falcon head and Anubis, the dark god associated with the underworld and death, whose jackal face looked ominous in black stone. It was becoming oppressive.

Natasha opened the door which carried in a waft of air. 'Here,' she said, 'you'll find a translation from *Papyrus Rollin*. This papyrus also relates to the conspirators. They are shamed in here by the *retrospective* removal of their positions of status. It's written as if they never held office.' She passed the book to Hingston, pointed to a particular line and explained, 'So, *this* conspirator is being described as *he whom God did not allow to be a scribe of the House of Life*, when in fact they *had* occupied that enviable role, possibly for many years.'

Hingston said nothing and swallowed.

'It's directly followed by the further insult, *insignificant and pathetic*. You can see the insult is repeated again further down in this section.' Natasha looked at Hingston who stared at the sentence. She was unaware it was the House of Life that held his attention. And for the rest of their meeting Hingston ensured she remained unaware of its present-day incarnation: a secret body which he now believed was actively involved in *taking life away*.

Chapter Nine
Marshmallows for Toasting

'You have a good evening too,' Remi said in her cheerful, professional tone.

Hingston heard her voice amplified from afar as he walked towards the ground floor staircase in the cold and tired Hampstead Police Station. The Petrie Museum library books were under his arm with his notebook.

'It was a pleasure,' a deep voice rumbled with gushing flamboyance.

Hingston knew it wasn't a fellow officer. Possibly it was a magistrate, except there was no reason for one to be visiting.

The man hadn't finished there. 'If all police officers were this charming, well, we'd live in a world without disorder!' He topped this with a laugh that sounded like three sharp squeezes of a vintage car horn.

'Well, thank you for the compliment.' Remi's voice had become louder since Hingston detoured away from the staircase.

'I do hope you reach a swift outcome,' the man added. 'Best of wishes,' he oozed and his tall, refined personage stepped outside just as Hingston saw he was younger and more fashionable than he sounded.

'We will do our best, Dr Yorke. Thanks again for your time,' Remi said as she closed the heavy door and Hingston visualised Dr Yorke skipping away up Rosslyn Hill.

Remi turned and saw Hingston heading in her direction. 'One of the more helpful associates of Dr Olson,' she said.

'He sounded *awfully* good and proper,' Hingston remarked. 'Trying it on a bit, wouldn't you say?'

'No. I don't think so, Jason. Seemed quite respectable to me.'

'Not another gynaecologist I hope,' Hingston laughed. 'Olson's choice of necklace was much more acceptable when I thought it was a stick man.'

***

Remi joined Hingston for an urgent meeting with Smythe. Despite the high ceiling and the generous span of Smythe's temporary office, his cologne had become noticeably stronger since the investigation kicked off on Wednesday. He was either dousing himself with it more often or it had already seeped into the fabric of the room. Whichever applied, Hingston found it as stuffy as the Petrie Museum.

'Okay. Petrie Museum visit,' Hingston began. 'There's a number of aspects to this. Main headlines: the Ancient Egyptian links we'd identified, were the tip of the iceberg, the likelihood that we're dealing with a cult has increased and forced suicide is of particular concern—Leanna Snow, Marchant, Sheila Baptist…' A raise of his eyebrows and a subtle opening of his hand indicated his speculation about further potential victims.

'Go on,' said Smythe as he repeatedly twisted his pen open and closed.

'Today's House of Life takes its name from the building where Egyptian priests would go about their daily practices which included the performance of magic. So, there's a direct link to an interest in Ancient Egyptology and to the wax figures. The words "insignificant pathetic" and the name Panik are written in specific papyrus records that relate to the assassination, or attempted assassination, of Pharaoh Ramesses the Third. This assassination plot is known as "the Harem Conspiracy".'

Smythe and Remi were both staring at Hingston. Their calm, straight faces were betrayed by eyes uncomfortable with the unknown.

'The conspirators to the murder were executed or forced to commit suicide. Mutilations were also inflicted. The conspirators were not named in the papyrus records. Instead, they were given alternative names and degrading titles, *Panik* being a prime example. The reason? So that they would be erased from memory and fail to reach the afterlife.'

Smythe huffed. 'I'm not dismissing the links. They couldn't be more obvious, *but*… why the fuck would this matter to anyone in twenty-twelve? Does this

Egyptian crap provide a motive for Olson's murder?'
Smythe shook his head.

'We're yet to ascertain that,' Hingston replied.

Smythe's colour was rising. 'A missing seventeen-year-old girl who's calling herself the demon. People being forced to commit suicide based on some ancient event that most of the population has never heard of! *What...* is Olson supposed to be the present-day Ramesses?' he ranted.

The room remained silent for a moment. 'Well, I think he's more likely to be an executed conspirator,' Remi said with a blink of her eyes that told Smythe his flippancy was unwelcome.

Hingston bridged the gap. 'I know, sir, it's all very obscure, but according to the museum curator it's evidence of an in-depth knowledge of the subject with a disturbing application. From the little I've learnt today, I believe the text message Emily sent to her school friends can now be understood.'

Smythe nodded.

'Emily was apologising for what she *had done*: presumably her involvement in the forced suicide of Leanna Snow, but potentially also for getting involved with the House of Life and other events that have stemmed from it—the extent of which we don't yet know. She names herself the demon and seeks forgiveness. However, her final words are concerning: "forgotten? Will you remember". Panik's real name was changed to erase him from memory and he was executed. Furthermore, the red ink used in Emily's diary is likely to indicate a curse. Is it likely that Emily will also be murdered, or that she is already deceased?'

Smythe leant back in his chair with such aggression it made a loud crack. He shut his eyes and massaged his forehead. 'So... do Emily's diary and laptop give us *any* leads?' he huffed.

'One last point of note from the museum, sir,' Hingston cut in, 'and this is a lead of sorts. The stick man necklace. It's a modern remake of an amulet used in ancient times. Increasing the probability that Olson gave these to Emily and Sheila, the shape relates to the female sexual organs.'

Remi glanced at Hingston and Smythe with a look of distaste.

Smythe frowned and folded his arms, his dark eyes fixed on Hingston.

'Protecting the wearer from miscarriages was one interpretation,' Hingston explained, 'and the stone it's made from was believed to magically enhance passion and desire. *According* to the curator, it's a *holistic* item.'

'Unless you're a present-day gynaecologist grooming your patients. Passion and *desire*,' Smythe scoffed. 'Noted. Remi, check whether the post mortem found Baptist to be pregnant. What else have we got?'

'I'll check. Right, it's my turn now,' Remi smiled. 'I'll start with the diary. Leanna Snow is subject of Emily's attention in early November. I'll read out a couple of the lines... "Leanna's more introverted than

I remember and becoming more pathetic by the day. Not the rebellious sort like *she* is and *Ani* will be surprised by how both have come together so quickly from such different starting points". It isn't clear who Emily is referring to as "she" because the diary focuses on a total of seventeen named girls in all,' Remi said. 'Additionally, we have this *Ani*, spelt A, N, I, who could be female or male. Possibly it's a nickname.' Remi looked perplexed. '*Ani* appears in the diary twice more. All three occurrences are on a Tuesday.'

'Right,' Smythe said and frowned.

'I wondered if Emily wrote about Ani in anticipation of meeting up with her, or him, on Wednesdays.' Remi upturned her palm and tilted her head, gauging the reactions of Smythe and Hingston.

Both men stared back, open to the possibility but unprepared to agree with this suggestion unless more evidence was offered.

'Emily appears to place herself in the inferior or subservient position when she refers to Ani. It's like Emily is the student and Ani is her teacher. It's made perfectly clear that Emily is looking to impress Ani,' Remi explained. 'Look, I'll read them to you.' She blinked with an air of impatience as she turned to the next page of her notes. 'Quote. "Ani should see how serious I am about speaking with him and how determined I am to make things right. I can convince anyone of anything! Once I've proved myself, Ani will be *impressed*". And the other entry reads "Ani was right. I will say so!"'

Smythe huffed with the loud expulsion of a long-distance runner and the crumpled face of a bad loser. 'Emily isn't helping us with all this ambiguity, Remi. She said these things *when*?'

'*October*. Before Leanna gets mentioned in conjunction with Ani.' Remi gave a stony look which Hingston and Smythe were both familiar with; she was preventing herself from swearing.

The object of her anger flared his nostrils and dropped his gaze. 'Okay,' Smythe said and adjusted his bullish tone. 'This *Ani* needs to be identified. Where have enquiries led you so far?'

Remi's eyes widened as she relaxed: satisfied she had reigned in Smythe without blurring the line between boss and boyfriend too much. She had to be careful not to speak out of turn whilst on duty and especially in the presence of other officers—even if it was only Hingston. Had she been at home she could have been as blunt as she liked. 'Okay, my enquiries. I started with Mrs Britton, but you know how useless she is. Unfortunately, the school were also unable to suggest who Ani could be. So, Ani continues to evade us at present. The school, however, did confirm the named girls are all in Emily's year group. None are close friends with Emily but they attend classes together. They were already aware of tensions between most of the girls and Emily because this stemmed from their

125

shared psychology lessons. This goes back to Emily's remark about bringing punishment with the power of the mind and her fascination with depression, self-harm, et cetera.' Remi sighed. 'Emily allegedly tried to impose her views and give *advice* to other students, generally when it was not asked for. Hence the parental complaints on Facebook and general fallings out with other kids. The diary backs that up,' she said and looked at Hingston for his corroboration.

Hingston nodded. 'Have we any indication from the school about the vulnerability of the other girls Emily has named?'

'They are looking into the safeguarding side of things and will contact us if any of the girls' records show concerns regarding self-harm or suicidal thoughts, et cetera. They didn't consider any of them to be "rebellious" as described by Emily. They haven't recorded Emily bullying any students at all. It seems her behaviour was unwanted but not belligerent,' Remi explained.

Smythe scoffed. 'So, the headstrong girls told her to bugger off and *complained* to make sure she did, whereas the vulnerable girls kept listening and said nothing—like Leanna Snow, for instance.' Smythe adjusted his tie.

'Exactly,' Remi agreed.

Hingston displayed an expression of resigned disappointment. 'Mrs Britton believes Emily will become a very successful psychologist. She thinks

Emily will enter that career path on the back of an Oxbridge degree. Sad to have such a hopeless aspiration,' he remarked. 'So, this leads me on to Emily's laptop, sir. *No* reference to Ani. Caryl has been assisting me with the review of the content so I could prioritise the visit to the Petrie Museum. I am confident Emily had every intention to keep her social activities involving Olson and the House of Life *entirely* secret. Had we not found the evidence in her paper diary, we would have drawn a complete blank from her laptop. Furthermore, her emails and social media usage give very little insight into the Emily portrayed in her diary *and* to be fair to Mrs Britton, Emily's relationship with Harry appears little different now to what it was in the past. I have the impression Emily has been very restrained and probably cunning in what she has displayed online. She hasn't used her email account greatly, so I'm assuming she uses a messaging service on her mobile phone, which of course we don't have access to.' Hingston paused and shook his head in frustration. 'Her contacts on her laptop *do not* include Hugh Marchant. There's nothing to link her to Highgate Cemetery or Olson's murder. Nor is there anything to assist in identifying her present location, be that Islington or elsewhere. Nothing has yet been found to shed more light on her train journey to Cambridge in October, so it's all becoming rather frustrating as far as Emily is concerned.'

Smythe huffed again and Remi stared with an almost bleak expression.

Hingston pursed his lips in agreement and continued: 'High Tech Crime made me aware that they have received Leanna Snow's mobile devices and her computer. They're prioritising this for us, so let's hope a link between Leanna and Ani is revealed and we start to identify suspects from that line of enquiry.'

Smythe cleared his throat and leant forward, placing his fist in the centre of his desk. His cufflink clicked against the surface and a fresh waft of cologne caught Hingston's attention. 'Emily is intelligent,' Smythe said. 'That's what we're being told by Mrs Britton and the school. We know she's cunning and secretive and her interests, or perhaps we should call them *obsessions*, are potentially dangerous. However, to be *so* savvy in the use of her social media and emails, plus her continued missing status, indicates to me that this level of "intelligence" has been *taught* by someone well versed in evading detection. She is under the control of someone who's exploited her vulnerabilities and in turn Leanna Snow's vulnerabilities, and it appears *at least one more* of those seventeen students named in Emily's diary.'

Hingston nodded. 'Caryl obtained Emily's hairbrush this morning so her DNA is now being compared to that found at Highgate Cemetery,' he confirmed. 'The search of her bedroom was also carried out this morning.'

'Yes, we'll have an update on that at the briefing,' said Smythe and he ran his hand over his head. 'Come on, we've got...' His mobile had started ringing in his trouser pocket and he impatiently retrieved it, looked at the display and groaned. 'Barry. What is it? Briefing's in fifteen minutes, you know.' His shirt cuff slid partly back over his chunky Breitling watch and its large, round, ruby-red face peeked out in embarrassment.

Hingston and Remi shared a glance to acknowledge Smythe's rudeness and rose from their seats to leave him to it.

A flaming colour had ignited in Smythe's neck and was travelling up into his cheeks. '*What the*... How the bloody hell did that happen! No... no. I'm *fucking* annoyed is what I am... Yes. I will be making a call before the briefing... See you in there. *I* will handle this.' Smythe cut Barry off. He spat another expletive as he grabbed the receiver of his landline and looked in disbelief at Remi and Hingston who had failed to exit his office before Barry's call had become unavoidably intriguing.

Hingston thought it likely Smythe would order them to leave, but Remi blinked her widened eyes with an exaggerated expression of expectation and said 'Well?'

'Scientific Services,' Smythe replied in an exasperated voice, '*claim* the four wax figures... have *disappeared*.'

***

Skipping dinner was not part of Hingston's arrangement with Uncle Zack. If he'd been working out of Chiswick Police Station, he would have had no option, but the shorter distance from Hampstead to Euston gave them just enough time to meet for a gourmet burger and a glass of red wine before stepping into a jog to Stephenson Way. The side road was flanked by a mixture of Victorian and modern terraced buildings and crowded with clusters of cold, eager entertainment lovers. Couples, office parties and a few lonesome-looking singletons were busy looking up at the concrete facade of the Magic Circle Headquarters. The tall, double doors and window frames painted in a shade of police blue felt homely to Hingston. The floodlit flag suspended two storeys up displayed the Magic Circle logo complete with horoscope emblems and Latin text, otherwise it could have been confused with a police station.

The night air was cold, but above freezing and there was no sign of activity inside the warm, lit building, despite it being less than a minute to opening time. A clatter of footsteps were heard approaching from the Euston Station end of Stephenson Way. The flushed faces of Remi and Smythe soon came into view around the corner, just as the grand doors opened and an equally grand gentleman with a deep, magical voice welcomed everyone inside. An orderly queue formed with plenty of politeness. Hushed voices exclaimed excitedly and diminished as each person stepped into the wondrous interior with its "floating" spiral staircase and circular checkerboard floor.

At the back of the queue, Hingston and Zack watched Remi who reduced her pace and neatened her hair. She had exchanged her detective chic for a fifties-inspired evening ensemble that drew attention to her waist and slim legs. Smythe had opted for a dark navy corduroy jacket, matching coloured shirt, designer jeans and a bright, heavily patterned pocket square for a bit of flashiness, which Hingston decided was necessary to offset and detract from his teeth.

Hingston glanced at his own attire and knew that *Ted Baker* had not let him down; in the latest gentlemen's styling, complete with a skinny tie and elbow patches, he easily outdid Smythe. He smiled at Remi and unashamedly gave her the once-over.

Zack, whose anticipation got the better of him, walked forward and greeted Remi with a swift hug and a Devonshire laugh. 'Wonderful to see you, my girl! As gorgeous as ever!' He turned to Smythe and gave him a broad smile and handshake. 'What a stunning fifties dress she's wearing,' Zack remarked, 'but always a worry when you remember them from the first-time round, isn't it?' He laughed.

Smythe's lip began to curl. 'You're Hingston's uncle, I understand. But you haven't picked up cops' humour from him. Never mind,' he snorted.

'Too many years as an electrician,' Zack chortled. 'What was your line of work then? Never fancied being a cop yourself?'

Remi interjected before Smythe could muster a retort. 'We best keep up with the queue,' she directed and pointed at the group ahead of them who were nearly inside.

Hingston kept poker-faced. He leant towards Remi as they turned toward the entrance and whispered, 'Sorry about Zack.'

She gave him a wide-eyed gaze and looked at his tie.

'Good evening, madam. Good evening, sir. Good evening. Good evening…' the magician greeted each and every one with a festive glow in his cheeks and an excited smile. They were invited to explore the building in the next half an hour before the show was due to begin.

Smythe led Remi in the direction of the Club Room bar and Hingston and Zack went downstairs to the museum. The lower staircase and corridor celebrated the history of magic from the Victorian masters onwards. Posters burst forth with glorious colours and bold proclamations, but they failed to distract Hingston from reliving Zack's own performance with Smythe.

'That will be the first and last conversation you have with Rob Smythe,' said Hingston as soon as they set foot on the lower ground floor. 'Remi knew you were having a pop.' His complaint was mild because he secretly admired Uncle Zack's style.

'He doesn't suit Remi, Jason. He's worse than you'd described, my boy. He loves himself. It's written all over him,' Zack said in disgust. 'My jibes won't do him any harm and *maybe* Remi will think about what I inferred. He's nearer my age than hers!'

'Only just,' Hingston said to reign in Zack before he began to rant. 'Anyway, what's in here?' he said, nodding in the direction of an open door on the right of the corridor.

A few people chatting and laughing overtook them, clearly on a mission to reach the museum. Hingston stepped up to the doorway and discovered a library with three magicians stood within it. The collection of books was immense and the magicians were talking inaudibly. It only took a moment for one of them to look up. He was a young man with thick blond eyebrows and wavy strawberry-blond hair styled away from his forehead with glossy gel. An older magician wearing a fez immediately began to walk towards Hingston with an apologetic look.

'The museum is further down the corridor,' the magician said in a commanding voice. He gestured with one hand whilst the other entered his pocket, almost as if he were performing a trick and intended to keep Hingston's eyes directed down the corridor. Of course, the magician had no idea he had a detective stood before him.

'Amazing library,' Hingston said looking over the magician's shoulder and taking another glance at his hands, one of which was now on the door. 'So, all magical secrets can be learnt by reading in this library?' he quizzed.

'In theory, yes, but with around ten thousand books it's knowing where to start.' The magician beamed at Hingston. 'No public access to the library, apologies,' he said as he began to close the door. 'The museum is just down the corridor,' he reiterated. 'Enjoy the evening!'

The heavy door clicked closed and Hingston turned to Zack who had joined him to peer into the depths of magical illusion and mystery.

'Must've forgotten the time, I reckon. That would normally be kept out of public view,' Zack chirped with contentment. 'Lucky to see it.'

In the museum another magician wearing a tuxedo was busily engaging with visitors and sharing his enthusiasm for the eclectic items it housed. He looked towards Hingston and Zack, scanned the room which was now comfortably full, and with a masterfully inviting, 'Welcome ladies and gentleman,' the crowd fell silent and all attention was his. 'One hundred and seven years ago, a group of twenty-three magicians assembled themselves for a discussion inside Pinoli's Restaurant on Wardour Street, London. Their objective? To form a magic club. That day, July the first, nineteen oh-five, the Magic Circle was founded.'

His deep, dramatic tone and Central London accent drew the audience in as if he were one of those original founders. 'One of the twenty-three was the acclaimed Mr David Devant who became the first president of the Magic Circle. Now, David Devant is a name I am sure many of you are already familiar with.' He paused.

A selection of positive responses were given. Hingston noticed Zack was joining in with the nodding. Hingston pursed his lips and raised his eyebrows at the seemingly endless breadth of Zack's historical knowledge.

'For those of you less well acquainted,' the magician continued, 'David Devant was *most unusually* both a performer *and* an inventor of illusions. Another name you are likely to recognise is that of Mr John Nevil Maskelyne, the father of British magic.' The magician cast his eyes across the captivated audience. 'Both men had been amazing audiences for many years before they worked together. Mr Maskelyne was the co-owner of Maskelyne and Cooke's famous Egyptian Hall, and David Devant performed there regularly from eighteen ninety-three.'

Hingston's attention was captured by the magician as if he'd cast a spell.

The magician swept his arm in the direction of an ornately carved, dark wooden seat and walked towards it like the chair was an actor being welcomed onto a stage. It was shaped in the classical style of Ancient Rome and its black leather cushioning exuded the luxury of high society Victorian Britain. 'This chair,' the magician said, 'once belonged in the front row of the Egyptian Hall, and here...' he stepped sideways to reveal a framed theatre poster, 'is one of David Devant's glorious advertisements.'

Hingston looked over and between the other guests' heads at the flamboyant illustration of David Devant sweeping back a drape of material to reveal a glamorous woman rising from a grand flower arrangement. "The Birth of Flora produced by David Devant daily at 3 & 8" was printed in hand-illustrated font.

The magician read out the caption with a rolling stage voice: '"A marvellous and beautiful development from a small square of silk suspended in mid-air",' but Hingston was not listening. He was reading the poster's header: "Egyptian Hall. Piccadilly. England's Home of Mystery".

For the duration of the remainder of the tour, no item of memorabilia, magical device or waxwork figure could hold Hingston's attention. At the close, Hingston jumped straight in when the offer of 'Any questions?' was made by the magician.

'Yes. I have a question for you,' Hingston said. 'Is the Egyptian Hall still standing in Piccadilly?' His anticipation was evident from his glistening eyes.

'Sadly not, sir,' the magician replied. 'Maskelyne and Cooke moved from the premises to another in nineteen oh-four. The spectacular Egyptian Hall was demolished and replaced with offices the following year. However, the building that now spans the site is called Egyptian House. It comprises offices and a few shops. Inside the lobby belonging to the offices there is a photograph of the Egyptian Hall and a plaque we presented some seventeen years ago. There is public access during the week should you like to see it. Numbers one hundred and seventy to one hundred and seventy-three Piccadilly. Easily found opposite the Burlington Arcade. You could even stop for a coffee in the cafe at number one hundred and seventy-one.'

Hingston's pupils dilated as he visualised Leanna Snow reaching out toward the Burlington Arcade as she beat on the window and he felt his heart sink with the same sudden heaviness as the moment she lost consciousness in his arms. 'Thank you,' Hingston said with diminished enthusiasm.

Zack didn't ask Hingston what the matter was. He too pictured the lifeless body of Leanna Snow laid upon the ground once owned by the Egyptian Hall. Zack, to his advantage, however, knew nothing of the dark depths into which Hingston's mind had just sunk.

Chapter Ten
There Must Have Been Some Magic

Hingston watched Remi and Smythe ascend the spiral staircase, some six people ahead of him in the queue. To his right, on the deep blue wall, he noticed the golden sandy hues of a mural that represented Ancient Egypt and the earliest origins of magic. He wondered if any of their practices were recorded in the basement library and to what extent, if any, the Ancient Egyptians influenced stage magic. The small wax figures belonging to Hugh Marchant brought to mind only malign intent with the "entertainment" limited to the secretive practiser of the dark art and any person who may have commissioned it. Of course, the disappearance of the figures after they had entered police possession was much more akin to a modern-day vanishing act or, as Smythe suspected, the sleight of hand of a corrupt member of the force. Hingston remained hopeful that they had been misplaced through incompetence and that come Monday, they would be found behind or under some other item that awaited testing in the lab.

'Oh,' said Hingston, noticing two women directly ahead had come to a stop part way up the staircase.

'Hold up,' he requested over his shoulder to Zack who was following close behind.

The women were reading and remarking upon a mural.

Zack was unimpressed. 'My goodness,' he complained in a loud voice that the women ignored. 'You're clogging up the whole staircase!'

'Excuse me, ladies,' Hingston said, having moved up to allow Zack and the grumbling queue behind him to advance another step.

Both women looked at Hingston. The nearest displayed a snooty look. The other acted surprised, smiled insincerely with squinted eyes and pulled at the arm of the other woman to make her move on.

The mural they had been so interested in was entitled "The Discovery of Witchcraft" and the words "Erroneous Novelties and Imaginary Conceptions" caught Hingston's attention.

'Arse,' he heard one of the women say.

He glowered at their backs and their long, heavy coats until they reached the grand, low-lit entertainment room on the first floor where he and Zack overtook them.

Straight away Hingston was absorbed by the invitingly mysterious ambience that had been created in the home of these world-class magicians. Shades of blue flushed the walls from strategically placed uplighters. Golden spotlights warmed sunken display cabinets that tantalised visitors with their windows into magic's history. Shadows danced about the walls and floors while silhouetted figures chose their seats in one of the four performance areas dispersed across the room.

'Ready for the tabletop magic, then?' Hingston said as he turned to Zack who was still shaking his head following the staircase absurdity.

'Let's avoid *those* two,' Zack replied. He scanned the room to keep a tab on the whereabouts of the two women, but they had already lost themselves into the dim lighting. 'This side of the room should do,' Zack directed.

Three rows back, close to the display of an embroidered magician's robe, Hingston and Zack sat down. Moments later, Smythe led Remi into the front row, reaching his arm around her shoulders as soon as she was seated.

'Typical,' huffed Hingston.

The magician with the gelled, swept-back, wavy hair walked to the front and busied himself with a pocket watch whilst the stragglers were ushered into the rows.

'Do you want to relocate? We could go over there if you prefer?' Zack offered.

'No, here's fine,' Hingston answered just as the magician slipped his watch into his jacket and said 'Yes, come to the front, please, and we will begin!'

Two long coats swept in as requested.

'Bloody hell,' Hingston muttered under his breath. He avoided eye contact with Zack for fear of prompting a remark or a last minute, disruptive relocation.

'*Ladies and gentlemen*,' the magician called to command everyone's attention. He paused to smile and clasp his hands together. 'I am *Joseph Kilkenny* and *tonight* I am the first of four magicians to entertain you. My colleagues and I will rotate around the audiences. You will see *all* of us perform. You do not have to do anything *beyond* paying close attention, laughing at the right places and...' A shrill, tuneful alarm sounded from his jacket and he pulled out his pocket watch, perplexed. 'Oh,' he said, turning the watch face toward the audience. 'It's not one minute to midnight! Cinderella can stay at the ball for *hours* yet! *Can't you... Cinderella?*' he asked of Remi.

Hingston knew Remi would have blushed. 'Well,' she said, always quick to respond whatever the circumstance, 'I hope so, but it appears I've come without my glass slippers, I'm afraid.'

There were a few laughs from the audience.

'Well done, ladies and gents,' the magician was keen to acknowledge their participation, 'that was one of the right places. *And before* I was so rudely interrupted by my good-for-nothing pocket watch, the third request I have of your kind selves this evening is... to volunteer!'

There was complete silence which allowed the other acts in the room to be heard.

The magician raised his thick blond eyebrows. '*Cinderella*, you'll have to help me out here.' He smiled at Remi with a wink, reached out his hand and she stood up, looking delightful.

There was a round of applause instigated by Smythe.

Zack, displaying a wry grin, leant toward Hingston. 'Well, this must be the first time Cinderella was accompanied *into* the palace by the pumpkin. These lights do nothing for bald, old Ken's complexion, my boy.'

Hingston broke into a smile for the first time since they had entered the building.

The magician bowed ceremoniously at Remi and his routine commenced with the production of a pair of ladies' tights. This prompted a snort and a long, strangled whine of a laugh from one of the two women in the front row. The magician looked away from the tights he held, pretending he suspected the noise came from behind him. He raised an eyebrow and displayed a bewildered expression, merging the unexpected comedy into his act and granting permission to the rest of the audience to release their laughter. The strange women, however, remained silent.

Swiftly the magician used his charm to coax Remi into parting with her wristwatch. She followed his instructions to blow upon the watch three times as he held it above the tights before allowing it free passage down one of the legs. He fed that leg down the other to double the strength. The magician chatted and bantered whilst he slowly swung the weight of Remi's watch back and forth, not to hypnotise, Hingston thought, but to distract.

The gasp that was emitted from both women at the front disguised any noise Smythe may have made when the magician applied sudden force to his swing. The tights stretched forth a metre, towards Smythe's nose and passed up and over the magician's head and behind, where the watch smashed upon a table.

Remi covered her mouth and blinked her wide eyes, but was no doubt tickled by Smythe's reaction. Hingston wished he could have seen his face.

Remi's eyes sparkled and Hingston found her looking straight back at him, ignoring her disgruntled Smythe until the magician commanded her attention with the jingle-jangle of broken mechanisms that slipped and slid about in the foot of the tights.

'I cannot *apologise enough*, my dear,' said the magician. 'That really *was not* meant to happen! You see the magic in this building takes over from time to time. If we laugh *too* much...' he turned his head to the women in the front row, 'things can start to become very strange indeed.' Whether he intended to prompt a remark or not, he got one—minus any snorts of laughter.

'I can give you strange,' said one of the pair and the other, probably the snorter, whispered something into her ear.

The magician did not falter. He winked at the women, turned back to Remi and said, 'But *you're* Cinderella and I'm *far* more accomplished than any fairy godmother. A broken watch is easily fixed.' He pulled a doubtful expression and jangled the tights again.

Noises of amusement were heard from Smythe. 'You mean I've got to buy her an even better one for Christmas,' Smythe quipped.

The magician's smile shone like the gel in his hair. 'As well as the ring I see she's also without, my good fellow!' he replied with a wink.

Hingston felt his neck getting hot and he forced his glare away from Smythe's tanned head to look at Remi. She was laughing, coyly, and as her eyes strayed from Smythe's, they met again with his. For that short second Remi appeared thoughtful and that look of doubt, regret or possibly sadness stayed with Hingston all the way to the interval.

***

'Double gin and tonic. Pink champagne for the lady,' requested Smythe with a flash of his teeth. 'Oh,' he said turning to the left and looking over Remi's head, 'and whatever these two gents' favour.' Whilst he was still brash and commanding, Hingston could see Smythe's focus was on having a good time: letting go of the

stresses of Op PYROLITE and letting his hair down—
so to speak.

Hingston smiled and having applied a firm grasp on
Uncle Zack's shoulder to remind him to *behave*, he
stepped up to the bar and thanked Smythe for the drinks.
'Yes, two glasses of red, please,' he said to the barman.

Zack positioned himself closest to Remi and asked
how they were enjoying the show.

Smythe had moved on from their strained
introduction at seven and spoke enthusiastically. He was
keen to emphasise how much better the mentalist would
perform in an interview room compared to any of his
detectives. 'How he could guess what I'd drawn on that
card *was not* down to luck,' Smythe said as Remi,
Hingston and Zack remembered the scratchy image of
the "skateboarding pelican" that had carved its way out
of Smythe's imagination. 'I went obscure all right,' he
continued with a sneer, 'and the mindreading bastard
still got it.' He knocked back his drink and ordered
another.

'D'you know where the gents are? Were they off
the landing on this floor?' queried Zack.

Hingston pointed him in the right direction and
seized the opportunity to brief Smythe and Remi on his
discovery in the basement museum. 'Tonight, has not
been entirely *extracurricular*,' he began and the straight
faces that stared back at him looked stony sober.

'Go on,' Smythe said.

Hingston produced his mobile and showed them a photograph of the David Devant poster. He zoomed in on the words "Egyptian Hall. Piccadilly".

Their eyes met each other's before they looked at Hingston for his explanation.

'*Leanna* died on the grounds where the *Egyptian* Hall once stood.'

Their expressions of realisation said it all.

'Shit,' Smythe whispered as quietly as his exasperation would allow. 'So, forced suicide. Controlled method. *And*, by the looks of it, controlled fucking location. *All* now pointing to the warped beliefs and practices of this...' He nodded at Hingston and Remi who knew the House of Life was at the tip of his tongue where it clung like bitter orpiment.

***

The four sat together for the second part of the programme: stage magic. Magicians' names were engraved on small plaques; one was affixed to the back of each seat in the grand upstairs theatre. Smythe, somewhat tanked up following the interval, was perturbed that none of the names he read were familiar to him. 'Putting aside Houdini, what about Paul Daniels?' he complained.

Remi rolled her eyes and blinked.

The show was introduced by a smooth-tongued, silver-haired magician who, in a predictable yet nonetheless entertaining display of chauvinism, selected an "assistant" from the audience. She was an attractive young lady who sported a natural tan and long legs. He must have spotted her when entering the theatre for no one could make such a lucky guess in the low lighting that now cloaked the audience.

It was readily established she was from Brisbane. The magician declared his skills in both magic *and* mentalism, launching into a fifteen-minute display of both. She proved to be an excellent choice, showering him with laughter and exclamations of "You're kidding me" throughout. If this was not enough praise, before leaving the stage she announced with a high-pitched squeal of delight that the magician was the highlight of her visit to the UK. "If I come over to London again, the Magic Circle will be top of my list!" she called out and planted a quick kiss on his cheek. Smythe had leant forward as soon as the man's mindreading powers had been made known, and at the close, he shook his head, none the wiser as to how this art was performed. 'She must have been a plant,' he scoffed.

A mime act followed, set to a variety of *James Bond* film tracks. The illusionist received periodic bursts of applause. He appeared to levitate; produced more than one deck of cards from his mouth; made fish appear in an aquarium; and performed a series of gravity-defying moves across the stage before a loud bang sounded and amongst a shower of ticker-tape, he vanished. In seconds, the audience applauded, cheered and whistled, realising he had appeared at the back of the theatre. He had changed into a dinner suit and ran down the centre gangway, bounded up onto the stage and bowed, unruffled and cool, like James Bond himself.

***

The curtain fell with a swing of heavy velvet. Zack leant across Hingston and attracted Remi's attention by tapping on the name plaque fixed to the seat in front of her. 'I used to play cricket with a chap called Chris Pratt,' he said. 'Not the same one of course, unless he kept his Magic Circle membership secret. Hmmm. Now that could explain why he was stonkingly good at poker.'

Remi laughed. 'Some may say you're a card, Zack,' she said.

Hingston smiled at the hushed banter taking place over his lap. It reminded him of the year of the Dartmouth Regatta when the three of them had travelled up the river to Totnes on a cruise boat. The captain spoke over his microphone intermittently to point out landmarks and entertain with local trivia. When he encouraged all aboard to wave at the passing Royal Navy officers and call "Hello, sailor", Zack and Remi's shared sense of humour was ignited. The hilarity that bounced back and forth between them made Hingston nearly choke on his crisps and Zack had to pull out a handkerchief to mop his tears.

The curtain rose again and silence was restored. The final act loomed. A female magician strode in from stage right and Hingston had to elbow Zack to prevent him from remarking too loudly, 'It's a *woman*.'

With her hair swept up in a chignon, the magician was reminiscent of Audrey Hepburn. Allanah Atkinson was her name. It wasn't long before the large wooden box that stood beside her on a tall plinth was also introduced. She proclaimed the box could make objects transform and disappear.

The missing wax figures flashed into Hingston's mind and the muffled grunt made by Smythe confirmed the same applied for him.

Remi placed her hand on Smythe's leg and Hingston forgot the wax figures. He averted his eyes back to the elegant Allanah Atkinson just in time for her to call 'Would the tall, dark and *handsome* gentleman wearing the *dapper* suit with elbow patches, please *stand up*.'

'That's you, my boy,' chortled Zack whilst patting him on the back.

Remi turned to Hingston and gave him a thumbs up.

Hingston, clearly enjoying the magician's compliments, stood up and to evidence he was the right man, held up an arm and pointed at one of the elbow patches.

'Ladies and gents, give this fine man a round of applause as he makes his way up to the stage!' she directed.

Hingston noticed Smythe did not join in, choosing to adjust his pocket square instead.

***

The spotlights glared golden-white and erased the audience from view. Hingston looked into the blackness and listened to the applause. Somewhere on the right was his vacant seat. A disconcerting wave of apprehension trembled through his chest, throwing doubt upon something indistinguishable. The words "insignificant pathetic" swept through his mind like a whisper of icy breath barely heard, just before his eyes adjusted and the front rows of the theatre became visible.

In her well-spoken voice, Allanah Atkinson instructed Hingston to put his hand into the box that stood on the plinth next to her. The feeling of apprehension evaporated and he discovered she had used her flattery to secure an individual who the audience would enjoy laughing at. His ability to laugh at himself was a gamble she had taken—unless she also possessed a high level of intuition or had mastered the "mind reading" technique that had fascinated Smythe throughout the evening.

Once Hingston's hand was dangled inside the box, she asked him to feel the item it contained, describe how it felt, provide his best guess as to its identity and how it would be used. When she dropped the side of the box, the item revealed to the audience was, every time, ill-matched to Hingston's conclusion—such as the, 'Toothbrush,' that had disappeared to be replaced by a loo brush. As Hingston peered around the box and beneath it, there was no clue as to how the trick was performed; even at close proximity it really did appear to be magic.

***

The queue that led out of the theatre was noisy with satisfaction as favourite moments were shared and the whole experience was praised with various repeated words of agreement.

Hingston waited with Remi just outside the doorway, breathing in the chilly air of Stephenson Way whilst Zack grabbed a quick word with a magician and Smythe made his way to, 'The little boys' room.' Remi seemed to run out of things to say about the evening as if she were either tired from the week or preoccupied with details of the investigation. The afternoon's briefing had been heavy going and Hingston had been fighting to keep from his mind a nagging degree of anxiety about the enquiries: the evidence yet to be obtained; the questions yet to be answered; Hugh

Marchant's developing symptoms of poisoning and declining health; Dr Olson's cold, lifeless eyes that looked through and beyond the cemetery shadows like an Egyptian death mask, knowing secrets that could never be spoken.

'You know…' Remi said with a mild frown and a deep look into Hingston's eyes. 'When I was called to the front by that blond magician and…'

Hingston leant towards her ever so slightly, listening for her next words.

'And he pointed out I was missing a ring,' she continued.

'Mmm. Yes,' Hingston encouraged. His chest tightened as he thought of her eyes meeting his in the audience, shimmering as they were now.

'When he said that,' she whispered, 'I thought of Dr Yorke.'

Hingston hesitated, stopping himself from touching Remi's arm. His mind raced back to Hampstead Police Station, the glimpse he caught of the flamboyant Dr Yorke and his gushing compliments that had travelled down the corridor like a nauseating version of Smythe's aftershave. 'Why did you think of him?' he asked.

'I don't know, Jason. He just popped into my head. Uninvited! *Smiling* and *courteous*.' Remi's frown lines deepened and her shimmering eyes moistened.

Hingston felt sick. 'Do you think it's just a crush on Dr Yorke or have you fallen for him?' He didn't know what else to ask and wasn't about to point out that such a relationship during an investigation was not permitted.

'No.' Remi looked shocked. 'No, you idiot! I think he's a *suspect*.'

Chapter Eleven
To Lay Before the King

Contemplation has its place. The fried egg on Hingston's Saturday morning breakfast plate did not benefit from it, however. The lukewarm yolk finally flooded toward the hash browns and under the streaky bacon. It reminded him of Hugh Marchant's poisonous paint; of last night's anticipation involving Remi and his gushing disappointment; of...

'Super choice, my boy.' Uncle Zack celebrated the bijou Chiswick cafe while demolishing his second grilled tomato.

'Yeah,' replied Hingston with otherwise convincing effort had Zack not known him so well.

'Unless you're in the dumps, that is,' Zack tagged on with an understanding tone that welcomed explanation.

Hingston still didn't fancy the egg and kept one side of the hash browns serving as a dam, to relocate some salvaged bacon behind it. 'It's the investigation that's doing it,' he sighed.

Zack gave a smile that signalled "and Remi".

'Yeah, that as well,' said Hingston, impressed by his uncle's management of his contemplative mood that he knew was providing poor company. 'I'm going to change the subject, okay,' he said resolutely. 'I'd like you to do a bit of research for me. History. Right up your street.'

Uncle Zack, eyebrows raised, placed down his knife and fork. 'This to do with police work?' chortled Zack in a mock American accent. 'Something to get my detective badge for?' He gave a wink.

Hingston shook his head and looked out of the cafe window toward his homely Chiswick Police Station. It stood on the opposite side of the road, beyond the flower market that looked suitably Christmassy with its handmade wreaths and mistletoe decorated with shiny red bows. A uniformed officer hurried past the cafe window with a couple of supermarket bags. 'Snacks for the team,' he pointed out to Zack and together they watched the young officer turn the corner and approach a parked public order van. A thumbs up from the driver and a big grin could be seen as the officer climbed inside and dished out the provisions to the team. 'They'll be heading off to a football match soon,' Hingston explained.

'What? In those boots?' Zack joked. 'Anyway, Jason, what's this research? What d'you want me to find out?'

Hingston reached to his inside pocket and withdrew the "Circus Death Horror" newspaper cutting and photograph.

The words made Zack frown. The photograph raised his eyebrows, then his eyes. 'You want to know who *he* is? Whether he's related?'

'*And* the girl. Anything and everything, please. Then I'll tell you how I came by them.'

'Mmm. "To the one I can rely upon, with love",' Zack read aloud. Hingston remained silent. 'This may be very interesting,' Zack added as he examined the photograph again.

***

Sherlock Holmes. A good Christmas read and one of his dad's favourites. This volume, printed in 1898, boasted illustrated plates... a rattle of the shop door, a squeak from its hinges and a gust of cold, Chiswick air interrupted Hingston's browsing. He looked up at the latest prospective customer who stepped inside, exuding enthusiasm to find an unusual gift in this tiny, antiquarian bookshop. Condensation rapidly formed on the man's glasses, prompting him to snatch them off and emit a self-conscious laugh as he pretended to bump into a bookshelf. The bookseller gave a peculiar smile, remarked upon the weather and floated her gaze in Hingston's direction where she scanned the shelves with great interest until the man walked past her.

It didn't take long for the warm scent of aged paper to recover its rich depth and, returning his attention to *Sherlock Holmes*, Hingston studied the original royal-blue binding and opened the book to a random page. It was as near to excellent condition as one could hope for over a century since its publication. That's what the bookseller had told him, anyway. He glanced across at Zack whose eyes had, for over fifteen minutes, been focussed on the shelves dedicated to the Italian Renaissance. It was true that this old shop, only yards from the police station, housed a world of literature. The shelves were fitted from floor to ceiling; they ran underneath the counter and more books were on display behind the bookseller's till. Hingston caught glimpses of classic titles, famous authors and poets, works he had never heard of and names of places he had never visited. From fiction to non-fiction, he had the sense that many of these first and second editions had sat for decades, largely unread, in grand houses within immense libraries and exquisitely carved bookcases.

Amongst the shimmering, embossed gilt letters stood a copper-coloured title on a dark leather spine. Its difference drew Hingston closer to make out the words *The Boy's Own Conjuring Book*. *Sherlock Holmes* soon found a place on a nearby shelf and Hingston eased the book from its crammed placement and turned to the front inside cover. This 1860 edition proclaimed its worth as "a complete hand-book of parlour magic… containing over one thousand optical, chemical, mechanical, magnetical, and magical experiments, amusing transmutations, astonishing sleights and subtleties…" and the list went on. "Illustrated with nearly two thousand engravings" and "intended as a source of amusement for one thousand and one evenings", this exciting book was printed in New York. *Yorke*. 'Bloody hell,' Hingston muttered. Dr Yorke conjured up anything but amusement. Remi's suspicions were now at the forefront of his mind and frustratingly, none provided sufficient grounds for arrest.

Last night, stood outside the Magic Circle Headquarters, Remi explained to Hingston that she was finding it difficult to detach from Op PYROLITE. It was bugging her more than any previous investigation, regardless of how challenging others have been. She was uneasy. Dr Yorke's behaviour made her suspicious of him: not at the time of meeting with him but retrospectively. What bothered Hingston was Remi's limited ability to recount her specific concerns. Yes, Yorke was a friend of Olson, she explained, but it was his charming manner, his flattery, his subtle attempts to, 'Connect,' with her, the sense that he was trying to draw information from her whilst seeming, 'Too helpful and too interested,' that didn't feel right. Yorke answered her questions, but she felt short-changed. She also thought, but couldn't be sure, that he had thrown in a subtle putdown along the way, but somehow, she had forgotten what he had said and the context of it. And why did Remi then whisper *that* word, 'Insignificant,' to play down her reasons for feeling uneasy about Dr Yorke? It prompted Hingston to remember Mrs Britton dropping her ashtray on her kitchen floor and sobbing, 'Pathetic.' The association of the two words made *him* uncomfortable and to his mind, this only served to elevate Remi's concerns about Dr Yorke to something *of significance*.

Unlike Remi, Hingston trusted intuition unequivocally. Since the Clarkes' case, his mind had become open to all possibilities, however illogical they may at first seem. He was therefore very direct with Remi when he told her that Dr Yorke, as a consultant psychiatrist, was attempting to control her. Furthermore, he decided that Yorke would be subject of a second interview: one which Remi will not be conducting alone. It was at this point that Smythe stepped out onto Stephenson Way, interrupted their conversation, ascertained work was being discussed and in the role of both DCI and boyfriend, took over.

'Let's wait until we get home where we can talk about it *properly*,' Smythe said and gave Hingston a long, thoughtful look which was soured by a sudden flash of jealousy. As Hingston returned an emotionless stare, he felt strangely empowered to know the feeling was mutual.

Now, alerted to his surroundings by a sudden pang of self-consciousness, the book came back into focus and Hingston took a quick glance about the shop. Zack was still engrossed. The bookseller was sipping a steaming drink with both her hands wrapped around the mug and the customer with the glasses was engaged in jovial conversation with another customer who appeared keen to shake him off. Satisfied that no one was watching him, he turned to the contents page of *The Boy's Own Conjuring Book* and blindly gazed at the print whilst his mind recapped the latest updates on Op PYROLITE that were shared at yesterday afternoon's briefing.

Hugh Marchant, the thirty-one-year-old whose arsenic poisoning caused his heart to swell and triggered convulsions on Thursday evening, remained in a serious condition at St Thomas' Hospital. Both a suspect in Olson's murder and a potential victim of the House of Life, Marchant was a computer programmer by profession. His role in the crime at Highgate Cemetery was being revealed as systematically as the messy layers of orpiment had been scraped from the crevices of his skin. The search of his home address had so far revealed that Marchant applied his mathematical mind to watching science fiction films, gaming and rigging up his computer with advanced security technology. He had also turned his hand to making the now elusive wax figures; the evidence of their making was at the bottom of his kitchen bin. Marchant was not a tidy person. The boot of his father's car was strewn with an accumulation of rubbish that comprised empty drinks bottles; carrier bags; chocolate wrappers; a dog-eared road atlas; plant debris; a winter road survival kit; old train tickets—none of which matched Emily's Cambridge excursion; a random dog lead, for Marchant had no pets of his own;

a hammer and a pen knife. At the bottom of some of the carrier bags were receipts and one recorded a purchase on Tuesday of this week, for spray-paint. The hardware store's CCTV had captured Marchant, alone. He wasn't wearing the dark green jacket that was found inside the car. The jacket's fibres proved to be a match for those attached to the ligature and the melted wax found in the cemetery, but the jacket's fit was three sizes too small for Marchant's wide frame. It was therefore suspected to belong to the bespectacled male passenger who had been seen whilst the car sped away from Highgate Cemetery in the early hours of Wednesday morning. Potentially, it was this male who had left his fingerprints behind on the chain cutters and his DNA at the scene. There was currently only one match that placed Marchant *inside* the cemetery: his shoes.

Marchant's parents were proven to be in Yorkshire since their arrival at a five-star hotel last weekend, only leaving when they were contacted by police about their son. There was no reason to suspect they were involved in, or aware of, Olson's murder. Their shock and continued bedside vigil had rendered them temporarily incapable of providing much information with which to build a profile of Hugh Marchant. His father summed him up as a, 'Very content, intelligent whiz-kid. A lonely sort, never one for socialising, but never depressed or suicidal.' Certainly, the contacts found on Marchant's mobile phone were few. His messages were limited to work-related communication and there was no record of Emily Britton's or Olson's mobile numbers to prove an association.

Turning to Dr Olson, CCTV from Tuesday morning provided no trace of him at Kensal Green train station, neither at his routine time for travelling to work or anytime later that day. Olson had therefore either made his diversion from home to south Islington on foot, by an alternative method of public transport, or possibly by meeting someone at an arranged rendezvous point. Circulation of Olson's photograph to all taxi firms, local private hire services and bus services was yet to provide a report of a sighting, leaving a large gap in the chronology between his departure from home and his first phone call made from south Islington at 4.37 p.m. to Emily Britton. His character, according to the accounts of all associations thus far interviewed, was beyond reproach. However, Olson had at least one secret beyond Emily Britton and Sheila Baptist: his Wednesday nights out. Despite the belief shared by his immediate colleagues, Olson was not a member of a table tennis league; there was in fact no evidence he had ever played the sport. His wife told PC Stoker that on Wednesday evenings he volunteered at a homeless shelter in Vauxhall, but again, when enquiries were made, that was also found to be a lie. It served to add some weight to the suspicion that Emily was meeting with the unidentified "Ani" on Wednesdays and that potentially, Olson was there, too.

Olson's home computer was yet another hefty chunk of data making its way through the workload of the High Tech Crime Unit, keeping the whole team on even more overtime this weekend. Whilst this phase of the investigation chugged forward, it was proving annoyingly difficult to obtain access to the patient records held by the White House Clinic for Emily Britton, along with any still held for Sheila Baptist. The likelihood of them containing any information beyond factual medical accounts was very slim, however, and Hingston was more interested in acquiring a better understanding of Olson's private life. The enquiry made at the British Museum was promptly responded to by their staff. A list of the talks Olson attended over the past four years showed his interest in Ancient History was mostly confined to the Egyptians with an occasional diversion to Greece and Assyria. A second list, comprising the details of all attendees at those talks in the past two years was soon to be received and checked against police systems.

Hingston smiled when he thought back to Barry's wide-eyed response to the, 'Surprising,' number of cemetery volunteers. All of their footwear prints had been checked against the unidentified sets of impressions found at the site of the break-in. Marchant and Olson had accounted for two and of the remaining four, there was just the one match. The feet were those of a prissy, middle-aged individual who volunteered as a tour guide. She told police that she had walked down to the gate on Tuesday afternoon after she had seen the cemetery visitors off site.

'I had a feeling, quite out of the blue, that I should just *check* the security over there,' she explained in a lilting voice. Presumably sensing the officer's speculation, she added, 'Yes. Psychic-like. But it's proved to be correct, really, hasn't it?' and gave a clever giggle. She then provided her alibi for the night of Olson's murder, which was a fortunate one for her, as it turned out. She was in A&E at St Thomas' Hospital at eleven p.m. and it wasn't until five thirty a.m. that she was discharged. She had been celebrating her sister's fortieth and between destinations—all of which were pubs, she fell down several stairs at Covent Garden tube station, breaking her wrist.

Reportedly, the officer who took her statement joked to the woman that too much alcohol must have drowned her psychic ability otherwise she could have avoided her accident. And reportedly, the joke fell flat. Whatever really was said by the officer, Barry did a fine job of plagiarising the mood-lifter. Hingston smiled and pictured Remi rolling her eyes at Barry's comments and then pictured her looking so stunning last night...

'Good book by the looks of it,' said Zack, who had sidled up to Hingston all of a sudden, peering down at the small print of the contents page. 'Mmm... *The Burned Handkerchief Restored... The Magic Shilling...* oh, not so sure about this one, my boy,' Zack pointed and squinted at the old ink. '*Professor Wyman's Great*

Trick of the Egyptian Fluids, or Impossibilities Accomplished!' He gave a laugh and Hingston was about to muster a response when his phone rang.

It was Smythe. 'Jason?' he said, having dropped his official tone.

It caught Hingston off guard. 'Yes, sir?'

'Can you get yourself to Islington nick?'

'It will take me nearly an hour, but yes.'

'Good,' replied Smythe, sounding resolute. 'Someone's walked in and wishes to be *interviewed*: Emily Britton.'

Chapter Twelve
Disperse the Gloomy Clouds of Night

Before Hingston took hold of the lightweight aluminium handle, he looked through the spy hole. Emily's face was obscured. She had her elbows on the interview table; her fingers pushed into her hair and spread wide. Her wrists were slender and they protruded from a shiny black puffer jacket which was unzipped, revealing a flash of turquoise top.

Smythe had briefed Hingston over the phone. Emily Britton was accompanied to Islington Police Station by a man who stated he was Alistair Britton: Emily's father. He had found Emily in his flat in Islington late yesterday evening after he returned from Brussels. He had been performing there with his band *The Wasted Revellers*. He had an arrangement with Emily that she could use his flat whenever she liked. He is estranged from Mrs Britton and she doesn't know that Emily meets with him. Emily had told him that her mum believed she was staying at Chloe's last night. It was not until this morning, when Emily started crying, that he, 'Got the truth from her.' Then, knowing she was missing, 'And in danger,' he brought her to the police station.

The "danger" that Emily had articulated to her father was just one of the avenues to be explored today, but it had prompted Emily to beg the station reception officer, 'Please don't contact my mother because she is planning to murder me.'

Through the spy hole Hingston could only see the arm of Mr Britton that was reached across his daughter's back. His sleeve was denim and his hand was the carrier of tattoos and numerous large, silver-coloured rings.

'Good afternoon, Emily; Mr Britton,' Hingston said as he stepped inside the room. 'I'm Detective Sergeant Jason Hingston.' He closed the door and Emily kept her fingers clamped close to her scalp, pushing out chunks of short chocolate brown hair at various angles.

Mr Britton tried to smile and stood to shake Hingston's hand. 'Emily's worked herself up into more of a state since we arrived,' he explained. 'One of your colleagues said we were going to be moved to a more comfortable interview suite. Is that what we're doing now?'

Hingston observed Mr Britton's shaved head, nose piercing and designer stubble. His obvious mismatch with Mrs Britton's appearance was considerable. Hingston wondered how long Emily had been meeting in secret with her father and whether he had ever moved to Australia as Mrs Britton had alleged, or if he had made it up to disappear, or if Mrs Britton had lied. Smythe had taken the decision not to inform Mrs Britton of her daughter's whereabouts until Emily's allegation about her was explored.

'Yes,' confirmed Hingston. 'This isn't an appropriate place. We're going to speak with Emily in a much more comfortable room than this. My colleague, DC Remi Armitage, is going to drive us there. Emily?' Hingston looked over at the teenager's unchanged posture. 'Emily, you're perfectly safe with us and we're here to help. If you'd like to come with your dad and me, we'll get ourselves ready to talk. How does that sound?'

***

The diesel engine rumbled into action and the wintry air sped into the cabin loud and cold through rattling plastic vents. The heating dial was already pointed into the thick band of red, but Hingston knew the job car would barely get warm before their destination would be reached. He turned the blowers down as Remi drove them out of the yard. He looked over his shoulder at Emily. 'We'll be there in about five minutes,' Hingston advised. He noticed Mr Britton leaning towards Emily who had clasped her hands together in her lap. Her eyes, lined with thick kohl, provided no reaction to Hingston's small talk and remained focussed out of the window. There was something a little eerie about Emily, Hingston thought, as the soft sunshine flickered on her pale, emotionless face and her dark brown eyes stared and stared.

Mr Britton, having given Emily time to respond, filled the void. 'So, the police own more property in London than the public would think,' he remarked.

Hingston could not crick his neck round to see Mr Britton, but he took this as an opportunity to keep an eye on Emily whilst making conversation, rather than facing back to the direction of travel. 'We have a small number of properties across the capital, yes.' He had already explained to Mr Britton the process and benefits of *Achieving Best Evidence* interviews for vulnerable victims and witnesses. 'The houses look just like any other residential property because that's what they are, but as we'll show you, we use one of the upstairs rooms for all the recording technology and the other is set up as a lounge for the interviews. There are no actual bedrooms in the house. The kitchen has the basics for making drinks and there'll be a reasonable selection of biscuits, maybe some crisps, and if we're lucky some chocolate, too.' His attempt to engage with Emily was failing.

'I've brought some provisions,' Remi chipped in. 'A *Cadbury* selection bag. I'll keep them away from Jason, though, Emily, as he's a greedy pig given the chance!' Remi glanced at Hingston and blinked her smiling eyes.

Mr Britton laughed, equally keen to relax the mood, and Hingston turned his head back toward Emily. Her demeanour was unchanged but her lips were moving silently. It was one or two words he saw at most and as she stopped, her eyes moved to meet his in a calm and confident manner. The resemblance to Mrs Britton was striking as she pushed her tongue behind her top lip. She looked down. 'Chocolate sounds good,' Emily said, sounding full of schoolgirl positivity which conflicted with everything Hingston had just observed. With a smile she returned her eyes to the window where Islington's terraced back streets became narrower and poorer and increasingly confusing as their journey turned and crisscrossed to its destination.

***

Hingston hurried from the car and glanced through the windscreen at Remi who was keeping the engine running and the conversation going. He fumbled to unlock the icy-cold bollard that reserved the only parking bay on this short, dead end street. The week suddenly felt very long, as did the list of questions for Emily that were buzzing around his mind like snippets of Christmas carols. The bollard's weight pressed into his palm. He gave a perfunctory thumbs up and a traffic officer's beckon to Remi whilst looking across the road to the boxy 1980s two-bed end terrace. The bay made this house a valuable little asset for the Met and put it at risk of being sold off in favour of a flimsy cabin-style interview suite that could be erected in a corner of a police station yard.

When Remi turned off the ignition, everything fell quiet. Traffic noise from neighbouring roads had been muffled by the tall, Victorian terraces that penned in and dwarfed the police-owned property. Bland and anonymous it stood, upon the land that used to be the back gardens of the period townhouses. They themselves had long since been divided up into a mixture of rented apartments and offices. A tiny council-owned patch of grass, a narrow walkway and the solitary parking bay had been squeezed in amongst this mismatch of original and modern architecture. Had there been space for just one tree, the street might have resembled a scaled-down garden village.

Before Remi got out of the car, Hingston scanned the windows that looked down into the street. He saw no activity and opened the rear doors to let Mr Britton out first and then Emily. Hingston watched Emily scan the windows, just as he had, and her eyes betrayed a fearfulness he had not witnessed until now. As they walked to the house, Hingston's thoughts returned again to yesterday afternoon's briefing. The search of Emily's bedroom had provided no new evidence to support her association with the House of Life and Emily's DNA was not a match for that found at Highgate Cemetery. What, Hingston wondered, would she reveal during her interview? Was Mrs Britton *really* planning to murder her own daughter? Would Emily tell the truth or did she plan to lie?

Upon entering the property, they were greeted with the warm smile of a Child Protection officer, DC Sharma, who had been called in to be second interviewer. She had already prepared the audio-visual equipment, got the paperwork together, the heating turned up and the kettle on. Remi, as lead interviewer, provided Emily and her father with a full tour of the house. She explained the interview procedure, showed them the recording equipment and answered their questions. Emily said very little, aside from being, *'Seriously* impressed,' by the, 'Covert spy,' earpiece through which Remi would receive prompts from DC Sharma in the second room.

It was in the second room where Hingston sat, ready to watch the interview on the computer screen and to convey messages to Remi via DC Sharma and the impressive earpiece. He reviewed the key points that he wanted explored:

- *Why is Mrs Britton planning murder?*
- *Why go missing Monday lunchtime and not before?*
- *Why take the photograph during assembly?*
- *Text message to Harry and Chloe.*
- *Leanna Snow.*
- *Olson.*
- *Necklace.*

- *Olson's associates? Yorke?*
- *Diary content:*
  - *Panik*
  - *Insignificant, pathetic*
  - *House of Life*
  - *Marshmallow choking article*
  - *Who is Ani?*
  - *Who is "she"—"the rebellious sort"?*
  - *Other named students—at risk?*
- *Wednesday nights.*
- *Cambridge ticket.*
- *Hugh Marchant?*
- *Sheila Baptist?*

With Mr Britton ensconced downstairs with a hot drink and a comfortable seat, the interview commenced. Hingston had a clear view of Emily and a profile view of Remi who had chosen to wear a pair of jeans and a black chenille jumper instead of her office attire. Without any notebook or pen in Remi's hands, the scene looked as relaxed as any regular winter afternoon spent chatting in a lounge. Hingston knew that Remi's keenly trained mind however, would be working its Christmas socks off as she proceeded with the introductory script.

Emily was responding clearly and confidently. She had removed her shoes and had tucked her legs up on the sofa. Her eyes moved up to the video camera occasionally. But when the lengthy preamble reached its end and Emily's understanding of truth and lies was confirmed, her body language changed. She began to pick at the elastic of one of her socks and she spoke over Remi. 'I do want to talk to you, but I'm worried,' she said.

'Tell me what's worrying you,' Remi encouraged.

'Too many things. I hate myself.' Emily pulled her sock up her leg and rolled it back down on itself. She wiped her eyes on her turquoise top, smudging the arm with makeup. 'But I hate my mother the most,' she added vehemently. 'I'm worried she'll kill me like she said she would, because she couldn't make me do it myself like Leanna. But...'

Remi picked up the tissue box from the coffee table and passed them to Emily. 'It's okay, you don't have to rush,' she soothed.

'I've been trapped,' Emily blurted, dry-eyed and angered. 'It's not my fault. I've been no friend, *no* friend,' she repeated. 'I can't tell you everything, I really, *really* can't.' Her pitch was rising. 'But I need your help because she killed him, too!' She released a laugh that pierced the air. Her eyes met Remi's. 'Why am I so pathetic?' she said as more tears fell.

Hingston looked at DC Sharma whose expression reflected his own. With no time to speak, she put her head back down and continued to scribe as if the page were a sheet of ice and her biro an Olympic skater.

Remi allowed Emily to continue, uninterrupted. 'She has a gun, you know? She *will* kill me because I no longer mean *anything* to her. I've done what they want.

They've got her and they thought they had me... and they did. They almost did, had he not loved me...' Emily began pulling at her sock again and her mouth was moving silently.

'Ask what she's saying,' prompted Hingston to DC Sharma, but Remi had already picked up on it.

'Emily,' Remi said, 'Emily, look up at me.'

Emily obliged. 'Pathetic,' she whispered and her eyes moved up to the camera in the corner of the room.

Hingston picked up his mobile and called the Control Room. 'Firearms licensing check, please,' he said, confident he had not seen a record of this kind for Mrs Britton.

In the interview room, Remi was attempting to obtain clarity from Emily, having explained that nothing would be considered pathetic. 'So, let's start at the beginning of what you've just told me and as we work our way through, give me the names of the people you've referred to. You said your mother couldn't make you do it yourself, like *Leanna*, and therefore she said she would kill you. Please tell me more about that,' Remi said gently.

Emily looked down at the floor and inhaled deeply with a noticeable shudder. 'Okay... Leanna. Leanna Snow used to be my best friend. On Saturday she died because she believed she had no choice. I've been told the same, but it's not what I want. Dr Olson said he would protect me, that he would make this all stop.' Tears streamed down her face, converging under her jaw bone. 'Mum is going to kill me *herself* because I won't kill myself. It's Mum's fault Leanna is dead. She told her how to choke...'

Hingston had confirmation from the Control Room that Mrs Britton did not possess a firearms licence. He passed a Post-it Note to DC Sharma which displayed his message for Remi.

'Remi,' said DC Sharma, seizing the moment while Emily was taking another tissue from the box, 'no firearms licence for Mrs Britton. Explore the gun. Could it belong to Mrs Britton's boyfriend? We *don't* have his name.'

'Are you okay to carry on, Emily?'

Emily nodded excessively. 'She... *Mum*, initially suggested I do the same, but Leanna took that method first. They can't all be the same or it may look suspicious, they said.'

Hingston stared at Emily on the screen, the words 'They can't *all* be the same,' pounding in his ears. *How many victims and how many of them children?* he thought.

'Who are *they*?' Remi said and let her question resonate in the silence that followed.

Whether Emily would name the members of the House of Life or the victims of the House of Life it was open to interpretation and her choice. She just picked at her sock.

'We *will* keep you safe, Emily. Who said it may look suspicious?' Remi persisted, focussing on the identification of the offenders first.

'The group,' Emily said and the reluctance that sounded in her voice pained her face. 'You're going to think I'm weird,' she cried, 'like some sort of nutcase.'

'I'm not going to think that at all, Emily, really it's okay for you to tell me,' Remi reassured.

'Those of us that... the group that meet. It came through them.' Emily pushed her hand into her hair and the look of anger that played with her young face contorted her lips and strained her unlined forehead.

Remi maintained her relaxed posture whilst, in the second room, Hingston hunched over his notebook and underlined his scrawled words "through them".

Emily struck the sofa with her fist and apologised with tears drying on her cheeks. 'Technically,' she said in a low voice, 'it's Madame Hesketh who said it would look suspicious. But you can't do anything to stop her. It's impossible! It's my mum and the two priests you should focus on.' Her anger drained. Emily stared at Remi with hopeless eyes.

'Tell me about Madame Hesketh first, Emily,' Remi said, her voice calm.

'You mean you don't know who I'm talking about?' Emily sounded genuine in her surprise. 'But it's a scandal!' she blurted. 'One that the police would know about because it was their fault!'

Remi hesitated; Hingston could tell from her changed posture. He felt equally taken aback.

Remi then glided into action, her hesitation well disguised from Emily. 'The police are a huge organisation, Emily, and Madame Hesketh is a name that's unfamiliar to me. Please, tell me all you know about her,' she said.

Hingston got back on his phone, requesting an intelligence check on the name, or alias, Madame Hesketh. No match: not known to police.

DC Sharma conveyed this information to Remi whilst Hingston leant across the desk to skim read her interview notes and catch up on the key points missed. His finely balanced multi-tasking exercise was fuelled by adrenaline. After a short preamble, Emily had stated that Hesketh "could communicate directly with"... He leant closer to DC Sharma's handwriting... "Ramesses the Third". As his frown knotted, he heard Remi's unwavering voice telling Emily, 'No, I don't think you're pathetic.'

Hingston's thoughts pinballed between what he had learnt about the Harem Conspiracy and the live investigation: the punishments for those who plotted to murder the pharaoh, the sinister name Panik assigned to Emily; the unidentified members of "the group" who presumably were one and the same as the House of Life; the murder of Dr Olson and the possibility that Mrs Britton had played a part; Mrs Britton's alleged threat to Emily's life; the unknown number of suicides, including those carried out and those that may yet come...

'Madame Hesketh,' Emily continued, 'is the only person who can speak with Ramesses. If the police hadn't arrested her there wouldn't have been the need for any deaths! Honestly, there *wouldn't*, because Ramesses would have risen to power again and the way to reach the afterlife would have been understood. Madame Hesketh was on the brink of conveying that special knowledge from Ramesses when she was arrested.' Emily began to sound uplifted, whipped up into a state of enthusiasm upon saying these words.

'So, where can we find Madame Hesketh?' Remi asked.

'You won't,' Emily stated with a peculiar smile. 'That's what I mean about the scandal. The police believed she was a false medium, some kind of fraud, but they were wrong and so was the jury. Madame Hesketh fell ill in prison. She died before she was due to be released in nineteen twenty-three.'

Hingston looked at DC Sharma's notes to check he hadn't misheard. No, it was 1923. His frown deepened and a creeping sense of familiarity disturbed his concentration. A glow of an oil lamp; the scent of cigar smoke; a touch of velvet... When he recognised his intrigue was drawing his attention away from the present, a loud slam, like that of a prison cell door, severed his thoughts. An icy coldness emanated from deep inside his chest as he recognised the mechanism:

this glimpse into the past, which he had not experienced since the Clarkes' case. He was not sure he welcomed it.

Emily was talking increasingly faster. 'The priests have contacted Madame Hesketh and she has started to allow *some* communication with Ramesses again, but it's come at a cost and that's why I need your help.' Emily sighed as though a weight was lifted from her. Then she looked down at her socks. 'I told you you'd think I was weird, didn't I?' and a strange laugh tumbled out.

Hingston felt his phone vibrate in his pocket. Incoming call: Smythe. He stepped away from DC Sharma and answered.

'Can you speak?' Smythe said.

'Yes, sir,' Hingston spoke quietly.

'We've had another suicide. British Museum, Egyptian Sculpture Gallery. Another Thomas Sprigge student, *known* to Emily. *Esther Watts*. Seventeen.'

Chapter Thirteen
You Better Watch Out

A growing sense of a lack of control gnawed at Hingston as he listened to Smythe's account of Esther Watts' suicide. He stared out of the window, down toward the dark grey job car. The windowpane was flecked with dozens of dried raindrops to which dirt clung. They were off-white like stale, muddied snow or stained, slushy marshmallows. He fought against memories of the unconscious Leanna Snow weighing down his arms. In the same way she was pulling and dragging his mind back to last Saturday. He ran his hand down his face. He *had to concentrate* on today's incident.

Esther Watts reportedly stood in silence facing a black statue of Sekhmet, the lion-headed goddess, and used a steak knife she had stolen from the British Museum's first floor restaurant to cut her left arm from her elbow to her wrist. Only when she collapsed, was she noticed. A nearby Portuguese tourist rushed over to discover the sleeve of her thick, black jumper was soaked through and a significant volume of blood had been shed over the statue's feet.

Hingston imagined the tourist's panic-stricken cries for assistance being amplified from an origin largely hidden by the crowds and obscured by the low lighting. He could almost hear them being carried above the rumble of voices and reverberating around the immense exhibition hall with its stone floors and pillar supported ceilings. Dwarfed by the overwhelming scale of the imposing Ancient Egyptian relics, Hingston visualised a shockwave startle the crowds and cause a commotion that played out beneath the undying watch of the giant-sized royals and their gods. He imagined those divine beings with their heads depicting the greatest predators, be they lions like Sekhmet, or jackals, falcons, crocodiles or hippopotami. He wondered too, whether Esther Watts' suicide had also been watched by one or more equally stealthy predators: those of mortal origin and representatives of the House of Life.

***

'When we go back in,' Remi said to Hingston, 'I'm taking *that* with me.' She pointed with a piece of southern fried chicken towards the evidence bag that contained Emily's diary. 'Esther Watts is one of the girls she's written about.'

Lunch was very late. Remi's rapport with Emily had flourished in the last hour of the interview and momentum had to be maintained until a suitable stopping point had been reached. DC Sharma lunched downstairs with Emily and her father whilst Hingston and Remi debriefed over their KFC takeaway to prepare for the second part of Emily's interview.

'*If* she's telling us the truth,' Hingston paused and raised his eyebrows, 'she'll tell us Esther Watts could be at risk.'

Force systems corroborated that Mrs Britton *could* have access to the alleged gun in the form of a rifle: a .22 centrefire owned by her boyfriend, Jonathan Dwyer. Emily stated that Dwyer was an innocent party, unaware of her mother's and her own association with "the group" that she finally, albeit reluctantly, named as the House of Life.

Mrs Britton's motive to kill her daughter was alleged to be in support of the House of Life's goal: to achieve justice for the death of Madame Hesketh and by doing so, to reinstate communication with Ramesses the Third, thus enabling him to rule in today's era through the practice of Ancient Egyptian magic. This, in turn, would provide society with superior knowledge and well-being, and provide believers with access to the afterlife through the practice of certain magical rituals. The motive, as perverse as it sounded to Hingston and Remi, was explained calmly by Emily. She spoke in a persuasive manner that made them recognise the potential Emily had to "recruit" her peers, as new victims, into the House of Life. Emily had proceeded to explain that to achieve justice for Madame Hesketh's death, it was necessary to replicate the punishments suffered by those who plotted to murder Ramesses the Third. When Remi had asked Emily how could she or Leanna Snow be considered responsible for Madame Hesketh's death almost ninety years ago, Emily explained they were not. Their deaths were required because the responsible parties were no longer alive and therefore "sympathetic magic" needed to be applied. Whilst Hingston had sat cold in his seat, Emily, without any evidence of fear, had stated that, 'Sympathetic magic works because those chosen to die hold a magically significant resemblance to those who should have died in nineteen twenty-three.' *What* was deemed a significant resemblance remained unexplained, but Emily was quick to urge that, 'Ramesses and Madame Hesketh make those judgements and the priests simply communicate them.'

'So,' Hingston said resolutely, 'Mrs Britton has allegedly masterminded Leanna Snow's suicide. What about her involvement in Olson's murder? Does it ring true to you?' he asked Remi.

'Emily's only given us what's in the public domain about the murder; no details that suggest she knows any more than that. No reference to other parties. It's possible she's guessing or making a false allegation, but if Olson *was* going to whistle-blow on the House of Life, and if Mrs Britton *is* as involved as Emily states, then yes, she could well be involved in the murder.'

'Emily's given herself a get out on the two *priests*,' Hingston said, changing the focus to the other suspects. He loaded this remark with a tone of scepticism about Emily's truthfulness. He knew it would encourage Remi to examine Emily's account more closely.

'Mmm,' Remi replied, 'but if they do wear these large wooden masks like she described, if they are an anonymous presence at the Wednesday night meetings and if all she knows is that one sounds male and the other female, then what more can we expect to get from her on that?' Her green eyes looked deep into his.

Hingston remained silent with a warm, challenging look holding her gaze.

'Oh,' Remi began to mouth. 'She hasn't yet mentioned Hugh Marchant! If his name doesn't come up when we talk about the other members of the group, then perhaps he is one of the priests. Perhaps there's more Emily can provide about the wax figures, something that may help us identify whether Marchant was one of the priests. But if he was, why would he need to commit suicide? Isn't that for lesser members of the group?'

'Why try to commit suicide at home and not at a place of Egyptian significance?' Hingston posed.

'Good point,' Remi said and sighed. 'What a hell of a job this one is, Jason.'

'Okay, on another tangent, this might help us. I decided to Google Ramesses the Third and *Cambridge*.'

Remi blinked hard and gave him one of her incredulous stares, just like she used to do when they were together.

It made him laugh. 'A bit like the Ashmolean Museum in Oxford,' he continued, 'I had a feeling there was a small collection of Egyptian artefacts on display in the city, and joy of joys, we've got the Fitzwilliam Museum. And what artefact could Emily Britton have been getting herself on a train to Cambridge to see? Ramesses the Third's sarcophagus lid.'

'Ooh. Now that is interesting. Have we got that train ticket with us?' Remi asked, her eyes sparkling.

Hingston enjoyed seeing his inspiration light her up. 'We have,' he smiled. 'Remember Marchant's parents live in Cambridge as well. It was Saturday the 13th of October. The museum should still have CCTV so I'm going to request local officers seize it for us. Maybe we'll find Emily paying good old Ramesses a visit, and *maybe* she won't be alone.'

'You don't trust Emily, do you?' Remi asked, almost rhetorically.

'Let's see what she says. Throughout the interview we've seen her distraught and at the other end of the spectrum we've seen a cool and measured Emily. She's not said enough about these Wednesday meetings. She's failed to state where the group meet.'

'But she is scared too, Jason. She has opened up to us a lot,' Remi defended.

'We must obtain the group's location,' he stressed and screwed up the paper bag that had contained his lunch. 'Watch... in the bin in one,' he boasted.

'Perhaps you should've brought your *Best Detective* mug along,' Remi remarked with a roll of her eyes.

'Olson then,' Hingston prompted, choosing not to further celebrate his hand-eye coordination. At the same time, his cheeky expression told Remi that he was enjoying using his rank to put her through her paces.

Remi gave him an unimpressed stare, but her eyes sparkled. 'Olson then,' she mimicked. 'It's a bizarre one.' She shook her head. 'So, Emily has stated Olson *loved* her. They met in a consultant patient capacity two and a half years ago. He took an interest in her because she talked about her A-Level aspirations which included history. Quote, "a subject dear to him". His "*childless marriage*" prompted him to take more of an interest in her than she thinks he would have taken otherwise. She didn't disclose to anyone that he had given her the necklace because she feared more would be read into their relationship than was actually the case. To Emily, the Isis knot represents well-being and protection.'

Hingston tutted. 'How generous and wholesome of him.'

Remi supported his sarcasm with an agreeable nod and a slow blink. 'Earlier this year, he offered to take her *and* Mrs Britton to meet with a group of people he knew. The purpose: to expose her to an environment that would be a useful learning experience for her studies in both history and psychology.'

'But the House of Life proved too intriguing for them both,' he surmised.

'Yes, the magic and mysticism as Emily put it, quickly made them become standing members of the group. This has been their Wednesday night routine since June,' Remi said. 'Olson attended every week, hence no table tennis and no helping the homeless. He and Emily shared platonic love only. Allegedly no sexual relationship.'

'And she says Olson decided he would whistle-blow on the group once he knew her life was at risk,' Hingston added.

'Yes.'

'But he took too much time getting round to it and met his murderers.' Hingston raised his eyebrows again. 'That could be true.'

'Agreed,' Remi said.

'But Sheila Baptist: the same necklace; the same hairstyle. Olson let her death happen without any whistle-blowing, as Emily puts it. Olson followed a similar course of events with Baptist, it appears. Platonic love I don't accept. She was too old to fill any childless gap in his marriage. And I don't believe that was all he shared with Emily either.'

Remi rubbed her left eye and checked her watch. 'Ten minutes and we're going to have to go back in.'

'Okay, I'll check off my list and propose an order.' Hingston flicked backwards in his notebook. 'Right. Those yet to be explored are: diary content. You're taking it in with you, but covering it *last*. We can challenge anything she's said that doesn't tally. I'll just number the rest...' His biro pressed firmly into the page and the circles he drew round the numbers could be heard whipping through the silence. 'So, first up is: Wednesday nights. Who else attends and *where*. Encompass within this Hugh Marchant, also Sheila Baptist. If Emily joined the group in June, that gave a few weeks before Baptist's suicide. Presumably Emily will have met her.'

Remi gave a tilt of the head in contemplation.

'Fourth point focuses back on her missing episode: why go missing at lunchtime and not before? Five: why take the photograph during assembly and post it on social media? Six: where did she go after leaving school? We know she ended up at her father's flat, but that's only corroborated from last night. Remember, the Panik graffiti fills her diary entry dated the first of December, the day of Leanna Snow's suicide. Did Emily know about Leanna's death before it was announced during assembly, did she come home after assembly to do this graffiti, or was the date coincidental? Eight: text message to Harry and Chloe. Nine: the rest of the diary content and let's see if that prompts comment on Esther Watts.'

Remi nodded in agreement.

'Final point of note,' Hingston added. 'I looked up Sheila Baptist's suicide location after I got home last night. The Victoria Embankment. I'll need to check the file, but I expect the area she chose was as near as possible to Cleopatra's Needle. Let's see if Emily can offer insight into any of the group's designated suicide locations and methods as well.'

***

Emily sat herself back down on the sofa, pulled off her shoes and tucked her legs up just as before. She had cleaned off her smudged eye make-up and, barefaced, looked much more childlike than she had before lunch. She smiled at Remi and as casual as a drifting snowflake her eyes floated a gentle gaze across the room. The angelic calm disappeared when the shocking pink diary that was sat on the window sill caught her attention. 'Is that my fucking diary?' she asked indignantly. The Mrs Britton in her came to the fore.

'Yes, Emily. It was given to us by your mum while you were missing. I've brought it in so we can talk about a few things a bit later,' Remi explained.

Emily made no response. She just stared at Remi whilst gathering her hair upwards. She held it in a tiny clump like a paint brush which she stroked back and forth. The silence continued.

Hingston wondered if Emily was planning ahead, changing tack now she knew the police had her diary.

'Okay, Emily?' Remi checked in a soft voice.

'Yeah,' she sighed. 'We'll talk about it later... sorry I swore,' she added. 'My diary's... um... it's got a lot of messed-up stuff in there, I guess.' She let go of her hair which remained back off her face. Her chocolate brown hair dye looked far too dark for her complexion. The energy-saving light bulb that hung shadeless, in the centre of the room was responsible for stripping her skin of its healthy colour. Through the window, between the gaps in the swivel blinds, the December afternoon appeared to have cloaked the quiet, Islington side street with steel-grey organza. Emily was focussed on one of the gaps.

'Are you okay to continue, Emily?' Remi persisted.

'Yeah... let's keep going,' she agreed.

'It's been very helpful, all you've told me already,' Remi encouraged. 'What's very important for us to know is where you've been meeting on Wednesdays.'

'Mum always drove.'

'Do you know the address?'

Silence. Emily's eyes darted up to the camera.

'Do you know the address, Emily?'

'It's in Islington. I don't know how far from here. It's the street with all the pairs of sphinxes outside people's front doors. I've never noticed a number. I know that sounds stupid, but the sphinxes are painted white and have very pale blue eyes. It's got all the intercom buttons for flats. We meet in the basement.' Emily started to bite the skin beside her index finger.

'Okay, describe the house to me: as much as you can about the outside and the inside,' Remi directed.

'The house looks like all of them on that road, with the steps up to the front door. You've got three floors above ground level, I think, and the basement. They're old. Terraced. Some of the sphinxes are painted black, others white. Some aren't there at all, some are damaged with broken noses, but these ones are in perfect condition. I haven't seen any other ones with blue eyes. The first time we went, Dr Olson took us. He pointed to the eyes. You know, as a means of identifying the right house. Perhaps there is no number, that's why I haven't seen it. You ring the buzzer marked Dr Anita Hesketh.' Emily resumed picking her sock.

'That's good, Emily. So, Dr Anita *Hesketh*,' Remi repeated. 'Is that the same surname as Madame Hesketh?'

'Yes. She is Madame Hesketh's only living relative. She allows the members of the House of Life to meet at her address. She's not really *involved* in what we do, but she has to agree that you can be part of the House of Life for which you have to be trustworthy, respectful and intelligent.' Emily drew breath and appeared to hesitate. 'If you've read my diary, Anita is who I call Ani.'

Remi did not confirm or deny. 'It's okay, Emily, just keep telling me about her.'

'The apparatus and all the artefacts belonged to Madame Hesketh. The priests use them with Ani's permission. These items aid communication with the afterlife. I wanted to become a priest because the abilities and power they have is just completely inspiring.' Emily's rush of enthusiasm increased her pace. 'When they channel magic from the gods, Ramesses appears in the room, like a vision, if you see what I mean, not a physical being, but he is *there* and the voices of the gods join us when we chant. Everything feels so immensely overwhelming and that's what I wanted to be part of: to be one of those who can make this happen.' Emily was tipping from jubilation to sorrow as she held her hands open to Remi, as if she were pleading for understanding.

'Ani only oversees proceedings, but I thought if I could convince her I was capable, devoted enough, she'd get me accepted as a priest... I don't really know how, but that's what I hoped for. But then, through the priests came the direction I had to die and that's when I resisted and Mum...' Emily burst into tears. 'I brought Leanna into this,' she cried. 'It's my fault she got involved.' Emily uncurled her legs and clumsily moved herself to the edge of her seat. She leant towards Remi and gripped the coffee table. 'I did the same with Esther Watts. You've got to help her, *you must*! She's called Esther Watts! She'll be dead too if you don't. Please help her!'

Chapter Fourteen
In Solemn Stillness

Richmond Avenue, Islington: affluent, chic and guarded by a unique row of sphinxes and obelisks. This swanky location was easily identified. The elegant Georgian terraces with their floral mouldings and decorative ironwork attracted homeowners who sought an exclusive type of kerb appeal. According to Emily, it also attracted those beguiled by Ancient Egyptian magic to congregate, in secret, in one of the basements: that allegedly used between 1917 and 1922 for Madame Hesketh's séances.

Mesmerised. That was the word DC Sharma muttered to Hingston while Emily described the basement occupied by the House of Life. The strange and disquieting impression conveyed to the three officers was not easily dislodged from the mind's eye. On taking her first step down into the basement, Emily's sense of smell was flooded with a sweet, thick and boozy incense. This, she was told by Dr Olson, was, 'The liquor of the underworld.' A few steps further down, Dr Olson closed the door from the hallway behind both her and her mother, depriving the narrow staircase of daylight. Oil lamps and candles cast a soft glow up the stairs whilst low, solemn voices hummed and chanted words that oscillated in a language unknown to her. She touched the embossed, turn-of-the-century wallpaper that dressed the walls in burgundy and could, 'Feel,' the last ninety years drop away, as if time had formed a heavy cloak which fell from her shoulders. As she descended and turned into the basement, Emily's eyes were drawn to the veiled and masked participants whose voices strummed the humid air relentlessly. They were seated around a long Victorian dining room table that was dressed in lavish emerald-green velvet and they swayed rhythmically, with every appearance of being entranced. A low, yet sizeable antique display case provided the table's centrepiece. Candles encircled the case, trembling and dancing dapples of light across the mummified remains of a body held within. Leathered skin could be discerned amongst the otherwise dusty biological matter which clung to discoloured bone. The skull had caved in beneath one of the eye sockets, part of the jaw had snapped and a few teeth remained. The exposed void was infiltrated by traces of fabric and brittle strands of long tangled hair. The mummy had allegedly been acquired by Madame Hesketh following an unwrapping party in the late 1880s which explained its poor condition. And despite Madame Hesketh's best efforts to preserve and honour the relic, exposure to air had caused further irreparable deterioration over the decades. Emily explained with disturbing conviction that the three-thousand-year-old remains were the conduit used by the priests to reach the spirits of Madame Hesketh and Ramesses the Third.

Emily described the reluctance with which she had first raised her eyes from the bodily remains: 'It took concerted effort to show courage and give recognition to the force that was watching me.' Her poeticism seemed to romanticise the threat she had felt exuding from the participants and from two man-sized, polished stone statues of the ibis-headed god, Thoth, and the jackal-headed Anubis. These statues were situated some distance beyond the table and were stood in front of thick, sapphire blue curtains. Mirrors on the adjoining walls created the illusion of an army of gods spanning infinitely to the east and the west, and, 'Their eyes penetrated like fire.' Thoth, Emily explained, oversaw the magical arts whilst Anubis protected the basement. The basement, she said, was introduced to her and her mother as, 'The tomb of Richmond Avenue.'

In front of both statues was an area of about a metre squared where the flooring had been removed and excavations reached down to the level of the foundations of the house. The earth that was revealed afforded the priests greater proximity to the underworld. Only from there could offerings of red wine drain down to Ramesses and the gods. Emily explained with great enthusiasm how the statues themselves contained magic which could be absorbed by touching them and by drinking water that had been poured over them. This ritual was carried out by all members of the group, and she and her mother were invited to participate at the end of their first meeting. From that point, Emily felt, 'Empowered and spiritually awakened.'

Situated between Thoth and Anubis, was a third original item from antiquity, which Madame Hesketh had allegedly purchased before the start of the First World War. The decorated wooden seat was not as grand as a throne, but served as such. It was now used by Dr Anita Hesketh, otherwise known as Ani.

Ani's appearance was always striking, according to Emily, who described her with adoration. Ani was a tall, imposing woman who dressed in the same robed fashion as her ancestor, over which she wore Madame Hesketh's lavish collar of turquoise beads, carnelian and gold that had been acquired by tomb raiders at the turn of the twentieth century. Ani oversaw the proceedings of the group, giving occasional authoritative commands and endorsements from behind a golden mask of the lioness goddess, Sekhmet. The officers deduced that this was probably the reason why Esther Watts shed her blood over the feet of the same at the British Museum. Emily stated that Ani spoke with an affluent London accent. However, at the conclusion of the interview, this reportedly grandiose figure remained little more than a name and a voice.

Emily declined to elaborate further upon the magical practices and exchanges that took place during the meetings. She maintained complete silence when

Remi raised the subject of the wax figures and she periodically flashed a glassy-eyed look of fear whenever Remi attempted to steer the interview in a direction she did not wish to proceed. However, Emily made it plain that the group prohibited conversation unrelated to the aims of the House of Life. Members were segregated such that each only knew the identity of Ani, and of the person or persons who introduced them to group. Finally, all forms of electronic communication were banned so that the group maintained complete secrecy: 'No trace beyond these walls, otherwise the link to the afterlife will be lost,' Ani had dictated. After their first meeting, Emily and her mother were provided with veils and thereon were as anonymous as all other members of the group. As such, the officers' hopes of learning more about Hugh Marchant and Sheila Baptist were snuffed out.

Emily's diary, which had prompted such a marked reaction from the teenager, provided a resource for asking direct questions and, it appeared, for obtaining direct answers. A chronology of events gradually came together. Emily stated that aside from Leanna Snow and Esther Watts, none of the girls named in her diary knew of the House of Life. They were simply subjects she wrote about, in pursuit of developing her skills of observation and practising her ability to interpret the human psyche. She admitted that had any of them been "suitable candidates" for meeting the House of Life's membership criteria, then she would have invited them along. Emily stressed how pleased she was now, that they were not.

According to Emily, Leanna Snow was perfect, being intelligent, open-minded, honest and cooperative. Emily stated that her mother also actively encouraged Leanna to become involved and she joined the group in August.

Emily introduced Esther Watts only a month later. She stated that Esther was the individual referred to as "the rebellious sort" in her diary. Esther was in foster care, had joined Thomas Sprigge High School at the start of the Sixth Form and was highly opinionated. Esther made classroom debates interesting. She was a deep thinker, yet very stubborn. She excelled at Art and Design and painted in a dark, gothic style which seemed to dissuade other students from befriending her. Emily stated that she saw Esther as "an experiment": if she could convince someone so strong-willed to support the House of Life, then she would have harnessed an individual who would be committed and passionate about its aims. She hoped to attain her own aspiration to become a priest by impressing Ani with her ability to identify suitable members and in turn, evidence her commitment to Ramesses.

When Remi challenged Emily over the comment in her diary that Leanna was "more introverted than I remember and becoming more pathetic by the day", Emily stated that the words "insignificant pathetic" were a spell. She did not consider that Leanna actually *was* pathetic. The repetition of those words served to cement the fate of the person who had been chosen to die and the more Leanna was associated with those words, the closer she would come to her death. As to why "insignificant pathetic" was scribed inside Emily's own pencil case, Emily stated that simply reading the words was sufficient, and therefore she could perform the spell throughout the school day in silence, unnoticed. At this point in the interview, Emily broke down again. She explained she had believed wholeheartedly that the suicides were necessary for the better good of society, and so did Leanna and Esther. Emily also stated that she did not think she, herself, 'Would ever be selected as one of those to die.' She thought she would remain untouchable and when the news was delivered by the priests, she went into denial. Ultimately, it was Leanna's death that shook her back to her senses.

The marshmallow choking article had remained in her diary from the point her mother proposed it to her as a method of suicide. Emily insisted that the diary page dated the first of December which was covered in the red biro graffiti, was not of her own hand. She stated that her mother had produced the crazed and morbid page to enact a, 'Curse,' to ensure that she, 'Would *become* Panik upon that day.' Hingston knew from his meeting at the Petrie Museum that this practice had some basis within Ancient Egyptian magical theory, even if it was only being tenuously linked to the historical facts of the Harem Conspiracy. Emily said she freaked out and believed that soon thereafter she would be murdered. She immediately sent her text to Chloe and Harry to serve as an apology for involving Leanna and Esther in the group, and an expression of her fear that she would soon be dead and "forgotten", just as had occurred to the original Panik in Ancient Egypt.

Leanna's death did not come as a surprise to Emily on Monday. She took the photo of the assembly to associate Leanna's death with her own disappearance and to signal to Dr Olson that she would be affecting her escape. She alleged she walked directly from school to her father's flat. Twice she went out to local shops, 'For essentials,' but otherwise stayed indoors.

Emily presented as surprisingly astute; she stated she went missing from school so that she, 'Would *have to be* reported missing to the police.' Emily felt that option was the safest; had she left at the weekend, she believed her mother would have reported her to the school as being off sick on the Monday, in order to give herself time to find her—and murder her.

Dr Olson, in Emily's opinion, was blameless and heroic. Whilst he introduced her to the group, he ultimately disapproved of the direction taken by the House of Life. Emily's cheeks were flushed when she stated, 'Dr Olson had tolerated the suicides of people unknown to him, but the prospect of losing *me* was too much for him to bear.' Adding validity to her account, Emily volunteered that they spoke by phone on Tuesday afternoon and evening. She stated that the first call was to confirm she was safe in her father's flat. The second was to discuss the next steps: that he was meeting another member of the group as he believed this person would agree things had gone too far and that together they would report the group to the police. Olson was due to meet with Emily later that night at the flat, but he did not arrive. She turned off her phone once she feared Dr Olson was dead, because she wanted to hide and stay safe.

The train ticket to Cambridge that was found in her diary was explained as a day trip to check out the city in which she hoped to study her psychology degree. She travelled alone and met no one. She corroborated Chloe and Harry's account that she used to date him, but split in 2011, and stated that her mother was aware.

Regarding her mother, Emily painted Mrs Britton in a very poor light. 'My mother has always *wanted* to believe in a higher power and the ability for humans to somehow tap into that power using psychic ability. Whether that power was to be harnessed for good or the opposite, she was equally intrigued. I'm the same, really,' Emily had admitted with a nonchalant laugh. 'I don't know, however, that *I*, as a young woman capable of giving life, would be so open to destroying it. But *she is*.'

Parts of Emily's interview sounded rehearsed. The three officers were in agreement that some of Emily's remarks felt like quotes from literature; well pondered words selected for maximum impact. Emily was certainly *different* to the majority of seventeen-year-olds. Her head teacher's observations and concerns that he had expressed to Hingston earlier in the week appeared fully justified.

'My mother *enjoyed* the concept of members of the group bringing punishment to themselves. She was keen to suggest suicide methods to them. It was almost like she wanted to feel personal responsibility for their deaths.'

Emily did not stop there. 'You must look under Mum's shoes. She has scratched Leanna's name into the soles of one pair, and the letters *mwt.t* are scored underneath it. That literally means *Leanna, dead woman*, and every step she took in those shoes was intended to stamp out Leanna's life like she was smothering a flame. I'm sure you'll find the same with my name,' Emily had added with a distant stare directed toward her pink diary that was on Remi's lap.

The drama peaked when Emily spoke about Olson's murder. 'My mother knew that Dr Olson was the only person that cared about me like a father would. When I went missing, she would have guessed he would help me. Mum believed my real father emigrated to Australia years ago. He *lied* to her, to escape her domination, you know. You can ask him yourselves. If those chosen to die *do not*, Ramesses *will not* rise and regain his power. Dr Olson didn't care about that any more, but my mother does. She *knew* Dr Olson loved me more than he honoured Ramesses, and she *hated* that! She would have got a message to Ani. On Tuesday night when Dr Olson met with the person who introduced him to the group, *they* would have been ready to murder him. Let's face it, what is Dr Olson's life to my mother when she is prepared to kill her own daughter?'

As fantastical as Emily sounded, there was an honesty in her fearfulness. Whilst Hingston watched her on the screen, in the back of his mind was the image of Mrs Britton: arrogant, dominant and intolerant. He had pictured Mrs Britton stood in her kitchen, just as he witnessed on Wednesday, and his mind replayed her sudden burst of emotion. As he visualised her falling tears, he remembered the crystal ashtray in her hands, and just at that moment Emily's interview interrupted his chain of thought with: 'Oh! I nearly forgot!'

Hingston listened as Emily continued: 'Mum smashes things. She smashes objects when performing spells. There *must* be evidence of broken china or glass in the rubbish. She does it to break the person: like stamping upon their name but with greater effect.' And Hingston remembered what Mrs Britton said over her smashed ashtray: '*Pathetic.*' Innocent coincidence it appeared not.

***

'Good work.' Smythe's huskiness sounded more pronounced over the speakerphone.

Hingston directed the mobile towards Remi whilst she reversed the Astra into a narrow parking space in the yard at Islington. Somewhere on the A1, Mr Britton drove north with Emily. A hotel in Hertfordshire was to provide suitable distance from the threat to Emily's safety which, despite her cooperation throughout the afternoon, remained only partially identified.

'Arrest enquiry for Mrs Britton underway as we speak,' Smythe boomed, prompting Hingston to visualise two uniformed officers presenting themselves at her pristine front door in the crisp night air.

In a moment of private amusement Hingston wondered whether Mrs Britton would shoot the same disdainful glance toward *their* feet and demand, "No boots past the lobby" before realising they weren't coming in: *she* was going out.

Chapter Fifteen
Shall I Play for You?

Enough was enough. At ten p.m. Hingston clicked the logoff button. He looked between the monitors and listened to Remi hammering at her keyboard. They were the only officers left in the report writing room.

'Ten o'clock,' he yawned loudly. 'You nearly done?'

'Just a... bout,' she replied whilst her fingers scrambled across the keys.

Hingston massaged his forehead and leaned back in his chair. He tried to reflect upon the day, but discovered an overload of information fighting for airspace like the voices of disc jockeys jostling amongst the fuzz of medium wave radio. He stood up and walked to the window where his reflection met him in the cold pane. He had started his working week in a similar way: staring into darkness. But now, Leanna Snow's death did not preoccupy his mind with pensive thoughts. The sense of personal responsibility that urged him to respond to Leanna choking in the coffee shop had evolved into fervid determination to identify all persons: victims and perpetrators, and to dismantle the House of Life. He mused over the strange letters "mwt.t", translated by Emily as "dead woman", and its conflict with the fact that Leanna Snow and Esther Watts were still children in the eyes of the law.

'Right,' Remi called out. 'Done!'

'Let's hope tomorrow *remains* a rest day,' Hingston said with a tired smile. 'I need a bit of time to look at these books from the Petrie Museum, never mind Zack who I've deserted for most of the week.'

'We've done as much as we can with Emily for the time being. It's been good progress,' Remi responded as she buttoned up her coat.

Hingston looked at her navy-blue woollen trench coat, the well-fitted classic that she'd been wearing since they were together. It didn't look any different for the years that had passed. As she picked up her car keys, the BMW badge caught the light and Smythe's white Series 5 might as well have run Hingston down, for his memories of 2008 were instantly squashed.

'Rob's updating the Deputy Commissioner first thing Monday,' Remi continued. 'Then he'll be at the Gold meeting in the afternoon. *So...* my rest day will be spent *sharing the stress*,' she laughed. 'I wonder what Emily's mother will say in interview tomorrow.'

'Well,' Hingston raised his eyebrows. 'I'll just have to wait for Monday to know that, but *you* will have the pleasure of finding out on the day,' he teased.

'I'm not sure *pleasure's* the word, Jason! Rob's never really off duty, you know. It can get a bit tiresome.'

'You aren't going to succeed in making me feel sorry for you,' Hingston quipped. 'While I'm doing my chores and cooking for Zack, you'll be having an à la carte Sunday lunch; cruising in that Beemer with its fancy heated leather seats; getting your Christmas decorations up; housework done by the DCI's maid...'

Remi smacked his arm with her gloved hand. 'Hey, it's not like I'm a footballer's wife!'

'*No...*' he stressed. 'But... if he was willing to share some of his fake tan...'

Remi rolled her eyes and flicked off the light. 'C'mon. It's time to get home.'

***

Uncle Zack's whistling and the warm aroma of the Salcombe Smokies he was grilling carried up the staircase early on Sunday morning.

'Get yourself down here, son!' Zack's boisterous volume was of military proportion, softened by his cheerful laugh that trailed back with him into the kitchen. He knew Hingston's alarm clock had not yet sounded. Hingston, who was accustomed to the quiet of living alone, had already been stirred ten minutes earlier by the clatter of dishes and cutlery. Last night, Zack specifically checked that, 'Police work would not be encroaching on the traditional day of rest.' Now, at six thirty a.m. it became apparent that Zack had all intention of doing the encroaching himself, and that was more than okay with Hingston. As he stepped out of bed he felt surprisingly revitalised by Zack's undisclosed plan for the day.

***

By eight a.m. the pair were on the road. Zack's Volvo had just over seventy thousand on the clock and most of those miles were accompanied by the sounds of the Rolling Stones. Today was no exception. The only clue Zack gave as to their destination, was the hundred and twenty miles that would be accrued, by the time they return to Hatch End.

'So, my boy, I've started that research for you,' Zack announced after *Angie* faded out. 'Thought I'd make yesterday afternoon productive by searching the British Newspaper Archive.'

'I thought you had to go to Colindale for that,' Hingston replied whilst wondering how Zack had found the time for it.

'*Used to*,' Zack corrected, 'but they've been digitalising their records, starting with the oldies from the nineteenth century. Very useful website for this little project as it turns out.'

Old newspapers. Hingston recalled the first time he read the words "Kallensee's Great Circus". How innocuous that name had sounded amongst the surrounding abundance of notices printed on that soft beige newspaper. How pleasing it had been to unfold that demure little wad, that intriguing time capsule that had been locked inside the musical box for almost one hundred and fifty years. He remembered the tremendous emotional shift experienced when Mr Kallensee, Mr Bibbings and Mr Crim, the Circus' Proprietor, Acting Manager and Clown were suddenly no longer faded shadows like the grey Victorian print; when he glimpsed between the circus tent canvas and recognised the criminal potential within their dangerous, debauched theatre which shouted out to him like the equestriennes' vivid spangled costumes and the Circassian girl's painted scarlet lips... 'Don't you miss the feel of the aged paper?' Hingston asked with a wistful tone to his voice.

'Well, it's still all there at Colindale, for now, at least.' Zack sounded a little perturbed that his nephew hadn't jumped in with an enthusiastic remark or a thanks for cracking on with the task. 'But digital is the way forward. Gives you faster access, Jason. Quicker results!'

'Yes, they're doing the same at work, but those old newspaper records are a bit different. Anyway!' Hingston realised his sentimental tangent was ill-timed. 'How did you get on?'

'As well as I had hoped.' Zack glanced at Hingston just before joining the A1.

Hingston wondered where Zack was taking him and began to calculate mileages in his head. 'Are we doing something related to your research today?'

'Today? On a Sunday?' Zack teased.

'You can't keep this up for another fifty miles,' Hingston laughed.

As Zack entered the national speed limit and they headed north, Hingston found himself and his thoughts accelerating toward Hertfordshire and Emily Britton. He thought about Emily's apparent obsession with the words *insignificant* and *pathetic* which she continued to intersperse during her interview. Her explanation that they constituted a spell now fuelled a suspicion that those were the very words she was mouthing in the car on the way to the ABE suite. Had she in fact, been practising the spell *knowing* that Esther Watts was in the British Museum preparing to commit suicide? Did she only mention Esther Watts once she knew it was too late to prevent her death? Could she still be a suspect? She vehemently denied knowledge of any proposed suicide locations and presented herself as a victim, helpless to the control of her mother, the priests, Ani and the overwhelming power of the group. Aside from her admission to remotely practising a spell that could, in reality, have no material effect, she stressed that she did not even discuss suicide with Leanna Snow or Esther Watts. She made no self-incriminating remarks that could be taken to suggest she had encouraged the suicide of either girl, or anyone else for that matter. 'The priests' communication is intended to be final,' Emily had insisted. Hingston pictured Emily picking at her sock. But had she been playing the police along?

Emily's strange behaviour made him restless. In Hingston's opinion, the adult members of the House of Life undoubtedly deserved the maximum penalty carried by the Suicide Act 1961, for which he believed fourteen years' imprisonment was still insufficient. In respect of Emily, if information came to light that suggested she may be a suspect, then she would have to be interviewed under police caution and in the presence of an appropriate adult. But for now at least, Emily sat safe with her father in a hotel room, while Mrs Britton breakfasted on a hard bench in police custody, listening to the grumblings and unattractive noises of Saturday night's prisoners, her view confined to plain walls, a heavy blue door and a steel toilet pan.

As they journeyed through the Hatfield Tunnel the soft yellow lights overhead illuminated the cabin in rhythmic, sweeping motions. Zack accelerated to overtake a lorry and stayed in the outside lane, missing the next junction.

'You *are* taking us north, then,' Hingston laughed and flashed a wise guy look at Zack.

'Thought you'd've worked that out after Barnet,' Zack retorted. 'Seeing that your newspaper clipping cited Royston, I'd expected you to guess. We're stopping there first. It would be wrong to do a drive-by given that's where your Circassian chap died. We've got two more locations after that. Those will remain a surprise, but so as not to disappoint, I haven't got anything on the girl—*as yet.*' Zack glanced at Hingston and smiled.

***

It was cool and crisp as they approached the small medieval market town of Royston on the northern edge of Hertfordshire. Open fields stretched up to small patches of woodland and into more arable farmland. Cables for a railway line ran parallel to the dual carriageway, but they were set at such a distance into the countryside they appeared almost miniature in scale. Hatch End with its suburban streets and busy roads suddenly felt remote. London compared to Royston was like the juxtaposition of an all-action computer game and an afternoon of quoits and draughts.

The sun was out as Zack turned off the Baldock Road into a chalky, bumpy side road that led to a small car park cut into grassy heathland. The air smelt fresh, and noticeably clean.

After stretching their legs and pouring coffees from Hingston's flask, they stood by the car and looked across the heath towards a golf course. Zack, sipping his steaming drink, began to tell the story as he now knew it, of "Augustus the tightrope walker" who plummeted to his death on the 27th of May 1866 during the evening performance of Kallensee's Great Circus.

'*Augustus*, a name meaning magnificent and exalted amongst other grandiose vocabulary, was all we had in this little newspaper clipping you gave me. *That*, and the town in which he died.' Uncle Zack gave a dramatic pause, just as he used to when Hingston was a boy and he was attempting to wow him with an account of his latest cricketing victory.

Hingston smiled and laughed to himself as he was taken back twenty years to his childhood holidays.

'Now,' Zack continued, 'just beyond this golf course, present-day circuses pitch up with their big tops and their fleets of vehicles. Where Kallensee's Great Circus situated their tents, it appears impossible to know. Either it was not reported or the relevant paper has not been uploaded to the British Newspaper Archive. I've discovered that most Victorian era adverts for circuses refer solely to Royston as the location, presumably because being a small town their presence would have been unmissable.'

Hingston nodded.

'However, it was also commonplace for newspapers to print very short notices that reported retrospectively on the arrival of travelling circuses. This is true of Royston. Some of these included the success or failure of their performances to entertain the public, and *some* identified specific locations such as the field belonging to a named farmer, or the meadow adjoining a specific road. I rather liked a description that read "in the meadow near the White Bear in the Gas Road". Sounds a bit like a cryptic clue,' Zack chortled.

'Sounds like some circuses may have arrived and set up without prior authority,' Hingston suggested. He imagined Mr Kallensee as somewhat the opportunist.

'Now,' said Zack in a serious tone, 'Augustus the tightrope walker wasn't famous like Blondin, but his death was so shocking that the papers reported on his funeral.'

'Okay,' Hingston encouraged, eager for Zack to continue.

'And that is how I so readily discovered his actual name: *Samuel Silverthorne.*'

Hingston was silent as he meditated upon that name, applying it to both the man himself and to the beautiful Circassian girl: the daughter of Samuel Silverthorne. 'Amazing! Well done!' he laughed. 'This is going to allow us to find out a lot more, isn't it?'

'It should do,' Zack said after he swallowed the last of his coffee. 'Come on. Back to the car. I've got a quick detour ahead of our next stop.' Zack was clearly in his element as he hurriedly packed up the flask, slammed the boot and started the car. He sported a broad smile and the sunlight highlighted his laughter lines and thick grey eyebrows.

They travelled past the golf course, noticing the Queen Victoria Memorial, and headed through the town centre with its trees decorated with strings of Christmas lights that would have looked cheerful had it been dark. Very quickly they were back out onto the main road north and either side of it were yet more fields that were undoubtedly little changed since the days of Kallensee and Samuel Silverthorne.

'This is nothing more than a point of interest, discovered when I was route planning last night,' Zack announced as they turned left ahead of a quaint wooden bus stop that had a tiled pitched roof. 'Felt like one of those little coincidences that you would like to see with your own eyes.'

'Mmm,' Hingston replied, interested as to what this could be.

The road became distinctly residential with a mix of original thatched cottages infilled by larger developments of the mid-twentieth century.

'Here we are,' Zack said as he slowed down and indicated left. 'Chiswick End.'

'Chiswick End,' Hingston repeated with intrigue in his voice. 'Well, this is a narrow road. It has a small stream,' he observed. Memories of Shuttern Brook in Newton St Cyres a year and a half ago were swiftly followed by the terrible vision he had experienced of the death of Samuel Silverthorne.

'Yes, it's a dead end,' Zack replied. 'We'll turn around here.' He manoeuvred the Volvo adeptly. 'Google Maps had emblazoned Chiswick End in capitals over this area of Royston, and in the centre of Royston, Samuel was buried. His resemblance to you and the association with the town in which you work seemed... well, a bit...'

'Unexpected,' Hingston cut in.

'*Spooky* I'd call it, my boy,' Zack corrected with a laugh.

***

The walk along the topiary-lined avenue up to the striking St John the Baptist Church with its flint clerestories and decorative tower was beautified by the rich, amplified, choral sounds of the Sung Eucharist. Hingston and Zack admired the architecture and the well-tended Priory Memorial Gardens that were the central focus of Royston. They noticed the stark absence of headstones which would usually weave a trail of centuries-old memories through the grass. Lichen, moss and pitted names upon crowded rows of weatherworn memorials had been the pair's expectation. Instead, they perused a number of headstones that had long since been relocated to lean safely against a wall, and the majority they found to be illegible.

Zack continued to relay the findings of his research. 'I will contact the church in the week to enquire as to the location of the burial plot,' he said. 'I was especially interested to read a local newspaper article which stated that Kallensee's Great Circus funded Samuel's funeral.'

Hingston was surprised. 'That must have been costly,' he remarked.

'Yes, and they may well have been short of paying for a headstone, but circus performers supported each other and their family members in times of great need.

A benefit performance was held and I have the *exact* location. That is where I'm taking us next.'

***

Their leisurely drive on this peaceful morning continued with a brief diversion off the A10. The village of Melbourn, which Zack pointed out had been listed in the Domesday Book, still resonated with times past. An old red telephone box and a war memorial embellished the foreground of a prominent corner plot belonging to All Saints' Church. A host of mature trees towered over the churchyard casting lengthy shadows over the gravestones which were illuminated by the winter sunshine. Members of the morning's congregation were still departing, finishing their conversations as they exited through decorative wrought iron gates. As Zack carried on past, Hingston imagined he was back in Royston at the springtime scene in 1866 when mourners walked from the funeral service to the final resting place of Samuel Silverthorne, wherever in the churchyard that may have been.

Zack did not stop at the park and ride that served Cambridge city centre. They passed the Cambridge University Botanical Garden and the buildings grew older, grander and more imposing. Architectural prowess and masonry skills were displayed in abundance, tested and proven by their longevity and celebrated by their preservation. Cambridge was itself a living museum and Hingston was eager to explore both Zack's destination and one of his own: the Fitzwilliam Museum where an ancient stone relic of particular interest could be met face to face.

***

A narrow side street provided a Christmas treat; resident permit holders only parking that did not apply on Sundays and a car indicating out of the otherwise full bays. In minutes they were at the edge of a large green expanse, segmented by long, straight pathways which also served Cambridge's many bicycles. Trees made it easy to establish the perimeter and the wooden guards that protected their trunks doubled up as convenient bike rests. A number of shabby, vintage cycles were only yards from where Hingston and Zack were stood.

'This,' Zack said with a degree of pride, 'is Midsummer Common. It borders the River Cam, is overlooked by a two Michelin Star restaurant which we're not going to be lunching at unfortunately,' he chuckled, 'and is situated only half a mile from the city centre.'

Hingston spied the blue signpost from where Zack had gleaned his last piece of geographical information.

'And,' Zack continued, 'is therefore a very desirable and profitable location within the annual calendar of events for Kallensee's Great Circus.'

'Remarkable,' said Hingston. 'You would think a benefit performance held here would have more than covered the funeral. I should get you working for me more often,' he added with a laugh. 'Shall we take a walk?' He indicated with a tilt of his head in the direction of the river.

Lunch was a hearty roast with all the richness of Cambridge's historic academic hub in which the restaurant held a prime location opposite the tremendous, gothic King's College and its spectacular chapel. It was also neighbour to the unique, modern timepiece known as the Corpus Clock. Atop its hefty gold-plated clock face stalked a black, mechanical, grasshopper-like creature which appeared far more monstrous than the gargoyles which surveyed the city. To Hingston's mind, its spiky gold teeth were inspired by the angler fish; it sported the sting of a hornet and blinked with dragon eyes. Zack, in his usual knowledgeable manner, informed him that this creature was officially named a Chronophage, which means "time eater". It was indeed gobbling up a great deal of tourism time both when they arrived and after they left the restaurant to walk further down the road to the Fitzwilliam Museum.

'So, what exactly is it that you're interested to see, son? Anything that's going to be up my street?' Zack enquired.

'Ramesses the Third's sarcophagus lid,' Hingston replied as he clasped his hands in response to the cold.

Zack gave him a look of surprise.

Hingston had to elaborate. 'This is not something I can discuss further because it relates to a case. There's no reason for me to travel up here during work time, so the convenience of stopping by is more a matter of personal interest.'

'You mean you're sniffing around? Being a stereotypical nosy policeman?' Zack teased.

Hingston tutted. 'I'm not evidence gathering if that's what you think. Nothing more than background research to better know my subject,' he said with a smile.

Zack gave him a look that suggested he thought otherwise. 'Well, we've got a couple of hours before closing time. Should be able to see a fair bit.'

***

He was the centrepiece: the ultimate image of regality; a giant, three-dimensional depiction of the pharaoh in the guise of the god Osiris. Displayed upright, fashioned in the form of a wrapped mummy, he was adorned by a tall, stylistic feathered crown and symbols of kingship. He had been carved from red granite and spanned the entire length of the monolithic sarcophagus lid. Ramesses the Third looked commanding, divine and eternal. Goddesses reached out from the relief-effect background design to protect and revere him with their delicate hands and slender, embracing arms. He dominated the other objects in the gallery as impressively as it may be imagined his earthly body once ruled over the land of Ancient Egypt.

Hingston looked up into Ramesses' pupilless eyes and observed their ability to cast a gaze from a multitude of perspectives. His face was pristine, although his plaited beard was partly broken off. There was a gentleness to his features which Hingston had not expected. He wondered if there had been a kindness within this ruler that had been exploited by those plotting his downfall. He couldn't help but think that the Harem Conspiracy offenders had unwittingly set up Ramesses the Third to be a repeat victim: exploited again thousands of years later by the false medium, Madame Hesketh, and again by a second group of murderous conspirators, in the form of the House of Life. The oppressive feelings he had experienced in the Petrie Museum and his lifelong aversion to the Ancient Egyptian fascination with death began to slip away. It was replaced by an increased concern about the practices going on in the basement of Richmond Avenue.

'You gonna take some photos then, Jason? Bit of a record to help you at a later date?' Zack suggested.

'Good idea,' Hingston replied. He took a few paces backwards, scanned the room and saw a CCTV camera affixed to a display cabinet. With a burst of optimism, he now looked forward to Cambridgeshire Constabulary's response to the enquiry he made yesterday. He wondered if Emily would be on the footage for the 13th of October and if so, with whom. He glanced through into the adjoining gallery and noticed a couple of art students sketching designs painted on decorative pottery vases from Ancient Greece. They were engrossed in their work. And then he felt *he* was being watched. He turned in a nonchalant manner and lifted his gaze in the direction of the doorway that led to the dim lit corridor and the softly illuminated staircase beyond. The face was instantly recognisable and with a fleeting smile passing over her lips, she stepped out of view. His heart raced, yet he wasn't about to tell Zack. Their day's exploration felt strangely complete. It appeared *Miss* Silverthorne wanted him to know she approved.

Chapter Sixteen
Freeze Thy Blood Less Coldly

'Morning, sarge.' One of the older, portly DCs acknowledged Hingston as they passed in the corridor. He held an empty cup in his hand and whistled on his way to the kitchen.

'Morning, Mick,' Hingston replied. He strode into the report writing room, keen to start the week.

The first floor at Hampstead felt invigorating. It was full of the drive and passion that the otherwise empty station deserved. It reminded Hingston of the first time he heard the musical box play after its long duration of silence. He considered each officer and member of staff to be performing their part like the pins on the brass cylinder inside the musical box plucking the steel teeth: a finely tuned mechanism that was systematically trundling through the investigation examining every piece of information from the opening few notes, through the multi-layered arrangements, to the celebrated finale.

Over the next twenty minutes everyone buzzed about the arrest of Mrs Britton and muted tones rumbled in and out whenever Esther Watts' suicide distracted from the headline.

Remi came round to Hingston's side of the desk and pulled over a swivel chair. Her patent heeled boots protruded from her tweed trousers as she sat down and crossed her legs. 'How was your day off?' she asked.

'Yeah, good. Went on a road trip with Zack. Ended up in Cambridge of all places,' he laughed.

'Ooh. Shame you couldn't have called into the museum to get that CCTV,' Remi replied. She glanced at his silver cufflinks, smiled and gave him a knowing look. 'But you went in there anyway, didn't you?'

Amused, he made her wait for a response. 'Cambridgeshire have emailed me. They're going to obtain the footage this morning. And *yes*, I've seen the CCTV camera with my own eyes, so I know Emily *will* have been captured if she went there. That aside, old Ramesses is quite impressive, you know...' Hingston got the photos up on his mobile and handed it to Remi.

As she flicked through the shots, Hingston emptied the Petrie Museum books from his satchel onto the desk.

'Ramesses is being adored by enough attractive young women, don't you think!' Remi exclaimed.

'And according to these text books, the Harem Conspiracy was led by one of his queens. I didn't get much reading done last night, but I discovered that Olson's White House Clinic shares its name with the Ancient Egyptian Treasury.'

Remi stared at him.

'Olson's interest in Egyptology goes way back,' Hingston said.

'As might his entanglement with the House of Life,' Remi surmised.

***

Smythe stormed along the corridor just after ten. Someone in the report writing room flagged his arrival, having caught sight of his personage speed past the doorway without looking in.

'No *good morning* from the boss, then,' one of the investigators quipped.

Hingston peered between the monitors at Remi who returned his look with a roll of her eyes and an expression that indicated Smythe was still in a bad mood. His meeting with the Deputy Commissioner had clearly made Monday morning miserable.

By the start of the briefing at ten thirty, Smythe had not improved. 'We're all aware there's a lot to do, so this will be as streamlined as possible,' Smythe said with pursed lips and a meaningful scan of the large room which was full to capacity with standing room taken at the back. He summarised the headlines from Emily Britton's interview and the fact that Mrs Britton remained in custody, professing her innocence and without an alibi for the night of Olson's murder. 'The Brittons' home address was searched yesterday. We have located three pairs of Mrs Britton's footwear with inscriptions on the bottom matching her daughter's allegation against her, and a muddy pair of boots which are subject to forensic examination this morning.'

Barry gave an affirmative nod.

'Her *boyfriend*, Jonathan Dwyer,' Smythe rolled straight onto the next headline, 'was interviewed yesterday. Due to the intermittent nature of their casual relationship, Dwyer claims no knowledge of her whereabouts on Wednesday nights, nor on the night of Olson's murder, for which Dwyer has his own alibi.' Smythe puckered his lips. 'He was at his work's Christmas party where he got off with a colleague and spent the night at her home address.'

Some exchanges within the room said it all. Having met Mrs Britton, Hingston was not surprised.

'The existence of Dwyer's rifle,' Smythe continued, 'is known to Mrs Britton, but he has not given her a key to his home address and the rifle is stored securely. Dwyer considers Emily Britton to be a bright girl who gets on well with her mother, although he has only met Emily on relatively few occasions.'

The focus moved onto Esther Watts' suicide, for which the press and social media had created a furore over the apparent ease at which the teenager had removed a steak knife from the British Museum's restaurant. Esther Watts' foster carer was of the belief that Esther was attending her local youth club on Wednesday nights and had noticed no changes in her behaviour, not even on the day of her suicide. Smythe acknowledged the impact two deaths would be having on all associated with Thomas Sprigge High School, and confirmed police attendance at a safeguarding meeting this afternoon at Ealing Borough Council offices.

Smythe's voice suddenly went hoarse. He cleared his throat. 'This leads us to DS Hingston's identification of a further link between four of our deaths. We now know that all took place at locations of Ancient Egyptian significance, not all of them obvious. Sheila Baptist drowned opposite Cleopatra's Needle. The cafe in which Leanna Snow died occupies a plot that historically belonged to an exhibition hall called the Egyptian Hall, also known as "England's Home of Mystery". Then we have Olson at the Egyptian Avenue and Esther Watts in the Egyptian Sculpture Gallery.' Smythe inhaled deeply. 'Hugh Marchant bucked the trend and proved unsuccessful in his attempt. We have some good news, ladies and gents: he stabilised this weekend and the hospital anticipate he will be well enough to be discharged for us to interview him later today or tomorrow.'

Some positive comments were muttered throughout the room.

'In light of the media interest in Esther Watts, may I take this moment to stress that it remains *confidential* that Leanna Snow's death is suspected suicide. The Coroner's Office has been updated accordingly this morning.' Smythe checked his watch and gave another stern look. '*Moving on...* Suspects. Dr Anita Hesketh.

Her address in Richmond Avenue, Islington, has been under surveillance since last night and it appears unoccupied. We have ascertained that the house is split into flats, but she has no current tenants. She owns no other UK properties and she is believed to be in the UK at this time. *Next up*, the male wearing glasses who was seen in Marchant's front passenger seat, driving away from Highgate Village. CCTV trawl has picked up the vehicle en route to Highgate Cemetery, we've got a good image, and it's been circulated to all forces.' Smythe pressed the laptop and the unidentified male appeared on the projector screen, looking indeed much smaller than Marchant.

Smythe's voice rose when he praised High Tech Crime for, 'Continuing hammer and tongs all weekend,' allowing the week to commence with access to the content of Olson's home computer, Leanna Snow's devices, Emily Britton's mobile which she handed over for examination on Saturday, and Mrs Britton's mobile and tablet. No mention was made of the missing wax figures, and eager faces and upright postures showed that everyone in the room was raring to return to their respective tasks.

'Any further updates we should be discussing that haven't been captured already?' Smythe asked with open hands.

The silent room indicated not.

'Any questions?' He paused. 'Good. Back to work. Return here at four thirty p.m. please.'

***

'Dr Yorke,' Hingston announced as soon as he returned to his desk.

'Yes,' Remi said, 'my charming *potential* suspect.'

'The overly helpful psychiatrist,' he mocked in a deep, well-to-do voice and mimicked the laugh he had found so nauseating.

Remi smiled. 'I spoke with Rob about him.'

Hingston remained silent and thought back to Friday night. He recalled Smythe's jealous look that was flashed his way outside the Magic Circle Headquarters and concluded the evening's alcohol had begun to dissolve Smythe's poker face. He smiled back to encourage Remi to continue.

'He agreed with you,' she said.

Hingston raised his eyebrows. 'Let's speak with him today.'

***

After a quick lunch and a check for any new emails, Hingston and Remi were ready to go. The day had already yielded some new information that the large and expanding team had been desperate to receive. A positive identification had been received from Cambridgeshire Constabulary for the passenger in Marchant's car. Thirty-four-year-old James Roe was known to police for his involvement in protests and he was convicted of a public order offence in 2008. Roe, a resident of Trumpington, the village on the perimeter of Cambridge through which Hingston had passed yesterday, was now subject of an arrest enquiry.

The British Museum had supplied the attendance lists for the talks frequented by Olson and on several appeared the name Dr A. Hesketh.

Hingston, a firm believer in knowing one's subject, had requested the 1920s Met Police file on the fraudulent medium, Madame Hesketh, along with the associated prosecution and Home Office files held at the National Archives. Scanned copies would be with him today.

'You all good?' Hingston asked Remi.

'Two minutes,' she replied as she hurried her belongings together and without telling him where she was going, she headed, presumably, to the loo.

Hingston, coated, rested up against his desk with his satchel strap loose upon his shoulder and watched the other officers and staff working at their computers, reviewing and processing information in this powerhouse that was fuelled with adrenaline and renewed optimism.

'Bloody hell!' hollered the DC who had greeted Hingston first thing.

The outburst in the room was met with the level of interest such an exclamation warranted. Heads were turned and only a couple of officers engrossed in phone calls did not down tools.

'*M W T dot T*! *Dead woman*! It's the name of a file on Olson's computer!'

Those sat closest moved round to look at the DC's screen.

'Shit. There's a document!' he continued. 'We've got names... *eight* names!'

***

Hingston and Remi pulled up outside Dr Yorke's clinic having filled the twenty-minute journey with speculative conversation about the race now on in the Major Incident Room. Sheila Baptist and Leanna Snow, were two of the eight names Olson had listed in alphabetical order. Emily Britton did not feature. Were the remaining six deceased or could any still be alive?

'You know, Jason, Olson's focus is on dead *women*. I'm thinking Hugh Marchant saw suicide as his only way out after he got involved in Olson's murder, *not* because the House of Life dictated it.'

'It's only women they're targeting?' Hingston paused as he considered the hypothesis. 'Could be. Would explain Marchant's attempted suicide location sharing no association with Ancient Egypt.'

'And it could support Emily's account that Olson was planning to whistle-blow which resulted in his murder. As a male, he should otherwise have been quite safe.'

'That would conflict with the Harem Conspiracy,' Hingston said, 'because male and female conspirators met their deaths. But this *is* a perverse interpretation of history that we're dealing with.'

They looked up at the clinic. Just over five minutes to spare.

'Oh, I forgot to tell you,' Remi said. 'Sheila Baptist wasn't pregnant when she died.'

The Edwardian building in which Yorke worked was painted white outside and in. Colourful, impressionistic paintings were suspended from the original picture rails. The clinic's short, bespectacled receptionist was refilling a glass at a water cooler when they entered. The machine glugged and bubbled noisily.

'Dr Yorke is just taking a phone call,' the receptionist advised after she returned to her chic, designer desk and ascertained their identities. 'It is unusual for him to be even one minute off schedule,' she said with a smile. 'Two o'clock is two o'clock as far as Dr Yorke's concerned, so he will be with you imminently!' Her cheerfulness was in abundance.

Hingston watched the receptionist with interest as she gave a wide smile. Her cheeks rose so high that her eyes nearly closed. Through her thick lenses it gave the disconcerting illusion that her eyes might have disappeared altogether. Then, somewhere in his distant memory, Hingston recalled a vintage cartoon that featured a mole emerging into sunlight. He smiled back.

Hingston and Remi took seats in the waiting area and looked at the various paintings.

The rattle of the receptionist's telephone receiver broke the silence. 'Well, I never!' she hooted. 'He's still on that phone. I do apologise for the lack of punctuality.'

Remi shrugged. 'Not a problem, it's only a few minutes,' she replied and turned to Hingston. She lowered her voice. 'D'you think he's going to try to postpone?'

Hingston gave her a contemplative look just as Dr Yorke's office door was flung open.

'Officers!' He greeted them with a cheerful voice and a commiserative frown. 'This is not my usual style, I can assure you.'

Before they had barely risen to their feet, Dr Yorke strode across and Hingston decided his first impression at Hampstead Police Station was spot on.

'DC Armitage, I assured you of my utmost assistance.' Yorke's giraffe-like eyelashes further softened the gaze he cast upon Remi and his Savile Row outfit complemented his square jaw and pearly teeth. 'As a man of my word, it pains me to greet you with an unexpected cancellation. My mother has just suffered a stroke and I have to rush to St Thomas' Hospital.' He glanced at Hingston and gave another commiserative frown.

'We're sorry to hear that,' Hingston responded, 'but we are used to emergencies in our business. You get yourself to your mother.'

Dr Yorke sighed. 'Thank you and sincere apologies. I know you have frantic schedules. I've got some time in the diary tomorrow morning if that's good for you? The receptionist can tell you when that is and get it agreed with my secretary.' With that, Dr Yorke strode back to his open office door, reached to a coat stand, flicked off the light and hurried back past them and out of the building with a leather jacket over his arm and car keys in his hand. 'Cheerio for now,' he called.

The receptionist was somewhat flustered by Dr Yorke's news and departure. 'Oh, the poor man,' she said with her cheeks flushed. 'Oh, where's his diary gone? Oh, yes. Right, here we are. *Tomorrow*. He can do before clinic opens at eight... or ten thirty... or three o'clock.'

Hingston spoke. 'We're going to have to check schedules back at the station. I know Tuesday afternoon is no good for me, morning may be okay, but what's Wednesday looking like?'

Remi shot him a glance and blinked.

'No time Wednesday, I'm afraid,' the receptionist confirmed. 'He only does Wednesday mornings and this one's fully booked.'

'Might he be open to a short appointment directly after clinic finishes or later in the day? We can meet him at his home address if that suits,' Hingston pressed.

'His secretary would have to advise, but it's my understanding that he has a weekly commitment. It's not like he has a free afternoon, so it may not be doable.'

Hingston met eyes with Remi.

The receptionist circled a number on a business card and handed it to Hingston. 'These are his secretary's details.' And her smiling eyes disappeared once again.

Chapter Seventeen
Sorrowing, Sighing, Bleeding, Dying

One in, one out. It just so happened that within minutes of Yorke's arrival at St Thomas' Hospital, Hugh Marchant was discharged. Marchant was immediately arrested and conveyed to Kentish Town Police Station where he was booked into custody shortly after three.

Stood on Holmes Road since 1896, the station may well have been home to many aspiring *Sherlocks* over the years. Indeed, Marchant may well have thought he was talking to the fictional great himself when he said the following words to the custody sergeant, expecting him to comprehend:

> *Ptah, the Lord of Justice, is just to me.*
> *He hath afflicted me with punishment.*
> *Be merciful unto me.*
> *I have seen that thou art merciful.*

Marchant had given the exact same words to his arresting officer, who, like the custody sergeant, asked him how to spell "Ptah" and to repeat what he had said, *very slowly.*

Those poetic words were now displayed on a briefing slide an hour and a half later for all assigned to Op PYROLITE to read. Smythe noted that Marchant *is* fit to be interviewed despite his "unusual responses" so far uttered, his rasping voice and his facial dermatitis. The latter two were the remaining afflictions caused by the thick orpiment he had painted onto his skin and the neat powder he had inhaled and attempted to ingest. Smythe also advised that Marchant's failed suicide attempt could have future repercussions on his health due to the carcinogenic property of arsenic, to which expressions of concern and surprise were shared around the room. Smythe relayed the custody sergeant's remarks that Marchant was compliant with wearing the anti-suicide suit and that he laid himself down on the floor of his cell, face up with his arms crossed over his chest in the fashion of an Egyptian mummy.

Smythe sighed and opened the window a crack, allowing the warm, crowded room a trickle of chilled air. 'While Marchant awaits the arrival of legal representation and the interviewing officers, his eyes have fixed a stare straight up at the ceiling. I'm sure it will be an interesting interview.' The grooves in his forehead concertinaed up like a Roman blind and he smiled at two of the detectives sat in the front row.

One of them laughed. 'If Marchant's going to keep speaking in verse, we'll have to take in one of DS Hingston's Petrie Museum textbooks and use it like a foreign language phrasebook!'

After a moment's banter, Smythe refocused the room. 'James Roe,' he announced with a well-contained yet nonetheless noticeable snarl, 'was arrested at his workplace which is a *reptile* centre. He is currently being conveyed.'

Hingston's requested CCTV footage from the Fitzwilliam Museum had been burnt to a disc and was travelling down in the same car.

'Roe,' Smythe continued, 'unlike Marchant, made a short and comprehendible comment to the arresting officer. I quote: "You've got no fucking clue". Well, I think we have, matey!' Smythe scoffed. 'Barry,' he commanded, 'the latest from Scientific Services, please.'

Barry, surprised by the pleasantry tagged onto Smythe's request, caught his breath which made for a wheezy entrance as he walked to the front of the room.

'I shall start with Britton *senior*,' Barry said having cleared his throat. 'Mrs Rosamund Britton and her muddy boots… negative result. Soil type not even close: Lake District. Her shoe size is a seven and we have unidentified prints of that size, but no evidence they belong to her. Fingerprints don't match the discarded chain cutters or the prints in Marchant's car. DNA result came back in the last half an hour and it's not a match with that obtained from Highgate Cemetery.'

There was a disgruntled snort somewhere in the room. Everyone knew that the likelihood of Mrs Britton being released on bail was rapidly increasing.

Barry continued. 'This brings me to Britton *junior*.' He coughed and gave a smile. His prominent eyes scanned the audience. 'As mentioned this morning, her DNA result was received first thing and does not match the DNA obtained from Highgate Cemetery. Fingerprints taken on Saturday,' he gave a nod to Remi, 'negative like her mother's.'

Smythe stood staring at Barry with a look that said "hurry it up".

Ignoring Smythe, Barry proceeded at his usual, moderate pace. 'I know we're not treating Emily Britton as a suspect at this time, but this girl has size five and a half feet. Just remember, she could have worn a slightly larger size shoe.'

'Any more *updates*, Barry?' Smythe said in a narked tone, unappreciative of his suggestions. 'I'm sure Mrs Britton could've put her size sevens in the size tens you've identified if she were that way inclined.'

Someone laughed, but Smythe did not smile.

Barry pointed at Smythe and displayed a superior look which was met with a flare of the nostrils. 'You need to *brush up* on your forensic science,' Barry taunted him behind the guise of a joke.

Thanks to Remi's insight last week, Hingston recognised the dig about Smythe's falling out with Barry fifteen years ago. He glanced at Remi who was sat next to him with her notebook and pen rested on her lap. Trying to disguise her amusement, she had partly uncrossed her arms and held her right hand up to her lips. She fixed an emotionless stare in Barry's direction.

'Putting aside the gender difference in the footwear,' Barry continued in his usual matter of fact tone, 'those size tens we've attributed to Marchant. He'd hidden them in a winter sports bag in his loft, wrapped up inside snowboarding trousers. Not a quick find, I can tell you. The mud in the footwells of Marchant's car is my next update.' Barry gave a faint wheeze. 'It's *also* a match with the cemetery.'

There were sounds of interest across the packed briefing room.

'Good work,' Smythe said, aware that amends needed to be made for his sarcastic remark.

'I've got a splendid team,' Barry replied. 'May I remind everyone that the mud found in the front passenger footwell is attributed to the feet of James Roe. The mud in the back nearside footwell could suggest an unidentified passenger, a...'

'*Fourth* suspect,' Smythe interrupted to steal the punch line. 'Someone who was *not* present on our CCTV footages *prior* to the offence. Someone whom the eyewitness may have missed when Marchant's car sped down his road *after* the offence. *Barry*. Continue.'

'Marchant's fingerprints taken a short while ago will be compared with those on the chain cutters, but you will recall the prints suggest smaller hands than Marchant's whoppers. *Naturally*, had the chain cutter prints belonged to Roe then we would've already identified him on the National Fingerprint Database; again, suggesting a fourth suspect.' Barry finished with a nod that was not dissimilar to a bow.

'*Before* you finish, Barry,' Smythe said, '*we* need to quickly brief everyone regarding the wax figures.'

Barry's straight face looked pensive. 'Okay. Do you want to take the lead or shall I?'

'Right,' Smythe boomed, 'I've had to make the Directorate of Professional Standards aware that the four wax figures seized from Marchant's address are missing. Thorough searches have been made since their absence from the exhibit store was noticed on Friday afternoon.'

The room remained silent.

'We are not jumping to conclusions or making allegations that any officer or member of staff has *stolen* them, but I am sure you are all fully aware of the implications if evidence has been lost, *regardless* of the reason.' Smythe looked at Barry, providing him with the cue to speak.

'As the DCI says, this is a serious matter and will be subject of a DPS investigation. Forensic work has already been undertaken and samples from the figures remain at the lab, for which we can be thankful. However, the figures should have been sat safely on a shelf in the exhibit store.' Barry's pale face showed some colour and his moist eyes looked larger than usual as he turned toward Smythe who gave a look of approval. Barry gestured a nod and set off at a stride between the rows of seats to stand himself at the back of the room.

The sombre mood persisted like low lying fog as the briefing continued. Even the progress made on Olson's list of "dead women" did not appear to shake everyone out of their state of reflection on the wax figures. Many thoughts could have been zipping through the ether: *Has someone stolen them? If so, who? Where else could they be found in the station? Could they have been thrown away in error? Did they actually make it back from the lab to the exhibit store? Surely, they couldn't have physically disappeared! What will DPS ask me?* And maybe someone in the room was asking *What should I do now?*

Olson's list revealed an unhappy prequel to the timeline of suicides. Four names corresponded with Met Police investigations. Associations with Ancient Egyptian themes had been quickly confirmed in the retrospective review, but had not been apparent to the police or to the Coroner's Office during the standalone investigations. Only two names on Olson's list remained unidentified at the time of the briefing, and they would be subject of review against records held by other forces.

In August 2012, two days before Sheila Baptist drowned, a twenty-five-year-old named Samantha Stephenson ran in front of a bus. She died at the scene, opposite Greater London House, the old Carreras Cigarette Factory that retained its original Art Deco

Egyptomania styling. Technicolour lotus columns and black Bastet cats dominated the backdrop of the scene of this young lady's death. In May 2012, a thirty-five-year-old commuter fell onto the tracks at Holborn tube station. Jemima Lewis-Smith was an unusual name. One of reviewing officers remembered the British Museum imagery that decorated the platform. A black and white photograph of a sarcophagus abutted the station's underground signage. Whilst it stared at the emergency response to Jemima Lewis-Smith's suicide, it appeared no more than an innocuous reminder that this was the closest stop for the museum. In February 2012, a fatal overdose of prescription medicine saw an unconscious fifty-year-old named Anne Johns blue-lighted to hospital from the pavement outside the old and disused Carlton Cinema in Islington. The building's facade was Egyptian again. In January 2009, now almost four years ago, twenty-three-year-old Carlotta Ferrario was stabbed whilst jogging. She died amongst the undergrowth close to the Crystal Palace sphinxes. Her murderer remained unidentified. Her name on Olson's list now reopened the case.

***

Hingston returned home with his head suffering from information overload.

'Glass of wine is just what I need!' he said upon entering the kitchen. As he looked at his crowded cooker top and smelt the tempting aroma of Zack's classical French cuisine, he laughed. 'I think you're showing increasing promise for entering *Master Chef*, you know!'

'The internet is a wonderful thing, son,' Zack announced as Hingston poured two glasses.

'What for? Recipes?' asked Hingston, noticing he had inadvertently picked up Zack's habit of asking two questions at once.

'That wasn't what I meant, but in a house with no cookery books it has proved useful!' Zack chortled as he stirred the contents of one of the pans. 'I was referring to my little research assignment, Jason.'

'How's it going?' Hingston rested his wine glass on the worktop and removed his tie.

'Samuel Silverthorne's daughter was called Talitha Rose. She was born in eighteen fifty-two.'

A pause in Zack's account prompted Hingston to picture the beautiful Circassian girl waving joyously in the golden meadow. *Talitha Rose.* She was young... 'And she died in?' Hingston asked.

'Eighteen sixty-seven.'

Hingston frowned. '*Only* a year after her father.'

'Just under a year. In the April.' Zack affirmed. 'Very sad.'

'I suppose the internet doesn't provide details of the cause of death?'

'No, but I've ordered a copy of her death certificate. It'll be coming to you rather than me. Might be here

Saturday.' Zack was travelling back to Dartmouth on Wednesday morning.

'Thanks for all your work on this,' Hingston said.

'I'm enjoying it,' Zack said with a smile.

'Changing the subject,' Hingston sighed. 'I've had to bring home a bit of reading. I don't want to spoil your penultimate night here by being poor company yet again.'

'Dinner's half hour away; make a start if you want,' chirped Zack. 'I can pop the radio back on. Not a problem.'

***

Hingston's antique desk with its gilt tooled, moss green leather top never failed to inspire him. The last time he placed copies of a National Archives' file upon it he reached a pivotal moment in his reinvestigation into the Victorian boy's murder. That moment led him to deliver a positive outcome for the Clarke family in the present-day murder investigation. As unlikely as it seemed, Hingston hoped the same may occur tonight.

Madame Hesketh was a very wealthy fraudster. Only in 1923 did this false medium's thirty-five year career catch up with her. No photograph of Madame Hesketh existed in the files, or perhaps it had been omitted when the paperwork was scanned this morning. The latter made sense to Hingston—the police may have requested the files, but they didn't need a mugshot of a woman who was eighty-nine years dead.

Hingston located the court papers first. The typed documents gave little impression of their age when compared to their modern counterparts until the words were read. Sentenced to nine months' imprisonment at Holloway in April 1923, "Madame" Myra Victoria Hesketh was convicted of the offences of *Conspiracy to contravene the provisions of Section 4 of the Witchcraft Act, 1735*, specifically *Pretending to exercise conjuration*; *Causing money to be paid by false pretences, contrary to Section 32 (1) of the Larceny Act, 1916*; and the common law offence of *Effecting a public mischief* on four separate occasions.

If the history recounted by Emily Britton was correct, Madame Hesketh would have died in Holloway Prison before her nine months were served. He flicked on through the bundle that was almost one inch thick. A typed statement from "N" Division caught his attention. The title of Edith Harris, "Woman Constable", did not take him by surprise, whereas the absence of a statement of truth in those days did, and after only two lines he found himself engrossed in her account of the 18th of December 1922:

"Acting on instructions from Divisional Detective Inspector Prout, I telephoned from the Post Office... to Madame Hesketh, whose telephone number is 115 Gerrard."

Hingston was unfamiliar with this telephone exchange and he imagined the shrill ring of the Bakelite phone piercing whatever bohemian venue was occupied by Madame Hesketh.

She answered the call and told Edith Harris to attend "36a Greek Street, Soho, W.1." at three p.m. and to "Ring and walk straight upstairs to the first floor; it is above the Egyptian Café".

Hingston inhaled deeply, took a sip of his wine and read on.

"I went up one flight of stairs at the side of the cafe and saw a door which displayed a sign in large letters which read 'Madame Hesketh.' I rang the bell and the door was answered by a girl, no more than 16 years, height 5ft 1 ins., dark bobbed hair with fair complexion dressed in green who said, 'Did you make the appointment for 3 p.m.?'... She showed me to a seat in the waiting area which had a window overlooking Church Street and a door to a second room. There were two settees in the waiting area and a small desk, under which a live cat was asleep. The girl said, 'Madame Hesketh will be with you shortly,' and within two minutes the door to the second room was opened by Madame Hesketh who said, 'Please come in and take a seat.' I followed her into the room which contained a small square table covered with a black velvet cloth. It was situated next to a fireplace with two seats. Also in the room was a desk and a telephone. On the table was an electric lamp with a shot silk shade in blue and a matching cushion. Madame Hesketh, age about sixty, seated herself opposite me across the table and she wore a silk Kaftan and matching turban. Her hands were covered by white silk gloves…"

A flash of green, heavily decorated feminine eyes broke Hingston's concentration. They overtook his imagination without warning: up close, more vivid than the officer's statement and intense in their fixed stare. They vanished just as suddenly. Startled, but undeterred, Hingston refocused on Edith Harris' account.

Madame Hesketh directed the undercover officer to place her hands, palms up, on the blue cushion. Hingston skimmed through the generic fortune telling patter that would undoubtedly have satisfied many unmarried young women in 1922 who aspired to meet a man, have a family and achieve an adequate or better income. Then the reading took an unexpected turn.

"Madame Hesketh asked me, 'Who are you mourning?' I said, 'My mother,' and she replied, 'Your mother worried about your health. She still does.'"

Hingston felt a degree of nervous anticipation growing in his chest. Had the young officer stuck to her pre-prepared backstory, designed for this operation, or was Hesketh drawing words of truth from her with which to manipulate her fears and desires?

"I asked, 'What do you mean?' and Madame Hesketh said, 'I can help your mother to help you. The most important messages are those most people cannot hear. Those are the messages from loved ones who have passed to the next life, because from there, knowledge, truth and foresight prevail.' I asked Madame Hesketh, 'How might I attain that?' and…"

The Richmond Avenue basement began to pull Hingston's mind down its dark staircase. The embossed burgundy wallpaper felt warm against his hands that were pressed hard against the narrow stairwell walls. He fought to resist the downwards drag towards the thick incense that was clogging his throat and the low, thrumming voices that had synchronised with his heartbeat…

'Jason!' bellowed Zack. 'Dinner's ready, son!'

Chapter Eighteen
I'll be Home for Christmas

Hingston left the remainder of the files unread that night. He preferred to think about the covert surveillance team that maintained watch over Richmond Avenue where the white sphinxes with their pale blue eyes guarded an empty residence.

Dr Anita Hesketh's whereabouts remained unknown. As the supposed leader of the House of Life, she was wanted on suspicion of conspiracy to murder Olson and on suspicion of encouraging a minimum of six suicides. What part she may have played, if any, in the murder of Carlotta Ferrario, was presently unclear. Search warrants were ready for the three flats that comprised the townhouse Hesketh owned. The policy decision made by Smythe was to wait to search the property until Wednesday night's meeting had commenced, '*Unless* Hesketh resurfaces before then.' Hingston recalled Smythe puffing out his chest before he closed the four thirty p.m. briefing with a clear mission statement: 'I want us to catch the whole bloody lot of them once they're down in that fucking *tomb* of Richmond Avenue.'

***

Yorke's secretary had been helpful when Hingston telephoned yesterday afternoon to rearrange the cancelled appointment. She advised that Yorke dedicates Wednesday afternoons and evenings to write reports for medical journals. He publishes several papers per year and whilst he normally refuses requests for appointments within his writing schedule, she considered the police would be an exception to the rule. Having obtained this information, Hingston did the "gentlemanly thing" and pretended to reorganise his own diary in order to meet Dr Yorke at a more convenient time when he wasn't writing. Importantly, it also reduced the delay. Tuesday at ten thirty was agreed.

Now, at 6.44 a.m., having stepped out of the shower, Hingston discovered a missed call and a voice message that had been left three minutes earlier:

"This is a message for Detective Sergeant Hingston. It's Sally, Dr Yorke's secretary. We spoke yesterday. I'm dreadfully sorry to cancel your meeting today. Dr Yorke's mother passed away in the early hours. I trust you will understand the situation. If you would be so kind as to call me back this afternoon. I should be in a position to agree a suitable appointment by then. My number is 020..."

Hingston cut her message and dropped his phone back on the bed. 'Damn.'

Caryl had clearly been waiting for Hingston's arrival when he walked into the report writing room just over an hour later. 'Jason,' she called and hurried over. 'Night turn made a start on the Fitzwilliam CCTV. *Roe* is on there.' Her eyes were wide and eager.

'That's interesting. *Not* who I was expecting, but good. Was he alone?'

'Apparently so, but there's a few hours left that I'm reviewing now. I'll keep you posted.' Caryl smiled and hurried on back to her desk.

Hingston looked over the monitors at Remi, who despite hearing Caryl's good news, looked a little sour.

'You all right?' asked Hingston.

'Yes,' Remi said. 'You?'

Hingston paused. 'Not the best start to the day, but I don't want to make you feel… well…'

Remi blinked and rolled her eyes. 'Rob's pissed me off, that's all. C'mon, spit it out!'

'Yorke's mother's died,' he said.

'Oh, for goodness' sake!'

***

At 11.02 a.m., Mrs Britton was charged with the offence of encouraging the suicide of Esther Watts.

Emily's diarised observation that Esther was "the rebellious sort" was not only accurate, but fortuitous.

253

The turn of events rested on the examination of Esther's mobile phone. Going against the rules of the House of Life, Esther had created a "trace beyond these four walls". A deleted video recording provided the evidence the investigation had been lacking. Almost a fortnight ago, Esther had smuggled her phone into a meeting. Holding it under the table, she secretly recorded Mrs Britton explaining the way in which to ensure a fatal outcome when taking a knife to the wrist. 'The last thing you want is to go in there *ballsing it up,*' were Mrs Britton's words of advice. 'You can wait until you feel confident,' she had offered. Esther was heard to say, 'Okay,' and then the video ended. The seventeen-year-old had followed Mrs Britton's instructions to the letter.

When presented with the video recording this morning, Mrs Britton finally admitted to her involvement with the House of Life, but maintained she had done nothing wrong and declined to comment further.

Roe had also spent the night in the cells at Kentish Town Police Station. From nine thirty a.m. his eyes had bored into the interviewing officers with a reptilian-like coldness. He had so far bludgeoned his interview flat with, 'No comment,' throughout.

Marchant was a very different detainee. His interview had commenced last night and continued today. Going against his legal advice and to the frustration of the interviewing officers, Marchant recited his verse about the "Lord of Justice" prior to every question he answered. During this time, he fixed a stare up at the ceiling which presented the whites of his eyes that were riddled with blood vessels. Periodically, whilst he answered his questions, he licked a tattooed cartouche on his hand. His heavily furred tongue lingered over the tattoo as he eyed the unfortunate detective sat directly opposite him. The officer diagonally opposite he ignored. Aside from slowing the interview process, it was uncomfortable to watch.

Some of the questions Marchant avoided with statements of, 'I honestly have no recollection,' but for the majority he was informative. Of greatest significance was the naming of James Roe whom he discussed at length.

According to Marchant, he met Roe twenty years ago at secondary school. They shared an interest in Heka—Ancient Egyptian magic. It predated their association and was fuelled as a consequence. Marchant alleged that Roe is still a virgin and as such, remains a highly competent medium. Roe introduced him to the House of Life, 'Six, seven, maybe eight years ago.' When asked if Roe held any particular position within the House of Life, Marchant declined to respond. Instead, he slowly spat on the table before spreading out the bubbling pool of saliva with his tattooed hand.

On Tuesday morning Roe had arrived at Marchant's house unexpectedly, 'When it was still dark outside,' and asked him to, 'Assist in the punishment of someone who has defiled us like we're his harem; someone who has used us for his base needs; someone who is going to sacrifice the honour of Ramesses for his own selfishness.' Marchant agreed to assist. He told the officers that he did not know who Roe was referring to and it is only since his arrest that he understands this to be Dr Sven Olson.

According to Marchant, he bought spray paint for blotting out the CCTV camera at Highgate Cemetery, but when he arrived at Swains Lane with Roe as his passenger, access had already been gained to the cemetery. This took him by surprise. Roe led the way through the grounds where they met Olson on one of the paths. He had another person with him who held a, 'Heavy-duty torch,' and then hit Olson with it. There was an immediate struggle and Marchant admitted to, 'Giving the muscle needed to force Olson into position towards the Egyptian Avenue.' The torchlight remained on Olson throughout and it blotted out the view of the person holding it. The rope was already in place above the Egyptian Avenue, tied to a sturdy structure that Marchant didn't see. Marchant explained he had expected to be assisting in setting up the ligature because Roe had briefed him, but everything was ready and the person who was to "have their punishment touch them" was already there which made him panic. It was Roe who fitted the noose around Olson's neck. Very quickly after that, Marchant managed to push Olson in the direction of the ledge and, 'He plummeted. There was no flex in the rope. None at all.'

In the meantime, a search team had been sent to Roe's maisonette in Trumpington; Emily Britton and her father remained in Hertfordshire; covert surveillance had nothing new to report from Richmond Avenue and at Hampstead Police Station data from computers to mobile phones and hours of CCTV footage from the British Museum were being reviewed at a pace. The hunt was on for any person or persons who may have been in the company of Esther Watts or who had otherwise been watching her during the four-hour window between her arrival and her suicide. A similar exercise had been conducted using CCTV from Piccadilly and identified no suspects in the vicinity of Leanna Snow, but that had been a much simpler task.

Hingston had conducted a check on 36a Greek Street to try to rule out any link between Madame Hesketh's old fortune telling haunt and the present-day House of Life offenders. The Egyptian Café was now a Chinese restaurant and the flat had been absorbed by the business. Hingston presumed it served as a storage facility or provided staff accommodation. Nonetheless, he requested the address be added to a list created by Intel: a list of all known London locations that could be associated with Ancient Egypt, past or present, should they become the scene of any future suicide or murder. Safer Neighbourhood Teams had been made aware so that their patrols could pay particular attention to these areas. The list had already been shortened by four locations when Olson's "dead woman" document was reviewed yesterday—not that the potential for repeat locations could be disregarded. Those that remained were the Petrie Museum; Sir John Soane's Museum in Holborn which houses a notable collection of artefacts including the sarcophagus of Pharaoh Seti I; the Victoria and Albert Museum where their support of Egyptologists continued into the mid-twentieth century, albeit their collection is no longer displayed; the famous Egyptian Escalator in Harrods department store; the Canary Wharf pyramid-topped tower; the former Daily Telegraph building on Fleet Street with its Egyptian facade; the offices at New Broad Street House which is decorated with sphinxes and winged sun discs; the mildly influenced Hoover Building in Perivale and the remainder of the "Magnificent Seven" cemeteries with particular focus upon Abney Park, Brompton, Kensal Green and West Norwood where the Victorian admiration of Egyptian Revival architecture had influenced many tombs and mausoleums, including the occasional headstone. None, however, were so striking as the location of Olson's murder at Highgate.

Lastly, Primrose Hill was listed. One particularly diligent intelligence officer had dug around in London's history and identified architect Thomas Willson's Pyramid Mortuary which had been designed to inter five million of London's dead upon the hilltop. Willson championed his proposal from the 1820s, but failed to obtain approval during the Burial Reform. Hingston was interested by this. Not only could it have changed the capital's skyline forever, but if it had, maybe the Egyptian Avenue at Highgate Cemetery would never have come into existence.

**

By the time Hingston commenced his drive home through the same darkness in which he had left the house this morning, his spirits had lifted. After a stressful day mucking in with the processing of information, the police were getting the upper hand. The evidence against Roe was mounting, Marchant's DNA was a match for Highgate Cemetery, and he was continuing to cooperate. That said, Marchant had added nothing more to Emily Britton's account regarding the House of Life and Richmond Avenue; at least, not *yet*. Emily Britton had not appeared on the Fitzwilliam CCTV and Hingston felt a pang of frustration as a result. An appointment with Yorke was, however, scheduled for Thursday morning and tomorrow he was due to meet with a representative from the British Museum's Department of Ancient Egypt and Sudan who was present for a number of the talks attended by Olson and Hesketh.

The White House Clinic had been asked whether Samantha Stephenson, Jemima Lewis-Smith, Anne Johns and Carlotta Ferrario had been patients of Dr

Olson and Jemima's name was confirmed. Hingston wondered if she could have been meeting with Olson at the British Museum directly before jumping in front of the train at its closest tube station. Combined with Marchant's interview account, Olson's predatory behaviour was being revealed and the true nature of his relationship with Emily Britton was being questioned once again.

As Hingston reflected upon his day, his car crawled along Hampstead High Street while shoppers hurried about and overtook on foot under a clear sky. The stars remained obscured by the queues of headlights and tail lights, the shops and restaurants that lit the pavements with their vast, glowing windows and the Christmas decorations that dressed the trees with a Milky Way of pale blue lights and white three-dimensional stars. The festivity had just started to penetrate his cabin when the travel report on the radio ended and the bugle call of *Stop the Cavalry* kicked in. At this rate, he thought, the investigation *could* be home for Christmas. He turned up the volume for his favourite Christmas pop song and as he strummed his fingers to the beat his thoughts turned to Remi and whether Smythe might still be *pissing her off.*

***

'Thought you might like to open it early, Jason,' Uncle Zack said as he handed him a sturdy red and gold foiled box which had saved him the trouble of wrapping paper.

'You know *me*,' Hingston laughed. 'Anyway, the tree's not up yet for it to sit under, so I may as well.'

At six thirty on Wednesday morning, having been out for a curry in Chiswick last night, Hingston was not expecting a surprise present from Zack ahead of his departure for Dartmouth.

The lid was a snug fit, held tight by the air that had been displaced when Zack sealed the box. With some prising, the lid suddenly released and Hingston's sharp reflexes prevented it from tumbling to the floor. *The Boy's Own Conjuring Book* from the antiquarian bookshop sat upon some tissue paper and its copper lettering gleamed against the dark leather under the artificial lights in Hingston's hallway.

'Oh, superb! Thank you,' Hingston said as he removed the book.

'I want you to have perfected one of those tricks when you visit for New Year,' Zack instructed.

Hingston flicked to the contents pages. 'Let me find something intriguing... what about *The Magic Handcuffs*, I've got a pair of those I could use, or... *Spontaneous Combustion*, hmm, might be a bit dangerous,' he laughed. 'Or... *To Exhibit the Magic Lantern*?' As he read those words his eyes were drawn down a few lines to *How to Raise a Ghost* and for a split second he saw a terrible, smoke-ridden face with drawn cheeks and dark eye sockets, and the smell of burning coal and incense caught his breath, turning his laughter to coughing.

As Zack told him to, 'Steady on there, son,' Hingston realised Madame Hesketh's unread files were beckoning.

Chapter Nineteen
Fall on Your Knees

Hingston's perception of the *Roaring Twenties* had always been influenced by the glamour of the decade: the flapper girls and the social freedom following the oppression of World War One; the iconic Art Deco buildings and evocative motorcars; the jazz movement; the emergence of a new era in crime fiction that would later be heralded as the *Golden Age* with mysteries and murders that captivated audiences then and now, including himself; and the ritzy setting of P. G. Wodehouse's *Jeeves and Wooster* that comically packaged up everything iconic and wonderful about the period. The publicity and propaganda portrayed the 1920s as a time when life was lived to the full: a decade to look back upon with fond memories had you been there and a decade to envy had you not.

Madame Hesketh's 1920s started, it appeared, in splendidly lavish style, but her fraudulent activities revealed to Hingston the vulnerability of those who were not wealthy or young, carefree and hitting the town partying. By contrast, the Met Police investigation revealed the women who were largely alone and still suffering from the bereavements of war.

Madame Hesketh was a stereotypical charlatan. Her séances were rigged with deceptions and theatrical devices. Her basement at Richmond Avenue was a place of entertainment for those seeking to dabble in the fashionable spirit world, and an addiction for those desperate to attend regularly in the hope of contact with lost loved ones, unaware they were paying for lies.

Business had been increasing exponentially for Madame Hesketh since 1920. She charged a hefty seven shillings and sixpence per person per evening, plus a "voluntary" supplement which clients were encouraged to place upon a circulating silver platter. The correlation between the size of the supplement and the time Madame Hesketh allocated to a sitter was obvious. Ancient Egypt had been a source of public fascination for decades and over that time Madame Hesketh had accumulated a collection of artefacts and a reputation that proved to be attractive and lucrative. However, the unique selling point that continued to beguile her clients was the stature of her spirit guide, Ramesses the Third.

As Hingston read the old Met Police file in the report writing room at Hampstead, he saw nothing but the printed words and he smelt nothing but the everyday mix of an office full of workers starting the day with fresh clothes, cups of coffee and a very tempting bacon butty that was wafting over from a corner of the room. He was actually quite pleased to have removed the files from his house where the memory of those heavily decorated eyes and the grotesque smoke-ridden face persisted.

'Found anything in there?' Remi called between the monitors.

'Not as much as the volume would suggest,' he replied, 'but it all correlates with the history Emily Britton relayed to us.'

'So, the police didn't seize the contents of Madame Hesketh's house in nineteen twenty-three, then?' Remi enquired.

'I haven't read anything about seized property so far,' he said.

Remi pointed at him. 'That's assuming Emily is correct that the mummified remains and all the *bling* is original.'

Hingston pulled a quizzical expression. 'Had she not died in prison, I wonder if she would have tried to continue her business?'

'Mmm…' Remi mused without committing to an opinion. 'Is there anything in there about her death?' she continued to question.

'Yes, there's a contemporaneous newspaper clipping in the paperwork. Cause of death *influenza*. Died the twenty-first of November nineteen twenty-three.' He looked at his watch and stared back at Remi. 'Briefing's in five minutes.'

***

During the time Hingston's tube train carriage rattled and whined its way in and out of the stations between Hampstead and Tottenham Court Road, he reflected on the latest updates provided by Smythe.

Roe's maisonette was found to be small and chaotically crammed with personal effects, including several vivariums containing snakes and a freezer full of mice and gerbils. It was a stuffy, claustrophobic property, *worse* Hingston imagined, than the tube carriage. Roe's bedroom walls had been hand-painted with crude imitations of hieroglyphs which gave the tiny space the semblance of a tomb. A collection of books on Ancient Egyptian magical practice, were the only possessions Roe had neatly stored. Officers had located one of the titles Hingston had been provided by the Petrie Museum, so Roe's understanding of the Harem Conspiracy was likely as good as any academic. The extent of his knowledge remained unknown, for even when he was charged with the murder of Olson, he rolled out a final, 'No comment.'

Also found amongst Roe's hoard of belongings was a mobile phone suspected to be Olson's. High Tech Crime were in possession of it this morning whilst PC Stoker waited for Mrs Olson to locate her late husband's PIN code which she believed he had, 'Written down somewhere.'

Marchant had also been charged with murder. In place of his routine recital about the "Lord of Justice", he spat on the custody sergeant and with a venomous baring of his teeth whispered something indecipherable whilst he fought against the grip of the officers who held him back. His facial expression reportedly looked, 'Demonic.' A charge of assault police was added to his record.

Emily Britton had returned to Acton and to Thomas Sprigge High School this morning, having expressed desire to resume her studies. With her mock A-Levels looming in January, she did not want to jeopardise her prospects of securing a place at Cambridge University.

The wax figures had not reappeared, magically or otherwise, since Smythe and Barry had addressed the matter head-on. There was now an underlying air of twitchiness throughout the station with the occasional speculative conversation doing the rounds about whether everyone was now being "watched" by DPS. Hingston, in his experience as a supervisor, was confident this would not be the case, but he was not about to dispel the rumour.

When it came to being watched, the CCTV from the British Museum failed to identify any person who may have been keeping an eye on Esther Watts last Saturday. It suggested she had fully succumbed to the control of the House of Life and that Mrs Britton had executed her terrible deed to perfection.

***

Before Hingston entered between the tall iron gates, he could hear and see a sizeable gathering on the grand stone steps that led to the entrance of the British Museum. Youngsters from a foreign exchange programme had congregated amongst an equally sizable congregation of London pigeons that cooed and pecked at discarded crumbs whilst flapping and milling around the feet of those who, like Hingston, were eager to hurry up and get inside.

Hingston was struck by the beauty of the museum's entrance hall, known as the Great Court. Daylight flooded the immense two-acre space through an enormous curved glass and steel roof set high above the majestic atrium which it crowned with its elaborate, geometric panes. A double flight of elegant limestone steps swept up and around the central circular Reading Room. The impression of knowledge and refinement was delivered by this architectural statement which felt as inspirational as the worldwide wonders that the museum housed.

Hingston presented himself at the information desk and received directions to the Department of Ancient Egypt and Sudan. He passed the hall in which Esther Watts took her life, detoured to catch sight of the restaurant and then located the appropriate large, wooden door in the quieter backwaters of the museum. He pressed the bell button.

Within a short space of time the door was opened by an individual most unlike the elegant Natasha of the

Petrie Museum. 'Detective Sergeant Hingston, I believe?' a small, fifty-something male said quietly with a smile. His face was showing signs of recovering sunburn, his rolled-up shirt sleeves displayed his tanned, freckled forearms and his fine, sun-bleached hair was short and somewhat fluffy. He shook hands with Hingston. 'Follow me,' he instructed, 'I'm Bernard Lane-Giles, by the way. I've been in Sudan for the past five months, but happily I've returned for Christmas and can be of some assistance to you as a result!' Bernard's chatter continued as he led Hingston around a narrow, unassuming staircase and through another door into the department's study room. 'Oh, you'll have to excuse this rather beautiful set of curtains we've got laid out on the floor here,' he said in a gleeful tone. 'We're in the process of evaluating them for a private client.'

Colleagues of Bernard were preparing to take photographs of the appliquéd Ancient Egyptian men and women that decorated the curtains' tremendous length in horizontal rows.

'What age are they?' Hingston asked.

'Oh, just over one hundred years. Egyptomania at its best!'

The modest room lacked the finishing of the public galleries, but the large windows that overlooked a broad courtyard afforded rafts of light for the banquet-sized table at which three members of the public were sat in silence, engrossed in the department's library books.

'So, can anyone request a visit to your offices?' Hingston asked as Bernard showed him through to a private room.

'Yes. The library is popular, but *any* object from our collection can be viewed upon request. The tiny proportion that is on public display is the tip of the iceberg, so to speak,' Bernard replied.

After a short conversation, Hingston launched into the purpose of his visit; the talks attended by Doctors Olson and Hesketh, for which Bernard was either the speaker or the facilitator for the events.

'Yes,' said Bernard, 'Sven Olson was a regular: a very engaging person, deep interest in the subject. The same is true of Allan Hesketh, although he attends on fewer occasions.'

Hingston frowned. 'Sorry, did you say *Allan*?'
'Allan Hesketh,' Bernard replied with a nod. 'Lovely chap, quite handsome actually... and much taller than me!' he laughed. 'The ladies can't keep their eyes off him. *Nor he them*. 'Twas most annoying!'

***

Remi's call to Hingston flashed onto his mobile phone screen. He answered.

'No trace on Voters,' she said.

Hingston's eyes scanned the old, chipped paintwork of the tiny room in which Bernard had left him. 'I'll be viewing the CCTV shortly, then we can pull him in,' he replied.

Dr Allan *Hesketh* was not on the Voters' Register. He was, however, expected to be viewable on the British Museum's CCTV footage which was two and a half days' away from its six-month deletion. Bernard's description matched the appearance and countenance of Dr Allan *Yorke*, who, mourning his mother or otherwise, was likely to find himself wanted by the police before the morning was out.

'Jason,' Remi continued. 'Quick update for you.'

'Okay,' he replied. He held a stare on the seat in which Bernard had earlier sat.

'Incident at Kensal Green Cemetery. *Two human ears* found at the feet of a small stone sphinx. The tomb itself is one of the points of interest for visitors, hence the discovery.' Remi waited for his response.

'Bloody hell,' Hingston sighed. 'Same as the Harem Conspiracy judicial punishments: *mutilation.*'

'So, you'd expect the victim is still alive?' Remi asked.

'*Not sure…* whose tomb was it?'

'You going to Google it then?' Remi was amused by Hingston's unyielding determination to know every minute detail associated with an investigation. It was something she admired about him, and Hingston knew it. 'I've got the details prepared for you already,' she laughed. 'Andrew Ducrow. Died eighteen forty-two. Circus performer.'

Hingston felt the silence plug his ears like they had been filled with expanding cotton wool and the taste of sawdust filled his mouth. He could not stop the nauseating sensation of irretrievable freefalling and loss that flashed through his mind and pulled him to the point of impact with a painful gasp.

'Jason?' Remi blurted down the phone. 'You all right?'

He coughed. 'Yes… just caught my breath.' He sniffed and took a steady inhalation. 'Thank you for that. I'll bell you back, soon.' He ended the call and reflected not only on the body of Samuel Silverthorne face down in the circus ring, but on the persistent tang of iron that lingered in his mouth and the uncomfortable sensation that *something* within this investigation was becoming personal.

***

At 11.44 a.m., Hingston made the positive identification. Yorke's involvement with the House of Life was indisputable. What part he played within the group was yet to be proven, but his assumption of the name Hesketh suggested to Hingston three distinct possibilities. Firstly, Yorke admired Dr Anita Hesketh or Madame Hesketh or both, and it gave him some element of satisfaction to use the surname in a public setting. Secondly, Yorke was in a relationship with Anita Hesketh and he took her name outside of work.

Thirdly, Yorke was the leader of the House of Life and the masked "Ani" known to Emily Britton was Yorke in disguise. Illusion, trickery and deception had flourished in the basement at Richmond Avenue for over a century and Hingston was prepared for any eventuality, however unlikely.

Hingston hurried through the Great Court and ran down the museum steps. Pigeons took flight ahead of his feet like a well-rehearsed magic show. They dispersed from his left and right in a style befitting a 1920s cabaret performance and with the same urgency as was being applied by the officers now deployed to arrest Dr Yorke. Hingston had just enough time to get across to Kensal Green Cemetery where he believed the crime scene would reveal more to him in person than it would via the scene footage at this afternoon's briefing.

***

Barry's lanky stature was unmistakable, even in a forensic suit. Hingston could see him from some distance as he walked along the cemetery's Centre Avenue towards the prestigious Inner Circle.

At Kensal Green, the bustle of midweek city activity encroached from all directions. Time had long ago robbed the graves of their original tranquillity and with the squeal of emergency vehicle sirens held in traffic and the rush of passing trains, it was hard to imagine the London of 1842 when Ducrow's family tomb would have been a fresh display of the flamboyance this showman adored.

Hingston's preliminary internet research conducted en route would have impressed Uncle Zack. The historical hierarchy that laid herein included Wilkie Collins, W. H. Smith and Isambard Kingdom Brunel. Hingston wondered if the latter may or may not have anticipated how immense his neighbouring railway would become. As well as Ducrow, who had been the famous equestrian of Astley's Amphitheatre, a second celebrated circus performer whom Zack had mentioned at the weekend had also chosen to be buried at Kensal Green: Charles Blondin the tightrope walker and acrobat.

As Hingston neared the crime scene, he could see Barry's team looking as busy as the design of Ducrow's mausoleum which crammed Ancient Egyptian iconography alongside Grecian and Western funerary symbolism. Taking the statement piece to another level was its personalisation with a pair of comedy and tragedy masks, and a horseman's hat and riding gloves.

Barry was stood watching the activity he had coordinated. 'I heard you were on your way, Jason,' Barry said as Hingston negotiated the scene tape. 'I hope you've got a trick up your sleeve for the non-forensic side of this investigation,' he joked. A wheeze curtailed his laugh.

Hingston smiled. 'What have we got to go on?' he asked as he scanned the undergrowth and scrambling vines that were intertwined into a matted conglomeration that almost surrounded Ducrow's moss-encrusted tomb.

Barry drew breath. 'The ears were deposited at the feet of *that* sphinx. They are now on their way to the lab. The cemetery is only open to the public during the daytime. Unlike Highgate, visitor movement is unrestricted. There is no evidence anyone made or attempted a night-time entry.'

Hingston nodded for Barry to continue.

'Going back to the ears, they looked clumsily placed, so the offender probably took a couple of steps off this path in broad daylight and literally dropped them down.'

'Okay,' said Hingston. 'So we're of the opinion the offender was here this morning?'

'Most probably so,' Barry affirmed and cleared his throat. '*Then...*' Barry paused for dramatic effect and stared at Hingston.

From close proximity, Hingston could see a redness about Barry's inner eyelids and a moistness that suggested he might be developing a cold. He stepped back.

Barry opened his palms and turned one hundred and eighty degrees, directing Hingston to look at a very grand memorial on the opposite side of the path to Ducrow's tomb.

'*Then*,' Barry repeated, 'we discover a wax figure, *unlit*, stood on this monument.'

Hingston raised his eyebrows.

Barry mirrored Hingston's expression and slowed his pace. 'And it appears to have been left unlit *for a purpose*... to show it's one of the missing four.'

***

"It is the fate of most men to have many enemies, and few friends." Hingston frowned at the opening words carved in memory of the individual whose tomb was embellished with reliefs of the iconic medicinal serpent wrapped around a staff. It seemed a strange pairing: the positive image of the Rod of Asclepius and the lamentable introduction given to the deceased.

Hingston read on, intrigued as to why the wax figure had been placed *here* as opposed to Ducrow's tomb: "Stranger as you respect the receptacle for the dead as one of the many that will rest here, read the name of John Saint John Long without comment". He pulled out his phone and took a photograph of the full inscription. An internet search identified this unusual name as that of an infamous Harley Street quack doctor who was convicted of the manslaughter of one of his young female patients in 1830. The inscription and imagery now made sense. Hingston, however, frowned some more as he thought about Doctors Olson, Hesketh and Yorke. He remained puzzled. *Who* was responsible for depositing the wax figure? They had made no attempt to disguise the laboratory marks left behind when the wax was sampled and therefore sought to taunt the police with their revelation of the stolen figure. Had that person also left a clue, intentionally or not, by drawing attention to the memorial of the quack doctor? Who was the victim of mutilation and where were they now? Were they still alive? The questions felt as mystifying as being asked by a magician to *Pick a card, any card,* knowing not where you would be taken.

Frustrated by the investigation, Blondin returned to Hingston's mind and, having seen all there was to see, he left Barry and his team to their work. He wasn't sure what to expect as he approached Blondin's red granite monument, but he hoped there may be a purpose to justify his detour before returning to Hampstead.

The boxy memorial was surmounted and dominated by an exquisite carved female figure dressed in drapes and it was personalised with marble cameo portraits of the great man and one of his wives. The figure's lofty eyes and lifted head drew Hingston's attention to the beautiful blue sky. As he watched the still, wispy clouds he thought about Talitha Rose and Samuel Silverthorne and yearned for a sight, a sound or a feeling that he believed he was due, but nothing came. He looked at his watch. It was time to return to Hampstead. The afternoon briefing was scheduled for three p.m. and Smythe never tolerated lateness. Being early was even more important today given the unexpected appearance of the wax figure and the importance of the raid, tonight, on Richmond Avenue.

Hingston found himself running again, circumnavigating the crime scene, back towards the main entrance on Harrow Road. To his annoyance, he saw two members of the public paying their respects when public access had been restricted to only those areas deemed essential for the day's funeral proceedings.

'Excuse me,' Hingston called to the mourners. 'Excuse me, please.'

Hingston was ignored, which made him huff under his breath. 'How the hell did they get in here?' he complained and then his right ankle gave way with a nasty pain that ricocheted up to his knee. He stumbled forward, horrified by the recognition of the scene he had experienced so vividly in Newton St Cyres the summer before last: the agonising moment that preceded Samuel Silverthorne's fall from his tightrope.

To Hingston's surprise and relief, he regained his balance without injury. He instinctively checked to see if his near miss had been noticed, and in doing so he saw the mourners had gone. There was no one in sight. The grave at which they had been stood was marked with a modest headstone. Warm from his running, he walked over and breathed in the cold air. The memorial read:

DR JAMES BARRY
INSPECTOR GENERAL OF HOSPITALS
DIED 25 JULY 1865
AGED 70 YEARS

The name was unfamiliar to Hingston. He tapped at his phone once again and the search result read "first female cross-dressing doctor". He read the words again and as he pondered over his earlier consideration that the charming Allan Yorke might be posing as the enigmatic "Ani" Hesketh his phone rang.

'Yes, Remi,' he said without sounding impatient.

'You need to get back here *now*,' Remi instructed. 'It's Richmond Avenue. There's been an *explosion*.'

Chapter Twenty
To Face Unafraid

The blast wave reached the van in which the surveillance officers had been sat. The debris appeared to be greatest at the rear of the property, yet the front door and ground floor windows had smashed across the pavement and one sphinx was decapitated. The emergency call was made before flames could be seen through the dust, but what was clear to the officers who had eyes on Hesketh's address was that the explosion had originated next door.

Richmond Avenue was now the site of a very public major incident led by the London Fire Brigade. In contrast, the major crime investigation remained confidential while an emergency effort was applied at Hampstead Police Station to repair the massive hole that had been blown in Operation PYROLITE.

When Hingston returned to the station he was briefed by another sergeant. It was presently too early in the fire investigation to confirm the cause of the explosion. However, the damage beyond the neighbour's terraced house was believed to be limited to Hesketh's adjoining wall. Yorke was yet to be located. His car was found at his home address and his small, bespectacled receptionist attempted in a strange, bumbling manner to obstruct police from entering his Clerkenwell practice office. Her efforts were reportedly quite comical, but nonetheless resulted in her arrest.

Smythe had postponed the three p.m. briefing to four thirty so that the changing operational priorities could be managed first. When everyone entered the briefing room, the impatient expression upon his face suggested it would be slick.

'Ladies and gents,' Smythe boomed. 'The headlines. Richmond Avenue. The source of the explosion is now believed to be a gas cooker. No one was injured by the blast. The homeowner, a Caroline Glossbrook, was out at work. She is a forty-eight-year-old stock broker. *Insists* she did not leave the gas on and is presenting shocked and distraught.' He gave a slow scan of the packed-out briefing room, meeting various people's eyes with his own. 'Health and safety, continues to prevent our access to Hesketh's address which is damaged at the adjoining wall. However, we are expecting the green light tomorrow, as soon as it is made safe. The security of the premises is unchanged.' Smythe gave an angered look and composed himself. 'Despite the local headline news, Hesketh *has not* lifted her head above the parapet. Ms Glossbrook and the neighbours who were evacuated possess no means of contact for *Anita* Hesketh. According to Glossbrook, Hesketh lives alone and is, in her opinion, "peculiar". She stated Hesketh has voiced opposition to modern technology on more than one occasion, despite their interactions being very infrequent. This explains why she is not registered with a mobile network provider and may also be the reason why she does not drive. Glossbrook then elaborated further, stating Hesketh hosts weekly meetings on Wednesday evenings. She believes Hesketh is, *in her words* "a religious nut" and that they may all turn up for this evening's meeting.' Smythe flared his nostrils. 'Well, we can scrub off those on remand,' he sneered.

One of the investigators punched the air, but Smythe made no comment.

'Yorke, the bastard, is presumed to be on the run. Anyone outstanding will likely be aware of the explosion and fail to show, but the surveillance team are remaining on location.'

Barry, stood at the back, gave a loud sneeze. 'Excuse me,' he mumbled behind his handkerchief.

'That's a suitable cue,' Smythe responded. 'Barry. Update on Kensal Green, please.'

Barry blew his nose and walked to the front. 'The ears…' a wheeze cut through Barry's voice and he took a sip from a small bottle of water that had been protruding from his fleece pocket. 'Sorry,' he said. 'The ears found this morning are small with double piercings to both lobes. We believe we have a female victim. No earrings were present. The lab should be contacting me any time now with their results.'

Smythe huffed. 'I'll put in a call if they're not forthcoming by five,' Smythe said with a glance at his watch. Another irritable expression began to gnarl up his face. He ran a hand over his head and remained silent.

Barry coughed and continued. 'The wax figure left in the vicinity of the ears is also at the lab for testing.' The significance of the wax figure was not mentioned. Only a limited number of supervisors were aware.

The suspicion that an officer or staff member was responsible for the theft of the wax figures was adding to Smythe's frustration. 'Okay, Barry,' he said, 'my understanding is that unless something evidentially useful turns up from the lab then this crime scene isn't going to help us one jot?'

Barry sniffed. 'The depositing was done without contamination as far as we can detect.'

Smythe simmered. 'And the fucking cemetery have been operating with a broken CCTV system. *Okay*, thank you, Barry. Next up, Olson's mobile phone.'

Barry sneezed again when he reached the back of the room. Hingston noticed a few expressions that indicated not only was the briefing unenjoyable, the prospect of a cold for Christmas was unsettling.

Smythe appeared of the same opinion. 'PIN code *eventually* received from Mrs Olson. Roe had deleted all the data, including Olson's contact list. High Tech Crime are retrieving the lot. We will be furnished shortly. And lastly, the remaining two women on

Olson's list of the deceased have been identified.' He mustered half a smile. 'Perrianne Blanchard's body was found in Egypt Woods, Buckinghamshire, in May this year. The twenty-five-year-old had suffocated herself using a plastic bag and cable tie. In October 2010, Erica Thomson, another Thames Valley suicide victim, checked herself into a National Trust hotel and spa. Thomson was found by another resident attempting to drown herself in the shallow water of the estate's Egyptian Spring. She was sectioned and in January *this year* she was found dead in her Aylesbury flat having electrocuted herself in her bath. Aged only twenty-two, she was found wearing a necklace identical to those possessed by Britton and Baptist, the water was highly perfumed with aromatherapy bath salts, and she had dressed the bathroom with lotus-flower-shaped candles.'

***

An hour and a half later, as the chill of early evening set in, Hingston could not shake off the visual he had imagined of a young, naked female manipulated into a death staged with millennia-old sexual imagery. His part in the revised operational order was in action. He tried to refocus his mind as he parked the Astra a few doors down from Marchant's empty home address which appeared to have receded into the darkness in shame. The adjoining semi glowed with festive cheer.

Hingston considered how much longer ago it felt than six days since his attention had been drawn to the number plate on Marchant's car in the now bare driveway.

Mrs Britton also seemed a distant memory in all that had passed since. He walked along the pavement to the Brittons' house at the other end of the street with his breath condensing into opaque plumes in the night air. In his hands were Emily's mobile phone and laptop to return to the teenager. Mr Britton had moved in with her so that she could be looked after in her regular surroundings, close to school. It was an ideal opportunity to make a house call without giving away the fact that the police were more interested in engaging with the teenager than they were in providing the prompt return of her property.

He rang the doorbell and heard a rumble of footsteps pound down the wooden staircase at speed. The door was flung open and Emily Britton gave a broad smile that immediately dropped.

'Good evening, Emily,' Hingston said.

'Hi,' she replied. 'Oh, you've got my stuff!' She reached out her hands.

'Is your dad there, Emily?' Hingston asked, keeping hold of her technology.

'No. I thought you were him, actually.'

Hingston expected Mr Britton to have a key.

'Oh, there he is now,' Emily laughed, and along the pavement strode Mr Britton with a large takeaway bag in his hand.

'DS Hingston!' he saluted.

Hingston bid him a good evening while he assessed the father and daughter in the warm light that flooded out from the hallway. His denim jacket looked insufficient for insulating against the December chill.

'We're just about to eat,' Mr Britton continued, 'but there's some prawn crackers going if you need to update us on Emily's mother?'

'Dad!' Emily complained. She rolled her eyes and then appeared to regret her outburst. 'Sorry,' she added.

Hingston smiled. 'Just a couple of minutes of your time. I shan't impose upon your dinner.'

Mr Britton led the way into the hall, giving no thought to the shoes that were now past the lobby. 'Harry!' he shouted up the stairs in a manner befitting a rock band singer. 'Give us a hand, mate! Cops are here.'

Emily scooped her hair away from her neck and played with the short ponytail she had created.

Hingston thought back to her interview. *Emily was not happy*.

At a steady rate, Harry dropped his way down each step. 'Hi,' he called with his blue eyes held steadily on Hingston. 'Getting Em back up to speed with sociology,' he said. 'Nice to see you again.' Harry smiled and took the takeaway through to the kitchen.

Five minutes later Hingston called Remi from the Astra. 'PNC check, please. What vehicle does Harry Whitson drive *and then*... was it on Harrow Road this morning?'

***

Hingston studied Marchant's empty address while he waited for Remi's update. His mobile rang sooner than expected. It was Smythe.

'Can you confirm Emily Britton is safe and well?' Smythe asked without saying hello.

'Yes. Saw her in the past fifteen minutes,' Hingston replied.

'*In confidence*. The lab results have *just* come back and indicate a DNA match between the ears and Emily's hair sample.'

Hingston shook his head. 'But Remi took swabs on Saturday at the same time as Emily's fingerprints,' he remarked.

'And the lab cocked up. Didn't process the swabs,' Smythe seethed in a low voice.

'Bloody...' Hingston began. 'So, hang on, who got the hair sample?'

'Caryl Pugh,' Smythe growled. 'She's on a fucking rest day. Have you tasked her with anything?'

'*Bugger*. The Fitzwilliam CCTV. She said Emily wasn't on there. She also assisted me with the review of Emily's laptop.' Hingston felt his face heating up. 'I've got Remi looking into Harry Whitson who's with Emily now. Something didn't feel right when I called round.'

Smythe let him talk.

'Bloody hell. If Caryl's covering for Emily, then Emily's *got to be* more involved.'

'I'll get the CCTV checked now,' Smythe said. 'I'll call you back. There could be three arrests coming up. Emily, Harry and *bleedin'* Caryl.'

Chapter Twenty-one
Do You Know What I Know?

Hingston checked his watch while he waited for the next call. He had put on his stab vest and his Airwave radio chattered. Time dragged against his adrenaline rush like he was trying to brush cat fur off velvet.

He thought about Caryl who had been so enthusiastic to check the Fitzwilliam CCTV. He remembered her cheerfulness throughout the investigation, including her helpful response to his call to check Marchant's number plate. He barely knew her, so how could he judge? *If* she is responsible for tampering with evidence and for stealing the wax figures, what else has she been sabotaging? What if it wasn't Caryl, but someone at the lab instead? Or worse, she *and* another member of the team were involved? He knew DPS would be all over this and that Caryl's rest day might be concluded in a custody cell in a neighbouring force area where she would be unknown to the officers. This brought him to the matter of the ears and the hair sample. Who was the victim?

The phone rang at last. *Smythe*.

'Right,' Smythe said. 'Caryl's in the shit. Officers deployed to arrest. Emily *was* at the Fitzwilliam. Harry Whitson's car *wasn't* on Harrow Road.'

'Damn,' Hingston complained. He was annoyed about Caryl and still suspicious of Harry.

'Intervention will arrest Emily. ETA four minutes.' Smythe was powering his way through the call. 'Make yourself present should anything kick off with Mr Britton. Harry's also being arrested.'

Hingston's heart raced. He *knew* he was right.

'Olson's mobile,' Smythe boomed, sounding almost celebratory. 'Harry was at Highgate Cemetery. Will explain later.'

***

Hingston closed the door to his semi at quarter past four that morning. 'Two hours' kip,' he sighed. That was all he would be getting before rising for another extended shift at Hampstead. As he brushed his teeth half-heartedly, he reflected.

Mr Britton had needed stern words and a firm grip on his shoulder to prevent an escalation of his indignant behaviour towards the arresting officers. Oddly, he was most vocal about the disrupted Chinese takeaway. The double arrest came as such a shock it was almost incomprehensible to him. Hingston had applied every bit of his authority and his negotiation skills to avoid the processing of a surplus detainee. There were greater priorities than this fiery, middle-aged upstart, including the outstanding arrests of Yorke, Anita Hesketh and Caryl. The latter, to Smythe's annoyance, had also done a vanishing act.

Emily and Harry spent the first of their uncomfortable hours alone in their cells whilst officers congregated for a late evening Op PYROLITE briefing. The room overlooking Rosslyn Hill buzzed with more enthusiastic talk than would be heard at a Christmas party at The Ritz, albeit without the laughter, the alcohol and the refinement. The projection screen displayed the paused video footage retrieved from Olson's mobile phone.

It proved to be a breathy monologue: a panicked record of an abuser seeking reform; a scared man sacrificing himself unwittingly in pursuit of saving his old friend, Yorke, and the victim he was besotted with. The footage began just inside the point of entry at Highgate Cemetery on the night of the 4th of December. Olson, alone, and equipped with a torch, followed the path that ran parallel to the brick wall perimeter. It was either his intelligence or an uncanny foresight that appeared to prompt the recording, during which he disclosed his intentions in a roundabout fashion. 'If Allan comes good… No, I'm being a fool. Trust, trust, trust… trust. We can… get through this… together.' He muttered something inaudible too far from his phone as he swung the camera to his right and shone the torch over the gravestones to the perimeter wall. The inaudible mumbling persisted as he checked the surrounding area chaotically. Walking ahead, Olson referred to Ramesses, justice and a need to, 'Come clean tonight.' It was then he began to utter sexualised ramblings about Emily Britton.

Hingston remembered the investigator who wisecracked, 'What genre is this? Horror or blue movie?' as well as the response Smythe blasted him with for being unprofessional. Perhaps DPS *were* watching.

It was then that Olson's footage reached the rendezvous point. He called, 'Allan?' and the camera trembled in his grasp. The footsteps that approached were light and a bright torchlight was directed at Olson. A well-spoken male voice said, 'He sent me,' and as the phone was removed from Olson's possession with a calm, 'May I?' the camera was directed up into the face of Harry, whose case would now be indefensible in court.

***

The search commenced at 1.50 p.m. on Thursday the 13th of December. Hesketh's address, arranged into three flats with her own accommodation comprising the ground floor and basement, held a combined market value of over two million pounds. A small team of officers were tasked with the search.

Hingston and two DCs took the basement. The light switch failed to operate. Their descent was tainted by stale, heavy incense and, for Hingston, the familiarity of the embossed burgundy wallpaper that looked aged, yet well preserved. It served as a reminder of both the long history of "the tomb of Richmond Avenue" and Hingston's aversion to it, which had developed since his reading of the Madame Hesketh files. Holding his torch, he attempted to blot out the fear that had made him push back against these narrow walls in his mind's eye.

At the foot of the stairs, Hingston turned and took in his first sight of the basement. His torch light found a glimmer of gold. He saw the presence of a grand dining table that matched Emily's description and he could almost hear the pulse of resonant chanting. Behind him to the street side of the property was a heavy curtain. He cast it back and the curtain tracks gasped as daylight flooded into the subterranean room.

'Bloody Nora,' one of the DCs uttered, astonished by the museum-like grandeur before them.

The mummified remains, central to the table, were guarded by the two statues that flanked Hesketh's wooden seat, allegedly used as a throne when she was masked by the golden lioness face of Sekhmet.

Hingston walked up to the statues and the mirrors which had been positioned to create the illusion of an army of gods and he noticed his own multiple reflections. He remembered Emily's ABE interview and the practice of drinking from the statue to absorb its magic. The stone surface of the ibis-headed Thoth was marked with traces of the minerals from London's hard water. At its feet was the sizeable excavation, purposed to allow offerings to drain to the underworld. He looked down and saw a small gold cylinder, not much greater than an inch in length.

'Evidence bag, please,' he requested.

The cylinder had a loose top which came away as he picked it up and it rolled around on the surface of his nitrile gloves. Inside, the cylinder was empty.

A voice from the hallway called down the stairs. 'Sarge! We've got a body!'

***

The top flat contained an unforgettable display of artistic talent and deepest melancholy. The once plain Georgian walls in the attic room that backed onto the grassy expanse of Barnard Park had been transformed by an enveloping mural into the Valley of the Kings. Depicted under a night sky, the spectacular painting extended across the ceiling. Beautiful stars surrounded Orion's Belt which was the dominant feature.

Four canopic jars stood in one corner and they stared blankly at the coroner when she remarked upon the uniqueness of the scene at Richmond Avenue. They were empty, but the presence of an antique embalming table and a collection of medical instruments suggested they had been assigned to house the organs of the female cadaver that had been found in the room across the hallway.

The room at the front of the property was painted black on every surface including the floorboards. The showpiece was a chest freezer that had been decorated to resemble a sarcophagus. A pair of eyes were painted on its side. Believed by the Ancient Egyptians to allow the deceased to see out, the wedjat eyes were large and distracting. To Hingston's displeasure, they were fashioned with green eyelids. They were a lifeless version of the heavily decorated human stare that had pierced its way into his consciousness on Monday night with an aggressive determination.

The victim inside the freezer had been positioned with her head in alignment with the wedjat eyes. She had not suffered any form of mutilation and her unclothed body was estimated to be between fifty and sixty years of age.

Atop of the freezer had been found a senet board: the game played by Emily Britton. Its pieces were displaced as if a game was underway. Hingston remembered sitting in the stifling Petrie Museum office, listening to Natasha tell him that senet was once played *with* the dead. He felt grateful to have been in the basement when his colleagues made the grim discovery. It made him contemplate whether the top floor was in fact "the tomb of Richmond Avenue" and that the theatre of the basement had been a purposeful distraction on the part of Emily Britton.

***

It was a delivery driver who found Caryl. While the search of Richmond Avenue was in progress, the driver exited the busy intersection near London Wall and pulled up underneath the Museum of London building. He saw Caryl wandering around the museum's restricted car parking bays in a state of distress, clutching her stomach. When he approached, he saw the knife she grasped. Its blade was pressed against exposed skin where her trousers were unbuttoned. On seeing the man, Caryl became hysterical and hurried to inflict a wound, but managed only a superficial cut. She dropped the knife to the floor and then herself, where she curled up face down, wailing, next to the lift access at the feet of a large statue. It was later ascertained that the two Portland stone statues that marked the underground access to the museum were the very same Osiris and Isis that once towered over Piccadilly from the first-floor facade of the Egyptian Hall.

Emily's interview proved as challenging as her mother's. She continued to blame Mrs Britton who she believed *still* wanted to kill her. Emily also sought to disassociate herself from any wrongdoing, but the evidence against her was mounting. The protection afforded to the teenager by Caryl Pugh was explored during Caryl's interview after her release from hospital where she was found to be four months pregnant.

Caryl was the most compliant of all those interviewed in connection with the House of Life, possibly because she still felt a sense of duty to the police family, possibly in the hope of achieving a lighter sentence, or simply because she sought retribution. Fully aware of the prison sentence she would likely be serving, Caryl voiced her intention to resign from the Met and admitted to being involved with the group for over a year. She stated she was introduced by her late friend, Jemima Lewis-Smith who died on the tracks at Holborn in May.

Caryl stated she "quickly became close" to Yorke and that it was possible he was the father of her unborn child. Her doubt in this matter was left unexplained and it was therefore speculated that Richmond Avenue was more than just a meeting place for magical practice. According to Caryl, it was Yorke who gave her the direction to commit suicide and it was only her pregnancy that held her back.

Caryl admitted that she had lied about the Fitzwilliam Museum CCTV footage. She was protecting Emily at the direction of Yorke because Emily had, 'Chosen to sacrifice Olson to protect the House of Life.' The fact that Emily had played Olson and traded his life in a selfish attempt to save her own was admired by Yorke. Emily's desire to, 'Impress,' had paid off.

Yorke was equally ready to disregard his own thirty-year friendship with Olson to protect himself and to continue the twisted machinations he so revelled in.

In conclusion, Olson's trust in Yorke and the cunning Emily was woefully misplaced. It appeared that Olson was far less intelligent than his doctorate would suggest. Had he gone straight to the police without pursuing a meeting with Yorke at Highgate, he would still be alive.

The interviewing officers had recoiled when Caryl explained that the hair sample and ears were those of Yorke's disabled sister who lives in Brixton. Caryl stated that the poor woman had been told by Yorke that she required surgery. He completed the procedure and dressed the wounds himself, committing the offence of grievous bodily harm. Police and the ambulance service responded to Caryl's report immediately and Yorke's sister was conveyed to King's College Hospital. Caryl denied having any direct involvement with the scene at Kensal Green Cemetery, but she admitted to removing all four wax figures from the exhibit store. She stated that she handed them directly to Yorke because he had expressed desire to, 'Play a little game with the police.' As to how the forensic error of using his sister's ears had occurred when they would undoubtedly be DNA matched to the hair sample, Caryl offered no suggestions.

Despite these revelations, the information Caryl possessed was slow to be released and it was not until

Monday the 17th of December that she disclosed Yorke's whereabouts. The control he held over Caryl, and presumably all of the other victims, was in keeping with that of a cult leader. Regardless of whether the House of Life fell under the definition of a cult, there was certainly evidence that this consultant psychiatrist had been deploying abusive tactics at a very advanced level.

Yorke was located hiding in a narrow boat along the Grand Union Canal in Greenford. He made no attempt to flee or to jump into the water to drown himself when the officers boarded from the towpath. Instead, he acted surprised and stated, 'Officers, what has happened? How may I help you?'

When he was cautioned, he said, 'This is a terrible misunderstanding. I am taking time to grieve for my mother in peace and solitude,' and then he began to sob like a child. It was apparent during his interview that he suffered from self-delusion. Yorke continued his attempts to flatter and charm. It was clear that he expected to sail through the trial with a not guilty verdict, despite the evidence against him.

The narrow boat belonged to Yorke's secretary, who was later arrested for perverting the course of justice. There was no evidence she held any association with the House of Life and after thorough investigation, the same applied for his receptionist.

Yorke's own arrest coincided with the publication of the scientific paper that concluded Ramesses the

Third had been murdered by the cutting of his throat. Natasha emailed Hingston the relevant link to the British Medical Journal website from her Petrie Museum account and wished him a relaxing holiday period. It was possible Natasha's input would yet be sought regarding some of the items seized from Richmond Avenue. This included the small brass cylinder which her reference books, yet to be returned, indicated could once have contained a written oracle to safeguard against danger.

The artefacts within Richmond Avenue were found to be genuine. Why these items were not seized by the police in 1923, the old Met Police file shed no light. They were accompanied by an interesting, relatively modern device known as a magical lantern, which was responsible for Emily's belief that Ramesses the Third *appeared* in the basement. In fact, had it been possible to borrow it from the exhibit store along with some of the coals used to create the smoke onto which Ramesses' image was projected, Hingston could have satisfied Zack at New Year with the performance of *How to Raise a Ghast* from *The Boy's Own Conjuring Book*. Its design was identical to that described for this complex, Victorian parlour trick.

Also identified in the basement was a fascinating mechanism which delivered the "voices of the gods" that had been described by Emily. A hollow, talking statue distorted and projected the sounds made by whomsoever spoke into its mouthpiece. The voice could be perceived as otherworldly if the listener was inclined to such persuasion. DNA taken from saliva stains found on the painted wooden mouthpiece matched Roe's profile and supported the police theory that he was most probably one of the priests.

The post mortem performed on the frozen body found at Richmond Avenue revealed a significant head trauma had been suffered prior to death. The old chest freezer had no mechanism to open the lid from inside; however, there was no indication the victim regained consciousness. The cause of death was suffocation. The identity was confirmed by odontology and an appendix scar, supported by a comparison with photographs. Given that the post-mortem interval is difficult to determine when bodies have been frozen, the professional opinion that Dr Anita Hesketh had been murdered approximately twelve to eighteen months prior to the search of Richmond Avenue had to be made in conjunction with other evidence. Hesketh had last visited her doctor's surgery in March 2011. She withdrew cash on a monthly basis at a local cash machine, presumably to cover food and sundries, and this routine ceased in November 2011.

Yorke alleged that Hesketh had been his partner for fifteen years and that they chose not to cohabit. He claimed that she had died only six months ago as a result of hitting her head on the corner of her kitchen worktop having fallen off a step ladder. He could not bring himself to part with her body and in order to keep up the pretence that she was alive, he facilitated the payment of utility bills and the like for Richmond Avenue using Hesketh's accounts.

Yorke claimed that the House of Life was a wholesome, holistic venture that, 'Gave hope and well-being to many troubled people.' He alleged that he had dressed as Hesketh since her death because that was the only way to induce the gods to act. Without the gods, support for their, 'Troubled clients,' would cease. A wardrobe was found at his home address which contained the outfits he had worn at Richmond Avenue to masquerade as Anita Hesketh. In the bottom was a mallet. The hair attached to it was tested, matched to Hesketh's DNA and Yorke was charged with her murder. The true circumstances that led to Hesketh's murder remained a mystery. It was speculated by the Op PYROLITE officers that Hesketh may have attempted to quell the spiralling criminality that had germinated from her great-great-grandmother's legacy.

There was no evidence the antique embalming table had been used since it was re-enamelled in its recent history.

***

After a heavy week processing and compiling evidence for the future trial, Hingston was anticipating the enjoyment of Christmas and New Year with the satisfaction of a job well done.

After viewing his face on the footage retrieved from Olson's mobile phone, Harry opened up. The eighteen-year-old stated that Emily had introduced him to the House of Life. He knew that Emily had been assigned to die, as Panik, and he knew that many others had gone before her. He was particularly keen to impress upon the interviewing officers that he didn't like Emily having sex with, 'That slimy bastard, Olson.' He had believed that she was clever enough to work out a way to save herself. Harry had also wanted to ensure that he remained alive himself, so he had been keen to assist Yorke with Olson's murder. For the same reason, he pretended to his girlfriend Chloe and to the police that he knew nothing. He stated he now regretted his involvement, although he had found the mystery, the sex and the danger addictive.

Harry's DNA was matched with that found near the scene of Olson's death. His fingerprints matched those found on the chain cutters and in Marchant's car. He said he had been kicking himself for failing to clean the chain cutters before gloving-up for the break-in, but that he hadn't, of course, intended to leave them behind. He blamed Olson's hanging for sending him into a state of shock, along with a last-minute change of plan involving the logistics for leaving Highgate. Harry admitted the green jacket was his own, but he then delivered the interviewing officers a revelation—the jacket had been worn by Emily. Yorke provided the transport to Highgate for Harry, and for Emily who was in charge of performing the spell associated with the wax figure. They were both supposed to be collected by Yorke, but after the hanging, Emily gave Harry his jacket back and Yorke told him to travel with Marchant and Roe instead.

The remaining footwear marks at Highgate Cemetery were matched with Harry and Roe. To Barry's discontent, this left one set presently unaccounted for. It could well have been Emily wearing a slightly larger shoe size or possibly someone innocent, perhaps a drunk or a curious person who wandered in through the open gates, oblivious to the heinous crime that was being carried out or had earlier taken place. Whatever the reason, the uncertainty was frustrating.

There was no evidence any police officer, police staff member or laboratory staff member had assisted Caryl. The failure to process Emily Britton's DNA swab appeared to be nothing more than human error.

There remained no sign of any other members of the House of Life attempting to visit Richmond Avenue. There was no evidence to suggest the existence of any persons yet to be identified. Yorke, Caryl, Harry and Emily had been charged and joined Marchant, Roe and Mrs Britton on remand for the vile crimes they had respectively committed. The suicides that had been encouraged were obscene in number. The Cold Case Review team were now actively pursuing new evidence related to the murder of Carlotta Ferrario.

As Hingston sat at his temporary desk in the report writing room on Monday the 24th of December, he watched Remi arrive. She was smiling and carrying a large tray of Danish pastries for the Christmas breakfast buffet. He decided that even tired Hampstead Police Station was starting to look mildly festive. One of the DCs had arrived extra early that morning with a large box of second-hand tinsel cut into short lengths. She'd affixed them along the top of everyone's computer monitors, including Smythe's.

Remi laughed when she saw the decorations. 'Jason! This is more like it!' She put the tray and her bag on the desk and unbuttoned her coat.

Hingston remembered the tree they had decorated together at his house in 2008, days before she left him for that bloody Will Finch. Four years on, Will Finch, was married to an Essex Police call handler with a baby son and another on the way, and Remi was living with Smythe.

Hingston agreed with her about the tinsel and returned to his emails.

'Can't believe we're here already,' Remi continued. 'I'm going to miss working with you when you return to Chiswick.'

Hingston looked up. 'I think I'll remain on secondment for a little while yet. Brace knows Smythe won't respond well to any chasing up!'

'*That* I can believe,' Remi said with a look of disapproval.

Hingston laughed and glanced back at his emails. IT Security had quarantined a message. 'Hey, look at this, Remi,' he said and beckoned her round. 'Someone has tried to email me *this*.' He pointed to the subject line which was entitled *The Weird Sphinxes' Spectre Guarded Road.*

Hingston telephoned IT Security. The email they released read:

In these huge chambers of the mountain's breast
The Theban monarchs kept their honour'd rest

Scenes of convivial mirth, or hateful strife
Clothe the mute walls with an immortal life

Yet while their annals in the depths of age
Hover, like phantoms, o'er th' historic page
Here, on the storied stone they ceaseless reign
And run their time-forgotten race again

Hence the weird sphinxes' spectre-guarded road
Conducts to Karnak's sumptuous abode

Oh! how the mind, bewilder'd, wanders back
*Along **the line** of **T**ime's mys**terious tr**ack!*

And speechless records tell, through endless gloom
Man's story from the cradle to the tomb

John Collett

Hingston found a copy of John Collett's poem on the internet. The Oxonian had written an anthology for which *The City of the Dead* was the title piece. The copy Hingston referred to was that of the second edition, published in 1860. He immediately ascertained that the sender had tampered with Collett's original work by splicing select lines into an abridged alternative. The sender had also lopped off one letter which changed Collett's application of the word "Thence" to "Hence". The result not only altered the context of Collett's poem, it created the illusion it could have been written *about* Richmond Avenue.

There were also eleven emboldened letters which drew attention to the line that read "**A**long **the li**ne of **T**ime's myst**eriou**s track!". The analysts were convinced the emboldened letters were an anagram, but they could not come up with anything meaningful in English.

The dark web and an encrypted email service were blamed for High Tech Crime's inability to identify the sender. There was also doubt over *when* the email was sent. The time displayed on the email would indicate there was an outstanding offender. However, it was plausible that any one of the prisoners had prepared a scheduled email prior to their arrest.

There was much speculation as to why Hingston was the recipient of the email when officers of higher rank, including Smythe, held more influential roles in Op PYROLITE. With a squint, Smythe observed, 'You *appear* to stumble upon evidence: got a nose that sniffs it out. But it feels like some things, *weirdly*, stumble *upon you.*'

Hingston felt both anxious and determined to find out *where* and *why* this had become personal. It was for that reason he now held a secret: the anagram spelt Talitha Rose.

By the end of the day, Hingston had considered his position carefully. As he switched off his computer and contemplated his cold drive home, he made his decision to remain as silent as a winter's night—as silent as falling snow.